Infraction

Annie Oldham

Infraction
ISBN-13: 978-1480009486
ISBN-10: 1480009482

To my readers, for helping me dream this book into existence

ONE

Jack and I have a range, a territory, though we haven't discussed it. It cuts a wide swathe west of the Puget Sound almost to the Pacific Ocean, south of the mountains. When we go west, I catch a glimpse of the ocean through the trees every now and then. In the distance, it is gray and immense and whispers a siren call, singing of familiar places. I can ignore the call. It used to be where I lived, but I still haven't found my home. I laugh to myself sometimes, thinking of life in the colony. My ridiculous father and all his aspirations for me. I wonder if he ever pictured me wandering through wilderness with a guy just a few years older than me, sometimes racing for our lives. Nope, I don't think he could have. It's a far cry from the sterile safety beneath the ocean.

Jack and I have an unspoken agreement—we can't roam too far from the magnetic pull of the settlement. That was the closest thing to home either of us has had for a long time, and what we felt there is still rooted deep in our bones. When I close my eyes at night, I see the hazy summer sunlight lingering on the oca fields, shining off the windows of the school building. Sometimes Nell is out back, dipping candles. Other times she's inside darning socks or making herbal tea. She's always happiest, though, when she has her hands deep in the soil, planting hydrangeas. Red is usually there beside her, a hand on her shoulder, on her arm, or lingering over her silver hair.

When I wake up from dreams of Nell, Red, Dave, or even Mary, I know why I haven't found home yet. I'm starting to suspect it isn't a place.

This realization also makes Jack both a comfort and a worry.

We find a small hollow surrounded on all sides by thickets of blackberry canes. We stash our packs up a tree and unroll our sleeping bags among the rattling brambles. The berries are long gone, and the dried, shriveled leaves will fall any day now.

We found the sleeping bags in an abandoned cabin in the forest. The cabin had been ransacked and almost every other usable item taken. There were a few bowls and plates left in the cupboard. We had no use for those. What good are breakable dishes when you have to stash them in a pack and tote them around? There was one piece of beauty left in tatters—a torn rug with a few tassels left intact. I took one beautiful red thread from the rug and put it in my pocket before Jack could ask me about it. I was kind of embarrassed to find something like a thread nostalgic or sentimental or whatever other word I could use. I don't think I could explain how the scarlet color touched me.

We eat a dinner of roots and canned salmon before the sun starts settling into the horizon. Yesterday we found the abandoned remains of a supply drop—tins of food, bottled water, and granola bar wrappers torn open by some animals. It was all scattered around a scanner, and we've been on edge since then because we can both guess what happened.

There are dozens of scanners out in these woods, ready to snatch any tracker data they can and send it back to the hungry capital. Their small black forms rise up out of the morning mist like ghosts. Neither of us have trackers, but we still shy away from them. Some of the scanners' black glass faces have been smashed in, small shards of glass glittering under the foliage.

"It's a federal offense to disable a scanner," Jack says, tentatively touching the small of my back to guide me away from one. We stay as far away as we can. They're like bad omens.

What would happen? I don't really need to ask the question; I already suspect the answer.

"You'd be put in a labor camp."

Of course. Slave labor. The government's solution to just about every infraction.

Someone with a tracker still embedded in their arm had been wandering around the scanners for too long, and the government found them.

I don't have a tracker—my arm is unblemished, and it's one of the markers that I'm not from here—and Jack doesn't have one either. His father cut it out for him when they escaped the midwestern city they came from. Jack's scar is small and neat. I study it when he doesn't think I'm looking—the thin white line almost fading into nothing and a few fine hairs cross it. Jack was lucky to have a doctor for a father, someone trained to use a scalpel and stitches. I've seen some tracker scars in my few months here that are twisted, puckering things. But no one minds the scar, not if it keeps the government away. Jack caught me looking at his once and asked what I was doing. Not in a

3

suspicious or unfriendly way, of course—I don't think Jack has a mean bone in his body—just curiously. I blushed. My pale complexion doesn't let me get away with anything, and all I could do was shrug my shoulders. Then I sighed when he turned his back. He was hoping it meant something more than it did.

So we're on edge, burrowed as deep into the hollow as we can manage, as far from the nearest scanner as we can be. The whir of machinery tells me these scanners are active, and there have been agents here within the last week or so. Jack barely whispers a word to me in the fading light, and there's not even the question of building a fire. It will be several days before we'll chance one again.

But Jack will write on my hand. He started doing it about two months ago. It wasn't out of pity for me, since spelling my words is one of the few ways I can talk to him. He does it when we need silence and because, I think, he craves the contact with me.

This is why Jack is a comfort—he is my companion, my partner as we try to avoid the government and other nomads like ourselves and tell ourselves we can't go back to the settlement. He helps hold me together when there are some nights all I'd like to do is curl up in my sleeping bag and weep.

He holds me together, and it's nice because I do the same thing for him. He's had a hard time in New America. People kill for a good doctor, and he has been the cause of death. There are times when I've heard the sleeping bag next to mine rustle softly with silent sobs.

We hold each other together. I'm grateful for that, grateful that I can help him as much as he helps me. It's even, fair. I never

4

had that in the settlement, when those good people did nothing but give and give and give. Now away from that, I don't just take.

But tonight as the sun goes down, as the shadows lengthen and then disappear altogether, and as darkness settles into the trees, I feel Jack's eyes watching me.

This is why Jack is a worry—Jack is in love with me. I'm almost sure of it.

I could love him too, easily. But I'm not ready for it yet. I can't let down this invisible wall I started building during my first vocation in the colony when I felt like everyone was charting me, studying me, probing me. It's a wall I fortified when I went to Seattle for the med drop and everything went wrong. I carefully checked all the chinks as soon as I saw Jack hurrying toward me through the long grass the day I left the settlement. When I came to the Burn, I had never been in love before—never even let myself contemplate being in love—and the first time I thought I was, it was a disaster. Now I'm more respectful of love, and I want to be careful. I don't want to hurt Jack if I'm not ready for it yet. Not Jack, who is my world right now.

So as I feel Jack's eyes watching me, I keep mine closed and try to keep my breathing regular. The crickets sing slowly as the weather turns colder. The night air chills over my face, and I'm so aware of Jack's body lying next to mine that my heart pounds against my ribs.

"Are you still awake?" he whispers so softly I wonder if he meant for me to hear.

I can't lie to him—him, out of everyone, I've promised I won't tell any more lies to. I've been building the courage to tell him about my past, tell him about the colony. I know it might mean I'll lose him, but it's something he deserves to know, something I want him to know. The thought of just coming right out and saying it—figuratively, of course—scares the daylights out of me. But I will tell him soon.

So when he asks me if I'm awake, I nod my head. Even if I don't know how to respond to him if he's in love with me, I can't lie.

"How long do you think we'll go walking on ice like this?"

My gut clenches. I'm not ready for this conversation yet. I unearth my hand from the sleeping bag and hold it out for his. The warmth from his hand eases into my cold one.

What do you mean?

"You know, Terra, sometimes I don't think you're afraid of anything."

I smile sadly because I'm all too afraid. Afraid of what I could feel for Jack, afraid of what he feels for me, afraid that if we go to sleep tonight, we'll wake up surrounded by wild animals, nomads who want our supplies, or agents. I squeeze my eyes shut and squeeze his hand just as tightly.

"You're afraid?"

I nod.

Jack nudges closer to me so that I can feel his shoulder through the layers of sleeping bag. "Me too." Then he laughs, and it has a haunted, hollow ring to it that makes me shiver. "I sometimes wonder if we'll ever stop being afraid. If one of these days, something will give and the world will be right again."

I sigh in relief. He wasn't asking about us, and I squeeze his hand more tightly. I should have known he wouldn't bring it up. He's been skirting around it for so long, waiting for me. I do love him for that—for his discretion, for his respect of my feelings.

Then I think about what he said, that the world will be right again.

Do you think it could happen?

"I always dream it might."

Something to hope for?

Jack releases my hand and burrows down into his bag. His voice is muffled. "Something like that."

And a pain twinges in my heart with everything he didn't say. The world righting itself is the only thing he can hope for right now.

Then we both hear a twig snap and we freeze, our conversation instantly forgotten. The night is completely dark now, and the trees let very little light filter down to us. I can barely see Jack who is twelve inches from my face, but still I strain my eyes, trying to see if an animal or something worse made the sound.

We lie in tense silence for so long my muscles ache to relax. We barely breathe, and somehow without my noticing, Jack's hand has found mine again, and I'm squeezing his so hard my fingers hurt.

I'm about to glance over and raise my eyebrows to see if he thinks all is clear, when I hear the sound of boots outside the thicket. Jack's hand trembles.

I listen, trying to discern the sounds that creep up around us. The crickets hush as the boots come nearer, stirring through soggy undergrowth and fallen pine needles. It sounds like more than one pair of feet. My legs ache to run, to sprint away as fast as I can—and I have become a good runner in the few months

I've been here—but running would most likely kill us both. The agents always have soldiers with them, soldiers with night-vision goggles and razor-accurate scopes. Even if they are just nomads around us, we could easily run right into their arms in the darkness. And the nomads I've come across haven't been friendly.

All I can do is lie here and pray.

The boots stop on the other side of the thicket by our feet, and I'm thankful our sleeping bags are dark green. I can hear heavy breathing and the soft throat rasp of someone trying not to cough. Then a whisper.

"Quiet!"

"I can't help it. We didn't make the last med drop, and this cough is getting worse."

Two men, though there could be more out there. I don't dare turn to look at Jack now. I don't want to make any movements in our fragile hiding place. The blackberry canes would rustle, and we'd be found in a heartbeat.

"You're sure they came this way?"

"Yeah, I saw them not more than two hours ago. They looked ready to camp down for the night."

"The guy and the girl?"

"I said yeah."

"Then where are they?"

I have to bite my cheek to keep from gasping. They're looking for us. Jack is paralyzed next to me. These men have been tracking us—who knows for how long.

"I don't know. Look, here are their packs."

I almost cry, thinking of our supplies we so carefully scavenged and then rationed. The beam of a flashlight flickers all through the blackberry canes, sending wild shadows bending across us. Through the thicket, two men stand close together. One holds Jack's pack, and the other holds the flashlight in his mouth so he can see while he rifles through my pack.

"Some cans of food. Some rope—that's handy. A piece of paper in plastic."

"What's it say?"

My heart sinks. The letter from Jessa. I've kept it all these months. I should have burned it or torn it in a thousand pieces after Mary found it and used it against me, but I haven't been able to. I close my eyes and feel the heat behind them as I try to keep the tears at bay. This is not how Jack should find out. He deserves to hear it from me.

"Does it matter? Check out the other pack."

I breathe deeply, thankful for this one mercy. Then I remember that Jack has mostly medical supplies in his pack, and if these are nomads looking to raid our supplies, they'll be looking for a lot more than supplies if they discover Jack's a doctor.

The man with the flashlight unzips Jack's pack, and Jack's breath catches in his throat. I long to reach for him, to comfort him somehow, but we both have to lie through this together but alone. I'm alone as I see Jessa's letter flutter back into my pack from one man's dirt-covered fingers, and Jack is alone as he watches to see if he'll be the cause of more death just because he's a doctor.

"Look at this. Bandages, rubbing alcohol, pain killers." The man holds up a jar half-filled with Nell's salve. "What's this?"

The other man leans close and peers at it, his lip curling. "Don't know. Looks nasty. Think they made the last med drop?"

"Could be. Could be that they know how to use all this stuff too."

"You think one's a doctor?"

"Could be."

"They wouldn't go far from their supplies."

"That's what I'm thinking."

"See, I haven't lost them. We'll just stick close and see if we can find them in the morning."

The flashlight flicks off, and the darkness falls on us so fast it's almost a shock. The sound of their boots slugging through the damp forest floor fades into the distance, and I finally risk bringing a hand to my mouth.

Nomads, then, and they'll be watching for us tomorrow.

TWO

The gray light of morning splays across my face, and I can't believe I let myself fall asleep. After the men had gone, the cricket song resumed and all the other noises of the forest woke up from some drugged sleep. It lulled me to unconsciousness. As soon as my brain is awake enough to think clearly, I freeze and can't move. I feel pressure on my hand, and I look down and see that Jack and I have slept all night with our hands clenched together.

When will we stop walking on ice?

My hand aches as I gently ease it from his. I flex my fingers, trying to will some feeling back into them. Jack's face twitches, and his eyes flutter open. I put a finger to my lips to remind him of our danger, but I don't have to. The fear etched deep in his eyes tells me he will never forget.

I stretch in the sleeping bag, urging my muscles to relax, but it's no use. I'm wound tightly around the threat the nomads pose to us, the nomads that lurk somewhere out there beyond the meager cover of our thicket.

I sit up slowly as Jack sits up in the opposite direction, and we study the woods through the gaps in the blackberry canes. Nothing. But neither of us is so trusting that we believe the nomads grew tired and simply moved on. We'll be watching for them every step we take. It's going to be a long few days.

Our packs are gone and our breakfast with them. Jack leans in close, his shaggy brown hair sweeping softly against my face. He used to trim his hair regularly in the settlement, but we had one pair of scissors in his pack, and we reserved them for medical use only. Jack didn't want to dull them on something like a haircut.

"We need to get moving. See if we can find food."

He's trying to distract me, talking about our immediate needs. I appreciate it though it doesn't help. I nod, try to smile, and roll up my bag. I take off my belt and use it to strap the bag to my waist.

Last night's cloud cover has blown away and sunlight filters through the trees, dappling the damp ground. We're lucky in one way at least—the soggy undergrowth is almost silent compared to dry, crackling leaves.

I swivel my head side-to-side as we walk west and Jack checks our backs.

It's not until the sun is high in the sky and our stomachs growl so loudly I think they might claw their way out that we hear any human sounds. Several male voices, muffled by distance and foliage. Jack and I freeze at once, both of us with the stiff, ready-for-flight posture of hunted animals. I move just enough to look at Jack. He nods, confirming my hopes.

The nomads are too far away to hear us or see us.

I cut southwest, away from the voices, hoping my heart will stop thrumming in my chest long enough that I can catch a decent breath and the knot in my stomach will go away. I step quietly, watching the ground more than my direction, looking for the quietest spots to plant my feet. I know the men are too far away. If they had heard us, they would have been all over us by now, but I'm still terrified.

I don't know if I'm more terrified for myself or for Jack. They would kill Jack if he didn't agree to give them medical treatment. Me, they might rough up a bit. I can live with bruises — I've had my share of physical wounds during my few months on the Burn, and I know I can take the pain. I couldn't live with myself knowing they hurt Jack.

I reach a hand behind me and Jack takes it. I squeeze his hand once and then drop it as we hurry faster through the trees. I can't hear the voices anymore, and if I can't hear them, they most likely won't hear us.

Then I'm running, flying through the forest, my pounding heart keeping rhythm for my legs. Jack's footsteps follow mine, and we lose all caution as we crash through the forest, away from the men that stole our packs and wanted to take us as well. My feet churn up the damp leaves, and the smell of decay floods my nose. The crisp air chills my cheeks and my nose starts to run. I swipe at it with my sleeve. Then a loud thud sounds behind me.

"Terra!" Jack hisses.

I whip back. Jack's legs are tangled in some brambles my running uncovered. I hurry back and kneel beside him. I pull the knife Gaea gave me from its sheath at my hip. This knife and freedom are the only good things she's given me. I could also say she gave me the gift of life, and while that's true, I can't call her mother. Suddenly my thoughts jump to sweet Nell with her fingers raking through the soil of the oca fields, pulling weeds, and making me smile. I draw a deep breath to calm the dull ache in my chest. She was more of a mother to me for the few weeks I was with her.

At least this knife is sharp.

I slice through the brambles, freeing Jack's legs. He shucks the dried plants off and jumps to his feet, but I don't have the energy to run anymore. He sees my hesitation.

"What's wrong?"

I just shake my head and brace my hands to my knees. Remembering my biological mother and then Nell brought me up short and now all I can think about is my exhaustion. I wouldn't even have tempted my mind to go there—wouldn't even have drawn the knife, if that's what it took—if I had known.

Jack takes one step in my direction, but I hold up a hand to him and then dry heave. He misunderstands, thankfully. He thinks my body has quit on me after running like a madman on no breakfast, but I can't bring myself to tell him about my mother. I need to. Oh, I need to. I need to tell him about Gaea, about the colony, about those pieces that make up who I am. Those are the things I need to tell him. But not yet. I'm so unsure if it'll just drive him away.

When my stomach stops cramping and my breath calms, I look ahead and see daylight bursting through the trees. There's

14

a clearing or some kind of break in the trees. I point, and Jack follows my finger.

"It stretches east and west," he says, "for quite a ways."

I tentatively step forward, unsure what this new development might mean. Could it be a barren town out there? If so, there may be supplies that haven't been scavenged yet or at least a bed in a derelict building that I could rest on for just a few hours. Towns are dangerous, yes, because they're easy to monitor from the air. But right now, I really don't care. I've been running for too long, and my body is ready to give out on me.

I walk the last distance through the trees, and the forest opens up to reveal not a town, but a smooth ribbon of pavement stretching east and west in an unbroken line.

A road.

Something about it, about its uniformity, triggers a warning, but my brain is too sluggish and stupid right now to puzzle through it and pinpoint why it sets me on edge.

The late morning light glistens off the road, making me squint. I peer left and then right. I turn back to Jack and shrug my shoulders. He puts a hand to the back of his neck.

"I don't know, Terra. Following the road would be easier, but for some reason I don't like it."

I nod, but the invitation of smooth road and no brambles clutching at our feet wins me over. I need food and water soon, and surely this road will lead somewhere—a town, a lake, anything. We've left the nomads behind. I'm sure of it. Even if we haven't, it will be easier to see them coming here in the open.

Jack frowns but steps beside me.

We walk long past noon, past what looks to be about three o'clock. My lips and tongue are dry, my stomach has long stopped rumbling, and my legs are ready to give out, when we see a small building. It's a small square of concrete set with windows shaded by a sagging canopy. Dingy, metal scanners stand beneath the canopy. At least they look like scanners, but they have hoses coming out the sides. Ancient scanners, maybe? I can't ask Jack what they are. Something tells me that if I were from the Burn, I would know. I'm reminded all over again of what I need to tell him, but he saves me by doing the last thing I expect—laughing.

"A gas station."

Jack lengthens his strides. He avoids the canopy; it looks like it could collapse at any moment. He yanks on one of the glass doors, but it's locked. He looks around, grabs a rock with his slender fingers, and smashes it through the glass. The violence startles me right out of my hunger fog. He has such beautiful hands; they soothed my wounded feet so gently. That's how I usually think of Jack—as a healer. To see him use his hands this way shocks me. I can't help but let out a strangled giggle. How else do I react to something so incongruous? Jack raises an eyebrow, but I think he's used to the way my laughter comes through at the strangest moments.

The shattered glass crunches under his feet as he reaches through the glass, unlocks the door, and opens it for me.

I marvel that the store hasn't been touched. Granted, there's nothing around—just the forest and this single road. Maybe when all the evacuees of local towns and unsanctioned cities were shipped off to Seattle, there was no time and no one to come here before us. But it's been decades. Could any of this food still be good?

16

A thick layer of dust coats every shelf. I draw a finger over the counter and leave a long, snaking stripe. A massive refrigerator that takes up the entire side wall holds some kind of bottle obscured by the foggy glass. Jack opens it, and rows of water bottles stand before us. The water might be stale, but the taste of stale water is the last thing to bother me now.

I swipe two bottles and open them both up so quickly I slosh some on my shoes. The water eddies around me in dusty swirls. I hand one to Jack, and our fingers brush as he grabs it. He lingers there just a moment too long, then pulls the bottle away and drinks deeply.

"It tastes horrible, but at least it's water."

I nod and sip mine. I'm too hungry and too thirsty. If I go too fast, I'll retch all over the floor. Jack may be in love with me, but it's still gross to watch someone puke. So I nurse my bottled water as I wander around the store. Too many of the cans are dented or bulging, and the food in plastic wrappers feels rock hard. I wonder if we'll find anything worth eating.

I notice a door at the back of the store with a small pane of glass. I push it open and can't contain a giggle. Jack takes a minute to decide if it's sincere.

"What is it?" Jack calls, stooped over some kind of candy, ripping open the packages and sniffing the contents.

I just laugh again and let the door swing closed behind me as I step inside. The people here obviously knew some kind of disaster was coming. There are metal shelves with toilet paper and soap for restocking the restrooms. But next to that are metal cans that read "hard red wheat" and "sugar" and "rice." Back in the colony during my failed attempt at culinary arts, I learned that the colonists kept several staples on hand in case of a disaster in the agriculture pods. Wheat, rice, and beans would keep for years without losing any nutritional value. I tried to learn recipes incorporating each of these, but my bread loaves were more like bricks and my beans could have been the mortar.

These people were also planning on a disaster. But can I open the cans? There has to be a can opener around here somewhere. And will there be a way to grind the wheat?

The door swings open behind me and Jack steps through. His eyes scan the room, but he doesn't understand what it means like I do. I grab his hand.

This keeps forever. Probably still good.

His eyes light up. "How do you know?"

Trust me. We need a can opener and grain mill.

We dig through boxes of first-aid supplies, silver pouches of water—these might taste fresher than the water in bottles—and rolls of paper.

"For receipts, probably," Jack says. "You know, I've never seen a receipt in my life. I only know what my grandma told me."

I find a can opener on a desk covered with stacks of paperwork. I get to work prying open a can of beans followed by a can of wheat.

Jack finds a metal contraption with a small chute at the top, a crank, and an opening at the bottom. I'm so excited that I hug him. His eyes shine brightly at me, and I pull away but return the smile.

"I take it that's what we're looking for?"

I nod.

He figures out how to clamp it to the desk. I find a paper cup in an old drink dispenser, and we take turns pouring grain in and turning the crank until the cup is full of coarse flour. Jack puts a hand on the back of his neck.

"I watched Red make rolls in the settlement, but I really couldn't tell you where to start. I liked to think I was better company, and they never offered to let me do it."

I laugh. *I've made bread. Not well.*

Jack squeezes my shoulders. "Well, that's probably better than I could do. How are we going to bake it?"

I look around the store. There are a couple microwaves. *Do you think the gas station is still on the grid?*

Jack shakes his head. "It might be. But we have no idea how carefully it's monitored. We could have agents on us in a heartbeat if it is."

We look at each other in silence for several moments. My stomach complains loudly.

"Here's what we're going to do. We'll gather up a few things. A can of rice, a can of beans, some of those medical supplies, some water. There was a display of packs up near the front of the store. We'll be ready to go. If we hear anything suspicious, we run."

You're sure?

He nods. "I know, it's dangerous." His mouth turns in a lopsided smile. "But the sound of fresh bread is too tempting."

Don't get your hopes up.

"But it'll still be warm."

I get another bottle of water and mix it into the flour and add a little sugar. I don't have any leavening, so this bread really will be a brick, but like Jack said, at least it will be warm. I put a lump of the dough into a small paper tray and open the microwave door. The light inside flicks on.

It's still on the grid.

Jack's hands clench closed. "We'll have to be very careful from here on out. It looks pretty deserted now, but it could have been a stop for government trucks."

We both know the risk of using electricity that may be monitored by the government. But hunger trumps our concern. The microwave sputters to life, and as the dough circles around the inside, Jack finds a small container of honey that is so crystallized he uses my knife to cut through the plastic and peels it away from the honey like a banana peel.

When the timer finally dings, I pull out the steaming mass of bread, and Jack holds the honey to it. The heat melts some of the honey, and when the bread is cool enough for me to pull a chunk away, I taste it. The bread may be dense, but with the honey it's almost palatable. I offer the tray to Jack. We devour the small loaf of bread before I have time to make another one and put it in the microwave.

After about half an hour, I feel like I have a rock at the bottom of my stomach and from the look on Jack's face, so does he. We slump to the floor in sight of the front entrance. I'm having a hard time keeping my eyes open, but Jack and I are both nervous that we've signaled the entire regime to our presence. The voice in the back of my head tells me we should grab our new packs and put some distance between us and the gas station, but after running this morning and then eating way too much heavy bread, all my body wants to do is lie here.

I put my head on my pack, Jack sits next to me with his hands crossed over his knees. The sun throws long shadows across his face, and the golden light of early evening shimmers through his hair. I blink and watch the dust swirl through the air. I'm so tired.

"Sleep for a while, Terra. I'll watch."

I shake my head. My mind shouldn't be this sluggish, and I want to stay awake with him. I need to talk to him.

He laughs. "Really, Terra. It's fine. I'll watch. I'll wake you in a couple hours, and then it'll be your turn." He turns a package of candy over and over in his hands, and the plastic crinkles as he turns it. He's keeping himself occupied, and I can't help feeling that I'm the reason he needs a distraction.

I need to talk to you.

He holds my palm and traces the words. *Not now. Just sleep. We'll talk tomorrow.*

It's important.

He smiles and his eyes crinkle as his cheeks turn up. He found a razor on one of the shelves here, and all his scruff is gone. His skin is paler where the sun hasn't been able to touch it. "Tomorrow will come, Terra. Sleep."

But I worry tomorrow won't come and things will be left unsaid. The need to tell him about the colony is almost overwhelming, but there's something on his mind, something he needs to puzzle through, and the distracted look in his eyes tells me he can't talk now.

I let my eyes slip closed knowing I'll be safe with him right there beside me.

But I don't sleep long.

I wake to moonlight on my skin and Jack's face inches from my own. He's shaking me awake, and before I can figure out what he's saying, I feel the rumble under me. All traces of drowsiness are gone in an instant, and I jump to my feet.

Trucks are coming. This gas station was being monitored by the government, and now they're on their way to investigate the unauthorized use of electricity. Inside I'm screaming at myself because I knew this would happen. We both knew it would happen, but we ignored it just for the sake of eating something half-way decent and enjoying a bit of shelter out of the woods.

The headlights slice through the dark. We sling on our packs and bolt through the supply room and out the back door. There's a fat, heavy moon tonight, and it bathes everything in light. Trees jump up to greet us only ten feet from the exit, and we're sprinting toward their welcome darkness before we even stop to ask which direction we're going. We stick to the deepest shadows, crashing between the trees, not caring about the noise we make. The screech of air brakes tells me that the trucks have parked, and I know we're still much too close. Light still filters through the trees behind me, and I'd feel much better completely surrounded by darkness.

Funny how I wanted nothing more than to get away from the darkness in the colony, how I felt like it was an oppressive force about to crush me. Now I'd give anything for that kind of black. I race beside Jack, and his breathing tells me he's starting to panic. Normally we can both run a fair distance without even being winded. I glance over, and his eyes are wide, his fists clenched so tightly the moonlight makes his knuckles look bone-white.

The bread sits too heavily in my stomach, and a cramp cuts its way through my side. I put a hand to it, willing it away. We can't slow down now.

Through gasps, Jack says, "They'll have night-vision goggles."

I nod. We have to keep running.

"We're too loud."

But where can we hide? Then I stumble over a fallen tree lurking in the shadows. I scramble in the wet leaves and try to right myself when I notice the dark space under the tree. There's a hollow barely big enough for both of us, and Jack sees it too. I look at him, his eyes shining in the moonlight fingering through the trees. He nods.

We burrow down in the hollow and scrape the bracken around us. I pile the leaves down against our legs and shiver as the dampness seeps into my pants. I'm pressed up against Jack, and his arm wraps around me protectively, before he can even stop to question—like he has on so many other nights—if I'd even want him to. There's no time for thinking, and when there's no time to overthink this, I realize I never want him to move his arm. But I can't follow that train of thought through to its conclusion because I hear footsteps coming toward us.

I reach my hand up to Jack's arm and squeeze it so tightly I'm sure he'll gasp, but he's silent and still as a tomb. I'm trembling, and even Jack's arms around me can't stop it. Nomads were one thing. They might kill us, but it would be quick. But agents? They would torture us to find out where we've been, how many other illegals we've come across, and what unauthorized settlements we've seen. They would probably kill us eventually, and there would be nothing quick about it. I look down and see the small thread of a tracker scar on Jack's arm next to the unblemished flesh on my own. Very few people have never had a tracker. What would the agents think of me, and what would they do about it?

I close my eyes and listen to the heavy tread of combat boots stirring up the leaves. I try to pick out the steps to count how many there are. I tap Jack's arm three times. He taps me back three times in agreement. Three soldiers armed with night-vision goggles and guns. Our only hope is that we've hidden ourselves well enough and that we have the patience to wait longer.

The boots get louder, and I swear they're close enough to kick me. The leaves shuffle by my head, and Jack grips me harder. Then a static click breaks the stillness.

"Anything?" comes a clipped voice.

"No, sir. Nothing. Maybe they didn't come this way." They're talking with an agent through some kind of communicator.

"But the back door is open." The voice trembles with impatience.

"Yes, sir."

"Which means, soldier, that there's nowhere else they could have gone. They wouldn't have followed the road, so the only other option is the woods. Spread out and keep looking."

"Yes, sir."

The static click sounds again, and then silence descends on us. All I hear is Jack's breath in my ear and the fainter breath of the soldiers. My legs and side are wet from lying on the ground, and the cold makes my muscles cramp. Jack tenses next to me, and I know he's feeling it too—the inane desire to burst from cover and run until we can't run anymore. When faced with fight or flight, we'd both choose flight. We're alike. We've always been alike.

The soldiers hover over us for a few torturous minutes longer, and just as I'm bracing myself to jump up and run, ready to feel the bullets whiz by my head, they leave. The footsteps fade into the distance, and I finally let myself breathe deeply. Jack's arm relaxes around me, and I let my iron grip loosen on his arm.

"That hurt, you know." He tries to say it with a hint of laughter, but his tone is all wrong.

I grab his hand. *Is it safe?*

"Is it ever safe?"

We wait at least ten minutes longer. We haven't heard anything, not even crickets, and the quiet is too much. I finally stretch my legs and groan as the cramps pinch every nerve I have. I'm shivering uncontrollably, and Jack chafes my arms with his hands.

"You okay?"

I nod. *You?*

He shakes his head. "I know you're trying to be strong for me, Terra. But I'd rather you be honest. I deserve that much. I'm terrified, and sometimes I think there's something wrong with me when you're okay all the time."

I turn to him. I had no idea. How little we've talked about how we feel. I know it's my fault; I'm the one who's pushed him away. The darkness and the stillness and the fear still linger, and I can't do anything about it now. We have to get away as quickly as possible.

We slide out of the hollow, and we've taken no more than ten steps when I hear the boots again, and they're coming fast.

THREE

There's no time for me to even look at Jack. We run. We run faster than we did from the nomads, faster than we did only a short time ago from the gas station. I bless and curse the moonlight—a blessing as it lets me run through the trees without fear of careening into one of them, a curse because the soldiers won't even need their night-vision goggles to see us.

The boots thunder behind me, and a deep, booming voice calls out.

"Stop now and you won't be harmed."

It's a lie. I don't even have to look at Jack to know he's not tempted. But I am curious why they aren't shooting at us, why they haven't used more force to capture us.

Another soldier appears to our left, rifle ready to fire, and he looks huge in the dark. We veer away until I'm sure we're running parallel to the road. Branches whip across my wet, cold legs and each slap burns worse than the one before. I will my legs to keep churning, and the adrenaline racing through me is in my favor. I'm sure I've never run this fast in my life, but I don't know how long my body will allow me to keep it up. Already Jack stumbles next to me. This can't go on forever.

I hear water up ahead. If we're lucky, it'll be a river and we'll be able to swim across—maybe even float downstream—before the soldiers can even take off all the gear they can't get wet. I pray it's a river. With the way we've run up against trouble the past few days, we could use a break.

Just as the pebbly, mossy bank comes into view, another soldier jumps out from the brush and we turn to the left. It feels all wrong, the soldiers jumping at us, driving us away. Part of me has already figured this out and knows something's not right, but I'm an animal now, all instinct to get away from the enemy that would have me as its prey. There's nowhere else to go. The soldiers press in on all sides, and Jack and I are herded back toward the road.

The darkness fades as more light shines through the trees ahead of us. My lungs burn as I run toward the light wavering through the trees. I'm not going to like what the light leads me to, but running is all I can do.

When I burst through the trees and out of the darkness, two trucks with tall sides and lots of wheels wait for us. There are also a dozen soldiers all with their guns pointed at our heads. I immediately throw my hands to the air, my legs wobbling underneath me. We walked right into their trap.

"It should have been broken up," Jack whispers. I look at him and raise my eyebrows.

"Silence!" One of the soldiers turns toward us.

"If it had been an abandoned road, it wouldn't have been so well maintained."

That explains the alarms that had gone off in my head, why I knew immediately that something wasn't right. I keep telling myself I'll figure these things out the longer I'm on the Burn, that these obvious things will make sense. Some consolation that is right now.

One of the trucks faces away from us, its headlights shining into the distance, offering faint illumination in the clearing. All the soldiers are dim silhouettes against the light. From behind the line of soldiers, a short man in a charcoal suit and black tie steps out. An agent. They all wear those immaculate suits. He motions quickly with his right hand, and two soldiers step forward—one at me and one at Jack. They flick their guns quickly to the left, and we step that way toward the other truck.

"Stop!" one of the soldiers barks. The soldier uses an iron hand to force me to my knees. "Hands behind your head!" he snaps. I thread my fingers behind my head and he clamps metal around both my wrists. He trains his gun on me.

I close my eyes, seeing nothing but red nightmares. Nightmares of firelight flickering over trees, of a circle of us gathered at mealtime. Of the stranger that steps through that circle, and brings nothing but terror with him. Of the way the gun feels in my hand when it discharges. The soldiers' guns bring on the nightmares. I can't ever look at a gun or even think of one without the visions of blood coming back. I even think I smell gunpowder on my hands. It's all too real how much destruction I alone have caused with one of them. I want the soldier and his gun as far away from me as possible, but I can't move. I can only kneel here on the ground like I'm bowing before the agent in reverence. The bile rises in my throat.

The agent puts something in his mouth. Then his eyes flash as the other truck's lights turn on, and I'm suddenly blinded. I turn my head. When I force my eyes open again, the agent has stepped forward. His hands are clasped behind his back, and he studies Jack and me. His breath comes out in shallow puffs, hang there a moment in the cold, and then melt away. I don't want to look at him—I don't want him studying me, prying into my brain with his sharp eyes—but I can't turn away.

"Nomads," he says with a smile. "It's a good night for nomads."

I don't know what that means, but the way he says it sends shivers over me.

"The cities were set up to protect the citizens of New America. And while most citizens do follow the laws, I'm always amazed at the number of nomads just wandering through the wilderness as if you don't want the government's protection. Or don't trust us."

I try to keep my face neutral, but I blink. My eyes are too dry.

His smile widens, baring glistening teeth. "Hmm. Trust is always an issue. I shouldn't tell you this, of course, but seeing as you have no future left, I think it's safe. The trust is what we're working on." He leans down lower, and I can smell mint candy on his breath. "You'll be a good girl and help us with that." He reaches for me, and I turn my head. He chuckles and pats my cheek.

I've only seen an agent one other time, at the med drop, and that woman was a kitten compared to this man.

"Into the trucks with them," he growls.

The soldiers spring at us. One grabs my arms and wrenches me to my feet. My shoulders blaze with pain, and I bite back a

29

whimper. The soldiers and that agent will get no satisfaction from hearing me cry. My only consolation is that Jack is still with me, and the soldiers thrust us into the truck together.

We stumble inside, and I fall to the floor of the truck, my cheek scraped up against hard metal. Murmurs fill my ears.

"Get up before you get us all in trouble."

"Are you okay?"

"Don't look at them."

"Get up!"

"It's them," a voice hisses.

My heart stops when I hear that voice. It belongs to one of the nomads who searched for us last night. I let my black hair fall between my face and the voice, willing myself to become invisible. Jack stumbles behind me. I hope he hasn't made eye contact.

A soldier nudges me with the toe of his boot, and I get up. He shoves me onto a bench. The heavy back doors of the truck creak closed, and then the engine roars to life. I'm wedged between two women—all the men line the other side of the truck—and my arms are cramped and aching behind my back. In the faint light from the lamp at the roof of the truck, I see that some of the women's faces are damp with tears, and everyone's faces are stony. Maybe they've moved past sorrow on to something else entirely, something that makes them look not quite human. Maybe it helps them feel not quite alive. It could help. I suspect we're on our way to a labor camp, and from what I've heard, I'd rather be numb to it as well.

The truck lurches as it finds its way back onto the road Jack and I followed. I bump shoulders with those around me, but I don't talk. I feel the eyes on me, the vicious stares of the nomads

30

who hunted us. Fortunately, Jack sits three men down from them. There is one soldier just behind the cab of the truck and two soldiers by the doors. If those nomads try anything, I'd like to think the soldiers could stop them. I close my eyes, though, because the thought crosses my mind: why would they even care?

I sit that way, with my eyes closed, not wanting to see the people around me, not wanting to see the soldiers' guns. Then closing my eyes brings on all kinds of new horrors: what the soldiers look like when they take their masks off. Do they have human faces, or are they like the fish that live at the bottom of the ocean floor—colorless eyes, gaping mouths with long, spiny teeth? Sometimes seeing the truth is better than what I'm able to dream up.

When I open my eyes, the nomads are watching me. Who knows where our packs are, the ones the nomads took. Searched probably, but then just left wherever the nomads were picked up? Discarded as common garbage? Jessa's letter is out there somewhere, my last physical reminder of my sister and my past life. Like a relic, I guess. I don't think I'll ever find it again. I have the most important parts memorized, however, and that will never be taken from me.

I just wish you would have told me so that I could under-stand. I want to understand. I love you.

Would Jessa understand *this*? That my dream was to come here, and now I'm being taken by these men and shipped off as a slave? No, she wouldn't have and neither do I. Yes, the colony has flaws, but they treat people humanely. Not everyone saw the colony as the prison I did. I glance at Jack. His head hangs from his shoulders and bobs with the motion of the truck. He looks inconsolable. People like Jack belong in the colony; people who are too gentle for this world. People like Nell. They deserve to be taken there and given a chance at a different life. But that will never happen. As far as I know, I am the only colonist on the Burn, and if I'm in a labor camp, no one will ever find the colony. Hopeless as it may be, though, a small fire flares in my heart. If only I could take a handful of these people to the colony and offer them a chance at peace and rest.

The first light of dawn filters in through the windows on the doors of the truck. The woman next to me slumps, and her head dips down to touch my shoulder. She jerks awake and refuses to look at me. Even the soldiers look exhausted. I wonder when they last slept. How long have they been out rounding us up and shoving us around?

When Jack's eyes meet mine, they are red-rimmed and wide. Somehow, we both know we're close to our destination, and we both know we won't like it.

Through the truck's back windows, I see nothing but a twist of road banked by trees. Then a chain-link fence topped with coils of barbed wire crops up behind us. Two soldiers flank the gate we drive through, and they swing it closed, locking it tight. The paved road gives way to dirt, gravel, and dust curling behind us. I can't see anything more.

The truck stops, forcing us all toward the soldier at the front, and we shy away from him, unwilling to get any closer. The woman next to me flicks her eyes at mine for just a moment as I back away from the front of the truck, and her look chills me. Her eyes are nothing more than hollow pools in the dim light. It's like there's nothing inside her.

Voices start up outside. They're muffled, so I can't hear everything, but I hear enough.

"How many?"

"Fifteen."

"Males?"

"Six."

"Nine females?"

"Correct, sir."

"Children?"

"None, sir."

Then the first voice says something that sounds like "Detox," and I brace myself against the side of the truck. We're crammed too close and the smell is awful, but here I feel almost safe compared to what could be out there.

The truck doors swing open, and I squint into the morning sunlight. The soldiers prod us out with the ends of their guns, and I stumble over myself and the others around me. Rough hands grab my arms and lift me out of the back of the truck and set me on the ground. Finally I blink my eyes open and look around. I'm in some kind of compound. Three concrete buildings form a square with the gate behind me. They surround a large patch of grass, and the whole compound is riddled with fencing and barbed wire. A line of fencing runs down the center of the grassy area almost to where we stand. Guard towers fill each corner of the square, and soldiers patrol the perimeter of the fence. Besides this small ragtag group of nomads and the soldiers, I can't see anyone else. The sky is perfectly blue overhead—not a cloud in sight—and it's too beautiful a day for where we are.

I look around for Jack. I lost sight of him when the truck doors opened, and I feel like I've lost my anchor when I can't see him.

There he is in the small line of six men. He's the youngest, and the oldest is probably sixty. The older man makes me think of Red, and I pray that he and Nell are still at the settlement and safe from the world. Jack keeps his eyes trained on the ground, but the nomad who was hunting us the night before last stares hard at him. I will him to look away, to ignore Jack, but he doesn't.

Then there's an agent in front of me, and she flicks my face with her thumb and forefinger. It stings fiercely, and I put a hand to my cheek.

"Hand down."

I drop my arm to my side.

"Eyes down."

I study the scraggly grass by her shiny patent pumps.

"You women will be taken to detox. You will shower and be treated for any communicable diseases. This is for your own safety as well as the safety of the others here. If you had been law-abiding citizens and followed the protocol to live within sanctioned cities, these measures would not need to be taken. Follow me."

As she turns, I look up. A male agent approaches the men. Where will they go?

The woman next to me nods toward them. "What about the men?"

The agent leading us stops, and the grass quivers under her feet. She doesn't even look back as she speaks. "You are not allowed to speak unless it is requested. Another infraction like this and you will be punished."

Then she resumes her pace, and we follow dumbly behind her. A soldier marches behind us. My cheek burns where the agent flicked me, and I wonder who is worse—the agent we follow or the soldier with his gun.

The agent leads us to the concrete building on the right, and I glance sideways and see the men have gone to the building on the left. My stomach sinks as Jack disappears into the doorway. How much of him do I remember, and will memories be all I have now?

We pass through the doors, and the smell of bleach, soap, and antiseptic burns my nostrils. The floors and walls are all tile, and we stop before a window set into the wall. An old woman stands there, and she looks more tired than anyone else I've ever seen in my life. Her thin, gray hair is loosely pulled back, and limp strands hang down around her face.

"This is Worker 143," the agent says, barely acknowledging the old woman. "If you show model behavior, you will be rewarded with positions like this one. Worker 143 is very happy here, aren't you?"

The old woman's gaze never wavers from the one discolored tile on the wall. Her eyes are dull, her hair is dull, and her skin is dull. She could never pass as happy.

"The detox procedure is as follows: first, hair. A breeding ground for lice and other vermin. Your hair will be shaved." As she says this, some of the women around me shift their weight, the most outrage they can safely express. The agent ignores them. "Second, shower. You will be hosed off and washed with antibacterial, antimicrobial soap. It may be harsh on your skin. Third, medical examination. A medical professional will examine each of you to ensure your physical health and determine if any inoculations are necessary." She clasps her hands behind her back. "Take off all your clothing and give it to Worker 143. No outside materials are allowed inside our facility. After showering, you will receive approved clothing."

I glance around at the nine women. About half of their eyes hold nothing—no emotion at what's being asked of them, no outrage at being treated this way. Two of them look more exhausted than angry. The rest look the way I imagine I look right now. Livid. I'm to strip naked in front of these people I don't even know? Get rid of these clothes that are my only possessions in the world right now? Wear something the government tells me I have to?

Anger flashes through my eyes. I'm sure the agent has seen it before because she crosses her arms over her chest, tilts her chin, and her eyes dare me to defy her. I'm not cowed by her look, but I know resisting is useless.

I take my clothes off. I try not to look at the others around me; I try to give them that little scrap of privacy. As I unzip my pants, I remember the single crimson thread from the rug in the cabin. It's too small and hardly significant, but it's one thing I'm sure I can hide and keep. Some small way I can claim something as my own. My eyes find the agent. She's not looking at me; she's watching one of the hollow women who fumbles with her buttons. I slip my hand in my pocket and hide the string between two of my fingers.

I give my clothes to Worker 143. As I pass them through the window, the first wave of expression passes over her face. Sadness. She takes my clothes and caresses them, as if she knows what they represent, and turns around, opens a metal grate, and dumps them down a chute. A blast of heat and a faint orange flicker tell me I'll never see those clothes again. I clutch the thread tighter, clinging to my last souvenir of the outside.

Once we've all given up our clothes, the agent leads us down the tiled hall to the next door. The tiles are cold on my feet, and I cross my arms over my chest and side-step to try to stay warm. I wonder if there's heating in this building because it feels just about as chilly as it does outside.

We pause before the door. The agent rests her fingers on the handle and turns to us. "Your hair will be shaved in here." She smirks, and I wish I could wipe that look right off her face. "Don't worry. This is just a one-time procedure to ensure no pests are transmitted to the others here. After this, you're free to grow your hair." She says it like she's doing us a favor.

I run a hand through my hair. It was about chin-length when I first came to the Burn. Now it's an inch or so above my shoulders. Jessa would have loved to see my hair this long; she always urged me to grow it out. Now I think of the way she looked that night a few months ago when she came to me on the Burn—her hair shaved as Gaea's price for helping me.

The agent turns the handle and motions the first woman forward. She looks back at the rest of us and then steps through the door. I can't see inside, but I hear the buzz of clippers and the soft hush of voices. Then another door creaks open, and the agent jerks her hand to wave another of us forward.

Finally the agent motions for me, and I step into the room. There is a small table set to the side. A pair of scissors and a comb rest there. A broom and dustbin wait next to a metal grate just like the one Worker 143 manned. That's where everything goes in this place—it all gets burned. The woman waiting looms over me, clippers in hand. She barely looks at me. The only part of me she sees is my hair.

I step forward and before I've even stopped, the clippers are up and scraping across my head. I watch the raven hair flutter to the floor, landing on my bare toes, landing next to me, stark against the white tiles. When the clippers finally rest, the woman speaks. Her voice is a hoarse rasp.

"Sweep it up and dump it." She nods to the metal grate. They take our clothes, take our hair, and then they make us burn it.

Numbly, I step forward and grab the broom and sweep all the hair into the dustbin. I cross to the chute and send my hair down. The smell of burning hair twists my stomach.

The far door creaks open and I step through. Another person waits for me. I think it's a woman, but she's almost nondescript in a plastic apron, gloves, and a surgical mask. She holds a thick hose with both hands. She tips her head toward the shower stall in front of her.

It's a three-foot square tiled area with metal walls extending all the way from floor to ceiling. Only the side facing the woman is open. There's a drain in the middle and a shower head straight down from the ceiling.

"I'm going to get you wet first," is all the woman says to me before she blasts me with cold water. I clench my fingers and arms together, and I shiver all over. I swear I'll get hypothermia if it doesn't end soon.

Then the water stops, and her monotone voice resumes. "The soap will come out of the shower head. There's a brush right there on that ledge. Scrub off until I say you're done. You'll want to close your eyes."

I find the brush and rub it across my palm. The bristles are coarse and unforgiving. Then the woman presses a button next to her, and yellow soap comes out of the shower head. I close my eyes. As soon as it hits my head, I cringe. My skin feels like it's on fire. I start scrubbing, hoping the faster I do this, the faster she'll press the button and use that awful cold water to get the soap off of me. I feel like I'm scrubbing off layers of skin, and I'm clenching my fingers so the thread won't slip from them and be washed away. Maybe the soap will dissolve me and I'll slip down the drain, and I can't help but wonder if that would be a better fate than what awaits me here.

Then the soap stops, the water hits me, and I gasp. My skin stings the way a cut stings when first dipped in water, but instead of a small paper cut, the water bites into my flesh all over. I look down, and my skin is bright pink, like the sunburn I got before I left the colony. I suspect these people won't offer me aloe to soothe the pain. But the thread is still between my fingers, and I think of Jack—of the way he held me as we waited for the soldiers to leave, the way he watched me every night as I fell asleep, the way he'd find little ways to touch me but would never tell me how he really felt—and I grit my teeth.

The roar of water fades to a trickle down the drain, and I don't know how many times the woman tells me to move on before I finally register that she's speaking to me. I look up and the door is open. I shiver and step through.

I enter a medical exam room. I stop on the rug by the threshold—thankful for the relief from cold tile—and wait. No one is here. There are two doors across from me, but neither are marked. One of them swings open, and a man in his twenties steps through. He wears a white lab coat and carries a digital notepad. He smiles at me. He's the first one here who's acknowledged me in any way as a person. I can't help smiling back.

"There's a towel there by the door." He nods to a hook on the wall that holds an immaculate white towel, warm from a dryer. I clutch it to me, wrapping it around myself, hoping the shivers will be lost in its fluffiness.

"I'm Doctor Benedict." He extends a hand, but I stare at him. He wants me to touch him? Shake his hand? Like we're business partners or equals?

I raise an eyebrow and step backward. He lowers his hand.

"I understand the mistrust. And I'm sorry about it. Please sit down." He motions to the table lined with paper. It crinkles as I sit on it.

"I just need to listen to your heart and lungs." He unwraps the stethoscope from his neck and presses it to my chest and back. He taps a few words on his notepad.

I crack my knuckles. His calm, kind demeanor sets me on edge. I'd be a lot more at ease if he were frosty like the other agents I've seen.

He smiles. "Nervous?"

I shake my head. I'm terrified, but even if I could tell him that, I wouldn't give him the satisfaction.

His smile broadens to reveal blindingly white teeth. He even has a dimple on his left cheek. Is he serious? They send a doctor with a dimple? I glance around me, waiting for the sky to fall.

"We're not all bad. The agents have their own idea how refugees should be handled. We don't see eye-to-eye on that one."

Refugees? He thinks we're fleeing to the government because they'll offer us protection or better care than what's out there? How naïve can Dr. Benedict be?

"You're very quiet. Why haven't you said anything yet? Most everyone else is either crying or ranting or yelling by now."

I roll my eyes. Of course he'd want me to open up to him, tell him my secrets so he can report back to his government. Wouldn't he feel like he hit the mother lode if he knew what secrets I could tell him about the colonies?

I open my mouth.

He frowns. "Oh. Oh, I'm so sorry." He bends over his tablet, tapping the screen.

I snap my jaw shut.

"You don't have to be embarrassed. I don't want you to feel ashamed of any deformity."

Is *that* what he thinks the problem is? Now I do glare, my equivalent of ranting.

"What's your name?"

I study him, study his fingers hovering over the notepad screen. I grab his hand. He tenses a moment and pulls back, but I look at him insistently and he relaxes.

Aren't you going to give me a number?

He smiles sadly. "No, I want to call you by your name."

I watch him carefully, searching his eyes. They're black, almost as black as my hair—or what used to be my hair. I self-consciously run my palm over the stubble on my head. I can't read anything in his eyes. Jack's eyes are hazel, but deep in their colors and emotion. Dr. Benedict's are reflective, bouncing my face back at me. I don't want to trust him, but he's the first kind person I've come across here. Should that make me trust him even less?

Terra.

"I like that."

I drop his hand.

"Now I just need to see your arm and get your tracker number."

I go rigid, all of me freezing to the exam table. He must see the panic in my eyes because his lips turn down and several creases appear between his brows. He tugs on his ear absently.

"This is standard procedure, Terra. We just need to record who comes through here, give trackers to those who have chosen to, um, remove them. Or make sure there aren't any phony trackers."

My fingers curl around the edge of the table, and I can't release them. I can't even blink.

"It'll just take a moment."

He doesn't understand my paralysis. How could he? Those who have cut out their trackers are pretty common, especially among the nomads. But those who never had one?

Dr. Benedict steps forward slowly, as one might approach a frightened animal. He lifts a hand, his palm up. He looks submissive even. I watch as his fingers inch toward mine. They brush the skin, and his hand is warm. He gently pries my fingers from the table, and then gradually runs his fingertips up to my wrist and turns my arm over. His eyebrows raise.

"You've never had a tracker?"

I feel the color drain from my face, and I shake my head.

"Were you born in a city, Terra?"

I shake my head again and pull the towel closer around me, wanting to hide from him and the other questions that will surely follow, but he surprises me.

"I think that's everything we need for this exam." He writes down a few more notes. "But you're not quite done here. You'll need to go through that door." He nods to the right. "They'll inject a tracker."

I'm to be branded. I'll never escape them now.

FOUR

Dr. Benedict offers a hand to help me down, but I ignore him and slip off the table. The tiles chill my toes, and I walk stiffly through the door. A nurse and an agent are waiting for me.

"No tracker?" the agent asks. She's middle-aged and heavy. I shake my head.

She smiles, showing the tips of white teeth that look unnaturally sharp. She looks like a bulldog. "You all think you're so clever cutting them out. It's ridiculous, actually. The trackers are our most accurate way of ensuring everyone gets the supplies they need, of measuring our population so we know how many we can sustain. And yet some of you insist on cutting them out. Hold out your arm."

My hand trembles as I raise my right arm.

The agent sucks in a breath between clenched teeth. "You didn't cut yours out, did you?"

I shake my head.

"I don't know how you avoided it in the past, but you're getting a tracker now. You won't be interrogated today—we have too many workers to process—but there will be more questions later on, I can promise you that." She sniffs at me, and her bulldog smile returns. "And you won't like it."

The agent motions to a metal chair and I sit. The nurse sets a small silver tray on the table next to me. A syringe with a thick needle rolls side-to-side. Inside I see the small cylinder. It has a blue light on one end. The nurse pulls on latex gloves and then rips open the foil package of an alcohol swab.

"Try to relax." Her eyes look like they could be kind, but there's too much hardness around the edges. "It'll hurt more if your muscles are tense."

I do my best to let my arm unclench, to ease my fingers open. I'm really not even worried about the pain; I'm worried about being marked, of always being afraid of the scanners in the woods—if I even see the woods again.

The nurse swipes the cold swab against my forearm. "You'll feel a little pinch."

I close my eyes. Jack's face floats before mine. I see his smile, and then I see the straight, neat scar on his forearm. Is he in a similar room right now, sitting in a metal chair with a nurse standing over him, ready to implant the device—it's only half-an-inch long, seemingly harmless—that will let the government follow him for the rest of his life? I never understood just how frightened people were of trackers, until now.

The needle pierces my skin, and I wince as the tracker slips through, embedding itself in my arm. I open my eyes and look down. A small drop of blood wells up, and the nurse slaps a square of cotton and a strip of tape over it. The tail-end of the tracker peeks out, forming a lump under my skin. Then the agent is practically on top of me, swinging a scanner over my arm. The tracker glows blue for a moment.

"Good. It's active. You're now recorded in the government archives. Worker 7456. If you show us that you can be a trustworthy citizen, you will be released." She's talking to me as if she's so bored she'd rather be picking the lint between her toes. "Once released, you'll be assigned to a sanctioned city and be approved for rations." I almost laugh at the way she makes it sound like a privilege. "Go through that door. You'll receive your clothing and your cell assignment."

I can't feel my toes or fingers as I stand and walk through the door. I don't think it's a side effect of the tracker injection. The agent's voice is so cold I should probably be numb all over. There's a window through the wall next to me, and I look back into the domain of Worker 143.

Worker 143 looks me over quickly and then turns to a wall of cubbies filled with neon yellow and gray clothes. She hands me two long-sleeved yellow t-shirts, two pairs of gray pants, two pairs of socks, and one pair of canvas shoes. She tries to smile at me, but her lips can't curve that direction, and the expression is lost before it even began.

I shuffle down the hall and wrap the towel tighter around me. A buzz sounds and a huge metal grate slides open. A soldier nods once to me, and I follow him—I think it's a him, it's hard to tell what's really beneath the mask—past rows of doors with a small window in each of them. He stops abruptly before one of them. He swipes a keycard on the keypad next to the door, and the lock slides back and the door swings open.

"In there," he says.

I clutch my few clothes closer and enter the room, and the door closes silently behind me. Garish light shines from a single bulb, and one square of daylight glows on the floor from a window three feet above my head. There's a bunk against one wall, a sink, a toilet, and one girl with lank blond hair. She cowers on the bottom bunk, her arms wrapped around her drawn-up knees, her head down against her chest. She doesn't dare look at me. I can't tell how old she is—she could be my age—but she's all sharp knees and elbows, I can't help thinking she's just a kid.

I walk to the opposite end of the bunk, put the clothes down, and pull on socks, pants, shirt, and shoes. I didn't realize just how cold I was until I got in here and there's no one to watch me, no one to hide my weakness from. My cellmate hardly counts. I've been here for two minutes now, and I don't think she's even blinked.

I put the extra clothes on the top bunk. I rub my hands on my pants, chaffing them against the rough fabric, trying to get some warmth back into me. I've been so cold ever since I saw Jack marched into that other building. I tip up on my toes and rock back to my heels. I don't know what's coming next, and my cellmate is the only one who can tell me. But I'm not going to terrify her by grabbing her hand just to start up a conversation. She looks like every day of her life is a terror.

I cross to the sink and turn on the faucet. A thread of water gurgles out, and it takes several seconds to fill my cupped palm. I gulp the water. I haven't eaten anything since the bread and who-knows-how-old water yesterday. It takes me a long time to gather enough water to finally slake my thirst. When I finish, the girl is watching me.

Her blue eyes are rimmed with dark circles, and I can't stop the image that crashes through my brain: a girl in an alley, clutching a box of medical supplies as it's ripped from her hands by someone bigger and stronger than she is. It's not the same girl; it can't be. This one is too slight, not quite as tall, but the similarities are striking. I feel a rush of pity so overwhelming it almost knocks me over. I can't speak to her, so I smile. She flinches.

I want to step closer, but if she's scared of a smile, she won't last through me approaching her. I slump down against the wall opposite the bed and just sit there, waiting for some kind of acknowledgement or invitation. She just stares at me like she's seen a ghost.

I don't know how long we would have sat there like that, but a crackle from one of the corners of the ceiling startles me. There's a small intercom box there, and a tinny voice fills the room.

"Work hours. Report to your assigned location." Then the lock of the door slides back.

The girl unfolds herself and walks out the door without giving me a second glance. I follow her. She winds down the hallways, through doors, and a trickle of other women join us. She finally leads me through a door with a window fogged over with steam. Inside, huge vats bubble. Everyone wears hair nets and rubber gloves.

The girl disappears through the steam, and I follow where I think she's gone, occasionally catching a glimpse of her hair. She stops at a desk, and I almost run into her. She holds out her arm, and an agent scans her tracker. She's given a hair net and gloves. As I thrust my arm forward toward the agent, I watch

48

the girl disappear between the vats. As the steam clears closer to the ceiling, I make out a narrow catwalk lining the perimeter. Two soldiers pace around it.

The agent's scanner beeps loudly. I look down.

"Ah, you're new." The agent's voice is so full of venom I almost step back. "And your tracker is new, I see."

I nod and reach for some gloves and a hair net. The agent swipes my hand away.

"You haven't had orientation yet. You have no idea what the cannery even is." She turns her head to the side, and her eyes fixate on another woman. "Worker 5932, over here."

A tall woman with red hair steps beside me.

"Worker 5932, please instruct our newest worker about the cannery." The agent picks up the gloves and hair net between her thumb and forefinger like they're contaminated. She drops them in my outstretched hands. "She'll receive her assignment in the cannery tomorrow—provided she can actually do the work."

Worker 5932 puts a hand on my elbow and steers me away. "Just ignore them. Most of them are like that, but I don't think they can actually do anything to you. Not legally. Well, nothing life-threatening, anyway. We might essentially be slaves here, but the government needs the work we do, and it wouldn't look good if there was no work being done."

We stand next to a huge pyramid of boxes.

"My name's Madge. What's yours?"

I motion to my mouth and then reach for her hand. Her eyes soften.

Terra.

"Well, Terra, this is the cannery obviously. We process all the food that comes from farming camps in the northwest. We really only work in the cannery during the late summer and fall because of the harvest. Don't worry, though, those agents give us plenty of other jobs during the rest of the year. If you ever wondered where the food for supply drops comes from, look no further. Though they'll never tell their 'loyal citizens' how much slave labor goes into it."

Up until that point, I thought Madge had managed to maintain some semblance of happiness in this place. The bitterness, however, cuts so deeply on the last sentence, that she now has my full attention. She smiles at me, but her eyes are flinty. She looks around her quickly.

"Don't worry. With all the pots boiling and people talking and the general noise of it all, they'll never hear us." Concern crosses her face. "Though you should still be careful. Always be careful." Madge puts a hand to her sweaty forehead. A hair net keeps her curly red hair from her face, and crow's feet stamp around her eyes. I like her; she's honest.

I nod earnestly to her, hoping she can trust me. I wonder if all the inmates here trust each other because we all have a common enemy, or if there are so many walls built up that trust is hard to come by.

I want to get to work, show her I'll help. I point to a box of ears of corn. I know corn—I tended the corn field in the colony. Surely I can do this.

"The corn? You can start there if you want. All you do is shuck it and then put it on that conveyer belt. That'll take it to the strippers." Madge laughs. "Not the technical name, but whatever. That's what I call them. They cut off the kernels."

I smile bewilderedly. I have no idea why calling them "strippers" is funny, and Madge doesn't look like the joke needs to be explained. It must be a difference between Burn culture and colony culture.

I grab an ear of corn from the box and pull open the husk. From a wisp of steam, my cellmate appears next to me, grabs an ear of corn, and uses her long, slender fingers to shuck it faster than I'll ever be able to. I wrestle with the long fibers and the silky threads and put the ear on the belt. She's already thrown five ears on by the time my first joins hers. Then we repeat it. Over and over again. After several hours, I'm able to shuck two ears to her five, and my fingers are sore. But she never looks at me. Her long hair, the color of the corn silk, falls between us. I wish I could speak to her. It would be less intrusive than grabbing her hand and writing words there. She's like a frightened cat: she'll come close if you ignore her, but one wrong step and she's gone.

Madge stops my hand before I can grab another ear of corn. She gently pries my fingers open, rubbing them where they're curled into fists that know nothing but corn shucking. She looks at me like she's not sure if I'm trying to win points with the agents or am just a hard worker. It wounds me that she'd think I'd try to get in with the agents.

"Give it a rest. They won't keep you on shucking long, anyway. I'll show you what else we do down here."

She nods to my cellmate. To my surprise, my cellmate nods back. Then Madge leads me into the thick of the steam where several workers stand over huge pots. Madge guides me to one in the corner. Her face tells me she has a secret.

"That pot right there?" She nods her head toward it. We're about twenty feet away, and wisps of steam swirl into the worker's face. The sweat pouring into my eyes makes my vision blurry and I squint at the worker's wrinkled face. She reminds me of Nell. Madge leans closer. "Blackberry jam."

I remember the skeleton blackberry brambles Jack and I slept under only a few nights ago. How we shivered in our sleeping bags. How frightened we were of the nomads. How he held my hand and we both fell asleep that way. Now I would give anything for that night again—fear and all. But I'm not sure what Madge's secrecy is about. I'm growing impatient with the games it seems everyone is playing with me. I wipe my sweaty face with my sleeve.

So?

"Have you ever gotten jam in your food rations? Ever even *seen* jam in a food drop?"

I shake my head. I'm assuming that's the right answer. I'm feeling light-headed from hunger, and the idea of sweet, sticky jam makes it even worse. In the several abandoned food drops Jack and I found in the wilderness, jam wasn't among the remains. But what is she getting at?

"Exactly. This jam isn't for anyone but the government." Her eyes flash, betraying that same fire she's so carefully veiled. "And do you see the obscene amount of sugar that Lily's—" a soldier walks right over our heads, and Madge glares at him "— I mean Worker 657 is getting ready to dump in?"

I look from the soldier to Lily. She holds a brown paper sack labeled *50 lbs. Pure Cane Sugar* under one arm, and she struggles under the weight. I'm ready to walk the few feet that separates us and help her. I wonder why Madge hasn't done so already.

But as soon as my foot so much as twitches, Madge puts an arm out to stop me, and her eyes freeze me to my spot.

"Have you ever gotten anything more than a few sugar packets in a drop? I used to save them up for my kids' birthdays." The anger in her eyes is suddenly replaced by such sadness that I want to cry for her. What happened to her?

Lily pulls a string at the top and the bag gapes open and sugar gushes into the jam pot, some spilling onto the floor.

Suddenly, there are soldiers everywhere.They jostle Madge and I out of the way as they surround Lily, and one rips the bag away from her. She raises gnarled hands dyed purple from the berries.

"I didn't mean to!"

The soldiers don't move until an agent parts them with her hands. "What's going on here?"

One of the soldiers jabs his gun toward Lily. "This worker wasted resources—sugar. She claims it was an accident."

The agent pulls a small scanner from her pocket and flicks her fingers for Lily's arm. Lily closes her eyes once and then extends her arm. The agent waves the scanner, the tracker lump briefly glows blue, and the agent reads the screen. She folds her arms and narrows her eyes.

"Not your first infraction, I see. Not your first by any stretch of the imagination."

Lily's eyes are wide, and she looks around wildly. "It was an accident! The bag is too heavy for me. It's fifty pounds. I was just trying to open it and pour it in. I didn't mean to spill some." She crouches down and runs her hands over the floor. "Look! Only a little bit spilled. Probably not even a pound."

The agent rolls her eyes. I know that look. The look before the storm. I try to step closer again, but Madge puts a hand on my chest to stop me and almost imperceptibly shakes her head. I glare at her. It's not fair. Lily had no business hefting that bag. Madge mouths, "I know."

I turn back to Lily in time to see the soldiers yanking her off the ground, and she yelps with the force of it.

"I think some time in solitary should get rid of your clumsiness," the agent says as she taps on the screen of her scanner.

"Please no! I've been down there too long."

"Get rid of her." The agent jerks her head to the doors, and the soldiers march Lily out of the cannery.

My hand slides over to find Madge's. *What are they doing?*

Madge waits until the agent has turned and disappeared through the steam. "Punishing her for wasting their excesses."

She won't say anything more to me. Her eyes are blazing and she grinds her teeth. She has a temper, and it takes all her willpower to keep it under control. I don't want to say anything more to her until we're away from the steam, sweat, and soldiers.

FIVE

After working in the cannery, my hands are so red and raw that I can hardly open and close my fingers. Everyone else who had cannery work hours looks the same way: red skin—not burned enough to blister, but still sore—and sweaty clothes. I follow the stream of workers down the corridors and into the mess hall. I spot my cellmate at the end of the food line and step behind her.

I'm starving. I haven't eaten since the pathetic bread in the gas station with Jack, and after working in the heat for hours, I'm swaying slightly.

My cellmate hasn't spoken to me, but she hasn't looked like she wants to get rid of me either. She keeps her head turned just slightly so she can watch me out the corner of her eye. I'm not sure if it's because she doesn't trust me, or she's just not willing to put out her hand and say hi. I'm the same way. If Madge hadn't started talking to me, I might be looking askance at everyone around me too.

I stand in front of the cafeteria workers—another set of harried-looking inmates. I'm getting the sense that the work isn't necessarily the worst part; it's the way the agents and soldiers treat you like an insect they'd rather squash that can break you faster.

An agent waits at the beginning of the line and scans my tracker. She barely looks at me as she nods me down the line. One of the workers slops some unidentifiable noodley stuff on my tray. Another dumps a meager pile of canned vegetables. I raise my eyebrows, and Madge leans in. I hadn't even heard her come up behind me. For my sake, I hope she's over her anger.

"I think it's supposed to be beef stroganoff."

I had beef stroganoff in the colony, and it never looked this colorless or congealed.

"We're on a weekly meal rotation, and after seeing it every seven days, I'm still not sure. That's what it kind of resembles though. You get used to the stuff."

I sniff it, and the smell turns my stomach.

Madge laughs. "But yeah, don't take too big a whiff. This stuff isn't for the faint-of-heart."

I get a cardboard carton of milk and follow Madge between the long tables. The linoleum is a dull gray. I can't tell if it's dirty or if that's the color it's supposed to be. The whole room is dingy. The cafeteria is full of women wearing the same yellow shirts and gray pants that I am. Soldiers with guns patrol the aisles, and there are some soft conversations, but no general chatter. I look at Madge.

Talking? I mouth.

She nods. "Just watch what you say. And don't talk too quietly or they," she glances up at an observation booth rimmed with windows half-way up the wall, "will wonder what you're saying."

I hadn't noticed the observation booth before. Two agents stand inside and survey us, their arms folded and deep furrows between their eyes.

I steady my tray on one arm and reach for Madge's hand. *Recording us?*

"Probably. Though I haven't seen any mics around here. There are watchers up in the corners, but I don't know how well they can single our voices out."

The small black boxes loom in each corner, and their shiny lenses watch our every move. I'm amazed I ever thought of the watchers in the colony as intrusive. Those were there to archive our daily lives for posterity—whatever that meant. These are here just to trap us. There are so many similarities between life in the colony and life on the Burn, but such different intentions. The unease spreads from my stomach up my throat.

Madge sits down, and I slide across from her. She gestures to the woman next to me. "Hey Kai, this is Terra."

The woman is probably ten years older than I am, and she smiles tentatively, barely showing the tips of her teeth. Her skin is the rich color of tree bark and her eyes are green. Her brown hair falls down her back in a shiny stream. She's beautiful, and her eyes are so alive she looks out of place here with all these hollow people.

I wave, and her smile broadens until all her teeth show.

"Terra can't talk," Madge says, shoveling some noodles in her mouth.

"I'm sorry." Kai says it carefully, her green eyes full of sympathy.

I shrug and try the stroganoff. I gag and choke—it takes three swallows just to get it all down—and take a swig of milk. I look up, and I'm shocked to see my cellmate next to Madge. I hadn't even noticed her sit down; she comes and goes so quietly.

"Told you it takes some getting used to." Madge takes another bite, and I marvel she can eat it so quickly.

"You can eat anything, Madge. I'm still not used to it, and I've been here two months." Kai pokes her fork in her noodles, creating swirls in the sauce.

Madge frowns. "You need to eat something."

Kai looks away. "I'm not too hungry."

There's concern in Madge's face, a concern deeper than I expected to see. I study Kai—her flawless skin, her full lips, her hair, and down to where her belly swells underneath the table. I grab her hand before I even think to ask for permission.

You're pregnant?

Her face twists in a grimace. "Yes."

I look at Madge, and the concern on her face hasn't lessened. "She's thirty-two weeks."

I don't know how far along that makes her, but it doesn't matter. I drop Kai's hand and grab Madge's instead. *Why would they bring her here?*

"She didn't register her pregnancy. You're too young to know, but you have to register a pregnancy within the first three months." Instantly the concern morphs into revulsion. "So the government can keep track of populations. That's the official face of it anyway." She glances up as a soldier marches by.

Then she lowers her head without trying to look like she's whispering. "I've heard that they're going to start giving newborns trackers."

My stomach falls. Citizens have to register their pregnancies? Infants injected with trackers? I push my tray away. My appetite has completely vanished.

"It's not like citizens have it any better, you know."

I shake my head.

"You were a nomad your whole life?"

I nod and push the food around my plate. I don't want to get into my back story right now.

Madge props her elbows on the table. "You wouldn't know then. I lived in a sanctioned city as one of those 'loyal' citizens. There are no wages—you're given a living space and you have to be sure to make it to the supply drops every month. Or you don't eat."

I do know about supply drops. I can still see Red climbing over the broken glass and twisted metal of old cars to go claim medical supplies for the settlement. I can still see the dark-haired man that wanted us all dead. Was he a loyal citizen?

Madge scoops up a forkful of stroganoff with relish. "At least here they make us dinner."

The vibrancy in Kai's eyes is veiled now, and she doesn't look at anything but her tray. I watch her push mounds of stroganoff around with her fork. Her vegetables are gone though. I look at the pathetic pile of carrot bits and grayish peas on my tray and quickly scoop them up and put them on her tray.

Kai smiles at me. "Thank you." She wolfs them down.

I ache for her. She's starving. I have no idea how many extra calories a pregnant woman needs, but I wonder if these servings are enough for even me or Madge. There's no way Kai is getting what she needs. Madge has a sharp look in her eyes but doesn't say anything, and I try not to squirm under her gaze.

Just as I turn back to my plate to contemplate my food, the lights dim and a screen lowers below the observation booth. I turn to Madge. She rolls her eyes.

"Just watch."

From the opposite end of the mess hall, a projector shines a moving image on the screen. It's a picture of a city: vibrant, green, with no broken windows in the buildings, and people walking peacefully and freely. They don't cower and they look each other in the eye. Where is this? Then a voice starts. Male, kind, and nondescript.

"Your government works hard for you. We're restoring your cities to be the kinds of places you would like to raise a family in." The film cuts to a picture of a mother, father, and two children walking hand-in-hand through a park with a sky scraper in the background.

Several agents have slipped into the mess hall so quietly I didn't even notice. They dot the room and watch us all intently. I try not to make eye contact with anyone and quickly look back to the screen.

"We've already made astounding progress on the Atlantic coast in the cities of New York and Philadelphia. We've provided jobs and housing for every loyal citizen in both of these cities. This vision of the future will soon be a reality where you live. Watch for restoration workers in your city."

60

Madge leans over to me. "And how do they think *we'll* see that? We're not going anywhere."

I smirk along with her. I would like to see where one of these cities is—if it actually exists—and talk to the people who live there. The whole thing looks set-up.

The male voice continues, the timber in his inflection increasing, and I can feel him coming to the end of his message. "And all this is brought to you by your government. Thank you for being loyal citizens of New America."

The lights flick on. The room fills with hisses and whispers, but there's one sound that shocks me: someone is clapping. My head whips around to find the source of it, and I'm not the only one. Everyone looks to see who could possibly be caught up in these lies. It's a middle-aged woman sitting two tables over from me, and her eyes glisten with tears and her face is alight with rapture. The agents descend on her, but carefully this time, with none of their trademark disgust. They gently lift her from her seat, and rest a hand on each arm as they lead her down the aisle toward the door. And good grief, are they actually *chatting* with her?

What was that? I mouth to Madge.

Madge's eyes have gone hard again. "Don't know. They show these little films just about every night, and every once in a while there's someone who buys into it. They're taken away, and we never see them again."

The door swings closed behind the woman and the cluster of agents. What in the world just happened here?

I turn back to my tray. I have no appetite for the mystery meal, not after the lies they've forced us to eat. But I'm not sure how much work I'll have to do tomorrow, so I make myself swallow the rest of my stroganoff. I'm actually not sure there will even be a tomorrow. The faces around me are mostly blank, like no one lives insides these shells of bodies. Only a few—Kai with her smile, Madge with the fire in her eyes—show any emotion. My cellmate is like the rest: empty. I suddenly wonder how long she's been here. If she had her hair shaved and now it falls half-way down her back, how long has she endured this?

After dinner we file back to our cells. My cellmate resumes her post on her bed, arms curled around her legs. I climb the bunk, lie down, cross my arms over my stomach, and stare at the ceiling. There's a long, jagged crack reaching from one corner almost to the window, like it's trying to escape. I follow it with my eyes to where it points out to the sky beyond. The last glimmers of sunset fade into violet black.

After several minutes, I hear the springs of the bunk creak as my cellmate lets go of her legs and slips beneath her brown blanket. I look over the edge. She hasn't taken her shoes off. Strange. That was the kind of thing Jack and I did in the wilderness so we could be up and running in a moment's notice. But here? What could she need to run from? And even if she could run, where would she go? She rolls away so she's facing the wall, and her blond hair spills out behind her and off the bed in limp waves.

It's dark outside, but the single bulb illuminating our room hasn't gone out yet. I roll onto my back and study the crack. I pull the red thread from my pocket and run it between my fingers. It is smooth and silky and softer than anything here. Softer than the concrete walls, the metal exam beds, the soldier's guns. Softer than the agents' eyes.

I let the thread fall to my lips, and it sends tingles down my arms. I briefly wonder if that's what it would feel like to kiss Jack. I roll over and force the thought from my head. Why would I think of something as ridiculous as kissing him? I spent the past few weeks hoping he wouldn't bring it up, wouldn't try. I've been stand-offish about it. I see his face and his hazel eyes and his lips.

For the love, Terra, focus on something else.

The blond hair hangs off the bunk below me. I decide my cellmate could be beautiful. I bet she was once too. When she could comb her hair, make it shine; when she could smile. I wonder when the last time was that she smiled. I hang my head over the side so I can see her better. Her back moves regularly with her breaths. She's already fallen asleep. Maybe the longer you've been here the easier sleep comes. And all that time, has she ever smiled? That will be my goal, the thing I want to accomplish here: to make her smile. I have nothing better to do.

My eyes flicker closed even though the room is still light, when music jerks me awake. It plays from the intercom in the corner of my room, and the echoes from the door tell me it plays in the hallway too. It's a triumphant, slow march that builds and swells. I recognize the melody Jack hummed in the cabin. It's supposed to inspire loyalty and patriotism. That's what Jack told me the anthem was originally about. But he was right. Whatever this stands for now, it just leaves me empty. I look over the bed again, but my cellmate hasn't even twitched. Maybe she tries to be asleep before the music starts.

As soon as the anthem is over, the light flicks out. The hall lights are still on, and they cast a ghostly glow into the middle of our cell.

I close my eyes, but as soon as I do, a horrible chorus starts. It begins as low whimpers and then builds to the screech of some monster birds of prey. The screams are in the cell next to ours, in the air, and down the halls. Are the screams what make people haunted, or do the screams come from the haunted? There are words in the pain, but they're so distorted I can't make them out. I grip the red thread tighter, like it's my only anchor to a world of sanity, to the world outside the chain-link fence, to a world of trees and rain water. The screams, cries, and moans that echo down the corridors, ripple through the concrete walls, finger their way into my ears shatter my calm.

I rub the scarlet thread between my fingers. I close my eyes and try to concentrate just on the smooth thread and the memories it holds: Jack in the cabin as we both scrounge up supplies. Jack.

It's not much, but it helps.

Still my cellmate sleeps. Maybe it wasn't the music she was trying to avoid. Maybe she tries to be asleep before this awful chorus starts.

SIX

The intercom crackles to life just as daylight creeps through the window and hazes across the wall above my head.

"Breakfast. Report to the mess hall in five minutes."

My cellmate is already standing and tucking her blanket around the edges of her mattress. Yesterday's clothes lie in a pile at the foot of her bed. I grab my extra set and change as quickly as I can. I should feel self-conscious stripping off all my clothes in front of her, but after the humiliation of detox, I don't know if anything could shame me. And honestly, I feel like I'm just about alone here anyway. My cellmate is almost a non-entity.

I rub my eyes. They feel like there's so much grit in them they'll never be clean again. I was able to fall asleep last night after the noise finally died away. The first hour after the lights switched off, though, were horrific. I heard every cry of pain imaginable: fear, heartbreak, loneliness, sickness, terror. I hid my head under the pillow to shut it all out. Then, one by one, the voices faded away. After the cacophony, the silence hung over me like a shroud. I wonder how in the world my cellmate slept. Maybe it's an acquired skill that comes through countless nights of enduring that noise.

I watch her put yesterday's clothes in a small metal chute by the door. They fall down, and I repeat the same procedure. I hope I'll get another set.

The door buzzes and then swings open, and we file down the hall. I join other women, herded along the corridors to the mess hall. The same lines form around the same food carts. The gelatinous beef stroganoff has been replaced by two rubbery pancakes (without syrup) and two dried-out sausages. I'm also given half an apple, another carton of milk, and a large water bottle.

Madge sidles up beside me. "To drink during the day. You know, because they care so much."

I follow her to the same table. Kai is already there. She's eaten all her pancakes and her apple. The sausages lay untouched on her tray. Without even thinking, I give her both my pancakes and take her sausages. Sure, the carbohydrates would probably do me some good, but she needs them more than I do. She squeezes my hand.

"Thank you."

I nod and take a drink of milk to wash one of the sausages down my throat.

"You'll get in trouble, you know." Madge cuts one of her pancakes into perfect squares. She doesn't even look at me, but I can feel that same sharp look she had in her eyes yesterday at dinner. Forget her butter knife—she could cut her pancakes with that look alone.

66

We must be having one of those "be careful what you talk about" conversations. I raise an eyebrow.

"We're not allowed to share food."

Why? I mouth.

"Afraid someone will get too strong? Afraid people will start fighting over it? I don't know. Doesn't matter. They just say we're not allowed to do it. They've enforced it before."

I frown and take a bite of apple.

"Hey, I'm not saying don't do it. I'm all for helping Kai out a bit. Just be careful." Madge flicks her eyes up to the observation booth and back down just as quickly. She has to be right about what she said yesterday—there's no way the watchers can pinpoint one conversation out of dozens, is there?

We don't say anything more, however, because two soldiers march right up to our table.

"Worker 7456."

I almost choke on the apple skin and nod, my eyes streaming tears. I glance over at Kai as she slips the last pancake under the table. They don't notice; they're too focused on me.

"You're requested for interrogation." They reach down and each grabs one of my arms, but I pull free and stand on my own. I still have a little dignity and they're not going to take it. I look at the remaining sausages and the milk on my tray. So much for breakfast.

My cellmate's eyebrows raise as I turn away, and it almost looks like she's worried. Then Madge does the last thing I expect: she reaches over and pats my cellmate's arm consolingly. Maybe my cellmate isn't quite the empty girl I thought she was.

Eyes watch me as I follow one soldier through the cafeteria door. The other follows behind, and we make a parade that terrifies me because I have no idea where we're going. I don't know what I'm to be interrogated about; I can't *tell* them anything. I also seriously doubt the interrogation is just about questions.

The soldier leads me down one gray corridor to another, and soon I'm so turned around that I have no idea how far into the building we are or how I'd ever find my way back. Then he abruptly stops before a windowless door and raps it with gloved knuckles three times.

The door opens and a cool, female voice speaks. "Enter."

The first soldier stands aside, and the one behind me prods me into the room. Then he leaves too, and I'm left in a brightly lit room with nothing more than an empty chair, a table, and two chairs occupied by an agent and Dr. Benedict.

Dr. Benedict smiles warmly at me. I can't bring myself to return the feeling, not with the agent—the same one who brought me to detox—sitting next to him with her arms folded and a scowl carved deep into her face. I stand and shift my weight to the other foot. Should I sit down? I don't want to get any closer to that woman than I have to, but after a moment, Dr. Benedict glances at the agent, bites his lip, and then gestures to the chair across from him. I sit.

The agent unfolds her arms and picks up a digital tablet. She taps the screen twice and then flicks her fingers over its smooth surface. Her eyes dart across the screen, and she raises her eyebrows.

"Terra?"

I'm not sure if she's talking to me or Dr. Benedict.

Dr. Benedict shrugs. "You know how I feel about names."

68

The agent rolls her eyes. "Stop taking your work so *personally*."

Dr. Benedict crosses his arms and looks away.

The agent purses her lips. "Worker 7456. You've been here almost twenty-four hours. Are your accommodations suitable?"

I nod. A little chilly maybe, but if I asked her to turn up the heat I doubt she would. She raises her eyes to see what my answer is. I study her hair. It's pulled back so tightly into a bun it raises her eyebrows at the ends, making her look angry all the time.

"Any conflict with your roommate?"

I shake my head. She wants to be a therapist too? I suspect she just doesn't want any fighting among the inmates—fewer people to work if there are injuries. All her terms almost make me laugh. Accommodations? Roommate? Next she'll be calling my ten-by-ten cell "guest quarters."

"Good. Now let's get down to the meat of the questions, shall we?" She leans forward and laces her fingers together. Her steely blue eyes bore into me, and I sit up and stare back. I won't be frightened, not now. I have to repeat it three times in my head. I won't be frightened. I won't be frightened. I won't be frightened.

"Tell me, Worker 7456, why have you never had a tracker?"

I swallow hard. The lies will start here, the lies that I promised I would never tell again in the settlement or to Jack. But lying to this woman with her severe bun and permanent scowl feels like a good deed. I motion to my mouth.

She purses her lips, and the expression cuts deep lines into her jaw. "I know about your tongue. Don't be condescending to me. I don't want you to forget for one moment that I know more about what's going on here than you do."

That's what you think, I tell myself as I fold my arms over my chest.

"Dr. Benedict?" The agent gestures to me.

Dr. Benedict stands and steps toward me with something that looks too much like a dog collar for my taste. I tense up and scoot back in my chair.

"It's okay, Terra."

The agent clears her throat when he says my name, but he ignores her.

"This will help you speak. It just goes around your neck, and it picks up the vibrations from your vocal chords and throat and transmits the data to a speaker just above the table." He points and, sure enough, a small black box hangs from the ceiling. "You won't sound like you, of course, but you can make words."

I'll be able to speak? I relax a fraction as he steps toward me again and wraps the collar around my neck, positioning a small lump just over my adam's apple. It scratches and presses uncomfortably against my throat, but he's being so gentle with me. His fingers brush over the thin skin of my throat, and his touch warms me. His careful hands remind me of Jack's. Unexpectedly my eyes are burning, and I can't help wondering where Jack is. Is he even still here?

"Worker 7456?" The agent's sharp voice cuts through, and I snap my head up.

How many times has she said it? Dr. Benedict looks at me like I've been lost for several minutes. I look at my hands.

70

"I said, why have you never had a tracker?" She sits with her fingers poised over the tablet, ready to make notations on every word I say.

I look at Dr. Benedict—the only thing resembling an ally I have here—and he nods slightly, encouraging me. Of course he'd want me to answer. He's with *them*, isn't he? But he's so different. Kind. I clear my throat, and the sound transmitted through the speaker comes out robotic and harsh. I glance up and take a deep breath.

"I was born in the wilderness." It isn't my voice. Dr. Benedict prepared me for this, though I wasn't quite ready for how inhuman I would sound. My voice has all the expression of a machine. Isn't that exactly what they'd like me to be?

The agent studies me, trying to divine the truth. "So your parents had trackers?"

I nod. I don't really want to hear that voice again.

"Say the words."

I look down at my hands. My fingernails are peeling from all the hot water in the cannery. "Yes, they had trackers."

"Did they have trackers when you were younger or had they cut them out?"

"As far back as I can remember, they had cut them out." There. Now there is no way for her to somehow search scanner records and find a way to track my fake parents down and figure out who I really am.

The agent smirks. "You know, I'm very good at reading lies, Worker 7456."

I swallow and do my best not to flinch away from her gaze. I need to be level; I need to stare unblinking back at her. The burning in my eyes worsens. I'm so used to being silent that I say nothing in return.

She stares at me a second longer and then looks down. "I see you had a flawless medical exam. Unusual."

Is it? My hands fall to my lap, and I pull at my pants. There's a nervous pit growing in my stomach, telling me there's more going on here than I'm aware of, hinted at by the way the agent looks at her tablet, stares at me, glances once at Dr. Benedict. He gives her a slight shake of the head. My brain can't quite put all the pieces together, but I know there's something very wrong.

The agent folds her hands under her chin, like she's trying to be coy. It's not a good look for her. "Anything else you want to tell me, *Terra*?"

I've never been so afraid of my own name before. I shake my head too readily, and I know I've given something away. I just wish I knew what it was.

"Hmm. Well, then. I guess we'll have to resume this discussion another day. You're due for more medical work with Dr. Benedict."

"But you said my exam was flawless." Forced silence hasn't gotten rid of my old habit of speaking before I think.

The agent's smile sets my teeth on edge. "Oh, it was. There's just more tests to run. Standard procedure."

Dr. Benedict shifts uncomfortably in his seat. I grip the edge of the table.

"Not to worry. These tests are mostly painless. A blood draw, that kind of thing. Right, doctor?" The agent turns to him with raised eyebrows. He looks down and nods.

"Well, then. You're both dismissed. Worker 7456, follow Dr. Benedict to the medical area."

She stands with a stamp of heels, and the door swings open for her. I hear the click, click, click of her shoes as she stalks down the hall. Dr. Benedict scrapes his chair away from the table.

"Follow me, please." He tries to say it with a professional tone, but I can tell he's as rattled as I am. Now I'm even more puzzled about him than I was before. He slides a hand through his dark hair and then hurries down the gray hall, like he's trying to escape from the interrogation room. Like he's as afraid of the agent as I am.

I rush to keep up with him, and I tug at the collar around my neck. It's scratching. He looks back and notices.

"It doesn't work here—there's no speaker to transmit to. But I've asked for one to be installed in the medical area, so you'll be able to speak to me there."

I grab his hand and stop us both in the middle of the hall. The windows lining the hall let in watery sunlight. Though they're wavy and warped, I can make out the grassy yard the truck pulled into yesterday. I think we're walking away from the women's wing toward the center of the building.

This isn't speaking.

"What do you mean?"

I sound like a robot.

His brows furrow. "But you can talk, right?" He really doesn't see it.

Makes me feel inhuman.

His eyes flash and then soften. "I'm sorry, Terra. If you'd like we don't have to use the collar. It'll make things slower, having to spell everything out. But if you'd rather not use the collar, you don't have to."

I nod and motion for him to take it off. He steps closer and reaches his arms around me. He smells like the woods and summer rain, and the smell reminds me of the months spent roaming with Jack. The smell I miss most is of Jack's warm body two feet from mine as we sleep beneath a canopy of trees. Dr. Benedict reminds me too much of Jack. As soon as he unfastens the collar, I pull away and put a good four feet of space between us.

"I'll hang on to it in case you change your mind."

I'll never want it again, but I smile for him. He seems to appreciate it.

Dr. Benedict leads me down a dark hallway with more flickering lights, and I dread what I will find in the medical area. He swipes a keycard in a keypad beside a door labeled "Medical Personnel Only," and when the door swings open, a flood of real, honest-to-goodness daylight spills out into the hall, and my fears wash away.

Inside is a small waiting area with a few chairs, an office set off by windowed partitions, and two exam rooms with open doors. A door between the exam rooms on the right and the office on the left stands open and all kinds of high-tech machinery loom in there. Every wall and every room has a window that lets in full, bright sunshine. The light warms me. We're on the second floor of the building, and I look out and see trees all around us. We must be on the back side of the building because I can't see the rest of the building or any of the yard below. All I can see are miles and miles of forest stretching into the horizon. With just a thin pane of glass between me and the wilderness, I feel almost free.

Suddenly Dr. Benedict is standing behind me, and I turn to face him. His dark, flat eyes stare out the window.

"Beautiful, isn't it?"

I nod. Does he have any idea I've lived in it for the past few months, that it was my home because it's where I was with Jack?

He coughs and turns away from the window to pull a digital tablet off his desk. "We'll try to keep this quick. I don't want to throw off your schedule too much. The agents like to keep you busy, and I make it a practice to stay out of the agents' way."

He puts his hand on the small of my back and guides me to the room with the machinery. I grab his hand.

What's all this?

"Just diagnostic equipment. I need to do a bone density scan. It's something I'm supposed to do with all the workers. If you've been living outside a designated city—which you have—your body may be malnourished. This will help me determine if I need to supplement your diet at all. Then after I'll just have to do a blood draw. Maybe an injection after that and we'll be done."

He says it with such unforced nonchalance that I'm put at ease. He sits me at a small table with a white machine on top of it. There's a space just the size and shape for a hand.

"You just put your hand in there, like putting on a glove. Then the machine will scan the bones in your hand, like an x-ray. It will show me how dense your bones are."

As I slide my hand into the machine, Dr. Benedict sits down across from me and presses a few buttons. The machine whirs to life, and I tense for a moment. Dr. Benedict touches my other hand so softly I barely feel the tips of his fingers.

"Don't worry. It doesn't hurt."

He presses one more button and a light shines out from the space where my hand is. Then it's over. The unease I felt ever since sitting down across from the agent fades as quickly as the light does. This can't tell them anything, can it? Maybe I'm just being paranoid.

Dr. Benedict smiles. "All done with that. Now if you'll just come over here."

He stands and leads me to a chair with a small tray attached to either side. We had similar chairs in the colony, perfect for propping up an arm, inserting a needle, and drawing blood. I sit down and offer my arm. Dr. Benedict wraps a length of rubber above my elbow and ties it off with a snap. I flinch.

"Sorry about that. I'm not good at that part." His tone is so guilty and vulnerable that I can't help smiling at him. I rest a hand on his and nod. *It's okay.* I think he understands without me even having to spell it out because he smiles back at me and takes a deep breath.

He places a small metal tray with a needle and four vials on the other arm of the chair. He removes the needle's protective cap. The sliver of metal glints in the light, and in my mind I see another needle: one that was meant not to take blood, but to take a life. I see two sleeping bodies in the dim room, their chests rising and falling in unison. I feel the summer heat from Dave's room, feel the sweat that beaded up on my forehead, feel the humidity like it was choking me. Mary's hair falls across her face, and her eyes twitch as she dreams. Her life would have allowed me to return to the ocean. Instead I chose to wander, and Jack chose it with me. I never regretted that decision, especially after Jack joined me. I had planned on going alone, finding my own place on the Burn, coming to grips with myself and

76

my choices. Then he followed me, and I never expected to be so grateful to someone in all my life. The sudden reminder stirs something in me. Do I regret that decision now that Jack's not with me anymore, now that I'm trapped here?

The memories catch in my throat and choke me, and I force myself to swallow them back down. I blink my eyes and look out the window where I'm separated from my freedom by a single pane of glass that seems such an insurmountable obstacle to cross. Do I regret it now?

"You'll feel a prick for just a second."

I watch the needle slide in. The first vial fills with blood. I haven't seen much blood since Jack healed my feet, since Smitty died, since the raiders were blown out of the water by the helicopter. The second vial fills with blood. I close my eyes. Blood brings too many memories with it.

"Are you feeling okay?"

I nod my head.

"Lightheaded, weak?"

I nod again.

"It's just the sight of blood."

You have no idea, I want to tell him. I've seen far too much of it.

"You'll be okay in a minute."

Do I regret it now?

Dr. Benedict pulls the needle out and puts a piece of gauze and some tape over the blood dot. "You're okay to stand?"

I stand without help. I need to get rid of this weakness. If this is where I am because of the choices I've made, I need to own up to it. I need to be stronger. He consults his tablet.

"Yes, I think we better do an injection. Just a one-time supplement to give you a quick boost."

I frown—the idea of being injected with some mystery serum nags at me—but I can't object. He's been kind to me. It's amazing what a little kindness will do.

Dr. Benedict turns to a small fridge with a glass door. Inside are rows of vials labeled with numbers. He strokes the tablet screen a few more times and frowns. He looks at me out of the corner of his eyes. His sudden uneasiness magnifies the nagging, but what can I say? I'm paranoid of another needle? I'm fully aware how powerless I am.

He rests a hand on the glass for just a moment and then opens the fridge and pulls out a small vial. He fills a syringe with the stuff and turns to me.

He smiles, and the dimple on his left cheek deepens. "Just one more needle."

I swallow and nod. The needle slips in, and the medicine burns as it's pumped through my veins. I wince.

"Sorry about that. I should have warned you."

I shake my head. It's nothing. It really isn't when I think about all the other types of pain I've faced. Dr. Benedict puts a bandage with ridiculous smiley faces over the injection site.

"Now you might feel a little funny after this."

I grab his hand. *Funny?*

"Headaches, nausea, dizziness, that sort of thing. If it gets really bad, tell an agent or one of the soldiers that you need to see me right away."

I almost laugh. Those are the side effects that just about anything can give you. He's probably obligated to tell me that. I'm ready to stand up again when Dr. Benedict steps closer. I smell trees and water again.

"I mean it, Terra. Please come see me if you need to."

My eyes focus on his. The plea I hear isn't "if you need to," it's "please come see me," and the way he's looking at me doesn't refute it. Could he be just as lonely as everyone else here? But the thought rattles me so much that all I can do is nod.

SEVEN

A soldier waits for me outside the medical area. As soon as I step through the door, he points with his gun and I follow him. I'm momentarily blind after leaving the bright daylight of the medical area and settle back into the flickering lights of the hallway. The soldier leads me down several corridors, and I smell steam, sweat, and over-cooked vegetables and know we're nearing the cannery.

He stops just outside the door and waits for me to go inside. As soon as I lose myself in the humidity, Madge squeezes my arm.

"You okay?"

I nod. I don't even know what time it is. With the concern on Madge's face, I'm guessing I've been gone for a while.

"I've been worried, Kai was worried, Jane was worried."

Jane? I ask.

"The girl you share a cell with?"

So that's her name. *She hadn't told me.*

Madge smiles and leads me toward the agent's desk. "No, I guess she wouldn't. Takes her a while to warm up." Madge laughs once, a little too loudly, and she glances up to the soldiers on the catwalk. She knows exactly where they are even though I haven't seen her watching them. "It should take me longer to warm up too, but I figure you'll either hurt me or you won't. You'll betray me or you won't. I might as well find out right off."

I hope I never betray her, even by accident. She's the first honest person I've come across here. Even Dr. Benedict with his kindness doesn't seem completely honest, and that worries me. I was so trusting in his care. Should I be more careful?

Madge drifts away as I approach the desk. I offer my arm, and the agent scans my tracker. "Worker 7456, follow me."

She leads me through the pots that bubble and steam straight to Lily's jam pot.

"We've had an opening here."

Of course. Who knows how long Lily will be in solitary confinement, and the government still needs its jam.

"The instructions are on this sheet." She points to a piece of paper in plastic tacked to the side of the huge heating element. "Follow these instructions exactly and there won't be any problems. Understood?"

I nod. She eyes me for a moment longer. I hate the way the agents do that—look down their noses like they're contemplating spraying you with bleach and wiping you away. I study her chin so she doesn't see the loathing in my eyes. The pores on her chin are big and she has several small blood vessels close to the surface. A sheen of sweat makes her shiny. Whenever I'd seen the agents before, they looked perfect. Perfectly made-up, perfectly coifed, perfectly dressed. But looking at her up-close gives me a different view. She's a person—a horrible, rotten person, maybe more of a machine emotionally—but a person nonetheless.

"Get to work." She turns and clicks away on the ubiquitous heels. Seriously, do they all have identical shoes?

I turn to the instruction sheet. "Measure 25 lbs of berries, mash in the pot, and bring to a boil with 1 box pectin."

I look around and see a huge box of blackberries. Next to it is a large silver scale, but there's nothing to put the berries in to move them to the scale. I remember Lily's purple hands. I dig into the box, gathering handful after handful of berries and moving them to the scale. I've seen the technology available here. Not quite as advanced as in the colony, but capable of making all this production automated. Yet they still want me to measure berries with my bare hands. Everything they do is designed to make me feel so beat down that I have no strength left for anything else. No strength for rebellion. That's what they're doing here. I don't know why it took me two days to realize it. I should have clued in during detox, one of the most humiliating experiences of my life. But why? What do they hope to gain from treating us this way?

I measure all the berries and then find a huge potato masher with a long handle. I squish it down into the berries again and again until streams of sweat trickle down my forehead. I swipe at it with the back of a hand and smear berry juice across my face. It wasn't this hot yesterday, but now I feel like the sweat pours out of me and my insides are starting to burn. It must be smashing the berries. Shucking the corn wasn't as strenuous.

82

I open a box of pectin. As I dump it in, I feel eyes on me, boring into my back, into my skull, into my hands as they study my work. I don't look up. I don't know if I'm being watched by soldiers or agents or both, and frankly, I don't care. I'm trying to do this so carefully because I know if I mess up, they'll pounce.

Next step: "Add 50 lbs of sugar." Here's where Lily stumbled. A mountain of sugar bags stands to the right of the pot. I reach for the top one, but it's at head level, and it's too heavy for me to heave off the top without smashing it into myself or dropping it on my feet. Instead I go for one at shoulder level, and I have to tug and pull until it inches free of the others. My arms are already aching by the time I heft it under one arm and bring it to the pot.

Why don't they have one of the men doing this job? Why are they making a girl of my size or a woman of Lily's age carry around fifty pound bags of *anything*? I wonder if they secretly (or not so secretly) want us to mess up. It goes along with what I've been realizing. They must get some twisted pleasure in punishing us. My mind rapid-fires through the images of a boot in a face, a boat blown out of the water, the way the agent watched as Lily was dragged away, like it was the best entertainment she'd seen in years. It makes me want to vomit.

I manage to open the bag and get it to the pot with only a few spilled granules—too small for the soldiers patrolling the catwalk to notice. The eyes are still on me, and I brush my shoes over the sugar, sweeping it under the heating element. The sugar falls into the pot with a soft shushing sound. I watch every granule, and it looks like snow: beautiful, sparkling, and sharp somehow. The sugar glistens as it disappears into the warming fruit, like snow melting. I don't realize my eyes have glazed over until I feel the empty bag compressing under my grip. How long have I been standing here with just a brown bag in my hands? I try to shake the fuzziness out of my head, but it clings. Maybe this is the beginning of one of those side-effect headaches Dr. Benedict warned me about.

Huge bubbles rise to the surface and pop with loud squelches. I stir the jam constantly—the instructions say five minutes, and I'll cook it to the second—bringing the enormous paddle around the side of the pot. I switch hands to give my right arm a rest when the intercom crackles on.

"All workers report to the yard."

All the cannery workers drop their utensils and file toward the doors. I can't just leave the jam, can I? Soldiers descend from the catwalk and follow behind, shepherding us toward the door. One sweeps by me and stops. I never noticed before, but his mask makes him look like a giant insect.

"Report to the yard," he barks.

I break my gaze from the bulbous insect eyes and gesture to the jam.

"Not my problem." He points toward the door with his gun.

I look back at the boiling fruit. I wasn't a success by any definition of the word when I tried food prep for a vocation, but I'm pretty sure the jam will be ruined if I leave it now.

"Get moving, worker!" The insect has a stinger and it jabs the hard tip into my ribs.

I wince and clutch my side. I turn off the heating element. I want nothing more than to glare at the insect, but that will just get me in trouble and my eyes are tearing from the pain in my side, so I glare at the floor instead.

84

I slowly make my way down the halls with all the other women. I've never seen so many of us in the halls at once, and I'm lost amidst the blank eyes, limp hair, and identical uniforms. I look for anyone familiar—Kai's dark hair, Madge's red curls, even Jane's stringy blond locks. No one. I'm adrift in an ocean of hopelessness.

As we filter down the hall, the flickering lights put off too much heat and I'm sweating again. Where did I put my water bottle? I must have left it in the cannery. My mouth is so dry my tongue stump feels swollen, and I roll it around to get some saliva moving. I lift the neck of my shirt up to wipe the sweat from my eyes. None of the insect soldiers are nearby, so I rest my hand on the cool wall for just a moment.

As I watch the women in front of me, suddenly their heads change and elongate. Horns rise up out of their hair, and the mooing starts at my left, but then circles around behind me and to my right, then gallops down the hall in front of me, and I'm in a cattle chute, surrounded by stamping bovine.

I shake my head, trying to erase the image. When I open my eyes, willing myself to see the other women, the cows are still there—a rainbow of colors this time, not just browns and blacks and whites—and one of the insects is charging up to me with his stinger brandished.

I cower against the wall. I try to push down the panic rising in my throat, but I don't want to be trampled in such a narrow space, and I don't want to be stung again. Then the insect surprises me. It doesn't sting me but grabs me by one arm and hauls me upright. It yanks me down the hall toward a light so bright I have to cover my eyes. I'm drenched in sweat, and I feel like I'm going to fly right into the center of the sun.

It drags me outside, and my eyelids flutter as I try to assemble the pictures in front of me. The mooing has quieted, and over there the cows are mutating back into women. The sunlight burns down on us like it's much too close. A huge fence separates the yard in two, women on one side and men on the other. Focus, Terra. Knowing where the men are means something, but what? I rub my eyes. Men. Jack.

I strain against the insect's grip on my arm. The insect. If the cows have become women again, is the insect still ready to sting me? I look at it, and the shiny bulbous eyes melt back into the black mask, and all that's pointed at me is a gun. It's amazing how harmless it looks compared to a mutant scorpion's stinger.

What is wrong with me? I rub my eyes, trying to make all the white spots floating in my vision disappear. I blink as my eyes fill with tears from the bright sun. What was I even thinking about before I watched the insect turn back into a soldier? And why am I so calm about what I saw?

I look at the fence and see a familiar halo of brown hair, familiar hazel eyes. Jack stands maybe thirty feet from me. He's so close I feel like I could just reach out and touch him, but the soldier's clamp above my elbow won't let me move.

"Hold still, worker. There'll be an announcement, and then you need to see the doctor."

Dr. Benedict? Why would I need to see him?

A hush falls over the crowded yard as an agent—the same agent who captured me and Jack in the woods—stands at a microphone. He's trying to keep his face solemn, but there's an annoying smirk playing with his lips. He's sucking on another one of those mint candies. I squint at him. He looks taller than the last time I saw him.

86

"Workers, I have some important information to share with you. We've received word from the capital that some of the inoculations you've received may have been contaminated."

I expect a whisper to ripple through the crowd or some kind of reaction, but there's nothing, almost as if the workers expect this. The agent gloats over us.

"Not to worry—there wasn't a large percentage of you given this particular lot number. But I would like any of you who received an injection over the past three days to report to Dr. Benedict. If you do not report to the doctor immediately following this assembly, you will be punished for disobedience."

There it is again—the desire to see us fail and to punish us.

"The symptoms of this contaminated inoculation are fever, dizziness, and hallucinations. Dismissed."

Women turning into cows? Soldiers with scorpion stingers? I've been hallucinating like it's going out of style.

"That's you, right?" the soldier says.

I nod dumbly. Dr. Benedict mentioned side effects from the injection, but nothing like this.

"Figured. Report to the doctor, understand?"

I nod again. The soldier steps away from me, back to the door where he lines up with a few others. They're getting ready to herd us all back inside. This is what we came out here for? Just to hear this short announcement? Why couldn't they say it over the intercom?

Then I realize how hard it will be to leave the sunlight on my skin and the blue sky. It's too cold to stay out for long—I already have goosebumps. After flickering lights and just the windows in Dr. Benedict's office with their offering of indoor sunshine, I don't want to go back inside. They torture us out here too.

I turn to the door and Madge is beside me.

"You feeling okay?"

I shake my head.

"You got one of those shots?"

I nod. Did I ever. It's hitting me again as I look at Madge's green eyes, and the irises start to coil like snakes. "Be careful. There's something funny with them. They make these announcements almost every other week. Seems like the capital could manage to make some shots that weren't contaminated. I had a few when I first got here. I screamed for days. They didn't give me another after that." Madge takes quick inventory of which soldiers are where, how far away the agents are. It's a skill she's perfected.

She leans in to me, and her snake eyes hiss at me, ready to strike. I want to stay as far away from her as possible, but I need to hear her. I tilt my head closer, trying to avoid the snakes. "I don't think they're inoculations at all. Not with the way they make people crazy and all the announcements after."

But if they're not vaccinations or nutritional supplements or whatever, what else could they be? I step away and I'm caught in the current of women going back into building. I only have enough time to turn back and see Jack at the fence. He sees me and he smiles. I'm relieved he doesn't distort into something vile. Instead his whole face lights up like a summer afternoon. He's as glad to see me as I am to see him. I wave once. I don't want to risk more than that. I suspect personal relationships are one more way the government can cause you pain.

88

It's enough, though. The look on his face as he turns his hazel eyes from me and walks toward the men's building shoots a burst of energy from the top of my head to the bottom of my feet.

Now I have to go see Dr. Benedict. Again.

There's a line of about twenty of us waiting to see Dr. Benedict. We stand single-file in the hall. No one talks. There's a soldier—mercifully without insect eyes and a scorpion's sting—on the opposite wall, watching us intently (or what I assume to be intently; you never know with those black masks), and no one says a word under his surveillance.

One by one the women file in. As they come out, they all have a new bandage on their arms. More shots? One contaminated injection wasn't enough? I'm going to feel like a human pin cushion if this keeps up.

Finally I'm next, and a nurse comes to the door. She scans my tracker, jots something on her tablet, and then beckons me to follow her in. She takes me to an exam room where Dr. Benedict waits. He's wearing latex gloves and already has a syringe in hand.

"You're starting to be a permanent fixture around here," Dr. Benedict says, holding a hand to me to help me onto the exam table.

I try to smile, but he sees the anger behind it. His laughing demeanor fades away, his dimple disappears, and he lowers his hand. I tell myself this is the government's fault. Dr. Benedict couldn't have known the medicine was tainted, but still he was the one who gave it to me. He sees the mistrust in my eyes and sighs. He nods to the nurse, and she leaves, closing the door.

"I'm sorry, Terra. Really I am. But just like you, I have to follow orders." He sets the syringe down on a tray and pulls back the sleeve of his lab coat. Fine dark hairs rise on the skin over a tracker lump.

"We all have them, even the agents. We're all scanned and given orders. I know it looks bad because I'm the one you're dealing with face-to-face." He steps toward me and touches my arm, and his fingers glide over my own tracker. The site is still sore and I wince, but he doesn't take his hand off my arm. I look at his black eyes, and for once they show emotion. Unfortunately, I don't have enough experience reading him, and I have no idea what his eyes tell me. His hand lingers, and his thumb traces an arc on the inside of my arm, and I can't help when I shiver under his touch. He smiles.

"We all have to do things we don't want to. This included." He reaches for the syringe again. His hand is slipping from my arm to take the cap off the needle when I grab his.

I shake my head. *No more nightmares.*

"You hallucinated?" His eyebrows arch, and the concern is gone and he's all professional. He grabs his tablet and starts typing. "What did you see?"

I look at the floor.

"Bad things? Terra, anything you tell me helps. There might be others who can benefit from what you tell me."

I know there are others. I heard their cries all night long. I grab his hand again.

The soldiers were scorpions. We were all cattle in a cattle chute.

Dr. Benedict rubs his chin and then types. "Thank you for telling me, Terra. I don't think the agents realize how important it is to provide the best care to all our citizens. Too often I feel like they don't listen."

He does genuinely seem like he wants to help, but as I study his face, his skin turns pallid. His black eyes flash at me and then swirl. His smile—meant to comfort a moment before— now arches up to an obscene angle, and his teeth elongate. He's a monster. I shrink back from him and hug my knees to my chest.

"Another hallucination?"

My hands tremble as he steps closer to me. The sweat breaks out on my forehead again, and I don't want him to touch me. I don't want that *thing* anywhere near me. I shove his arm away.

The monster grabs the syringe and it looks tiny in his hand. He pulls the cap from the needle with his huge teeth. I want to kick him and run away, but the thought of putting one of my limbs anywhere near him sickens me even more. I've shoved myself up against the wall as far as I can; there's nowhere else to go.

Then a sharp prick focuses my thoughts, and his monster face slips back into his normal concern. The long teeth are gone, his eyes black, his skin golden. He pulls the needle from my arm and slips on another stupid smiley face bandage. Now I have a matching set.

"I'm sorry," he murmurs. Then he reaches up and strokes my cheek. I might have let myself lean in to the touch if I hadn't just seen him as something inhuman. He sees the disgust written on my face. He clears his throat and steps back.

"That's all, Terra. This new batch should be better."

It better be. I slide off the table, and the nurse escorts me out of the medical area.

EIGHT

Dinner is subdued. No one wants to talk about the assembly or about those who had to go to the medical area. I push dry bits of chicken around my plate. Kai shakes her head when I offer her my applesauce.

"The chicken's the worst. No one wants to eat it. You need that for yourself," she says. I put the plastic cup on her tray anyway.

Even Madge doesn't have anything to say tonight. Her eyes are fiery. The anger she usually keeps so well in check bubbles over, and she doesn't dare say anything for fear of not seeing a soldier in time. Jane scoots closer to me until our arms brush. This startles me more than anything. I don't know what changed, but she feels the need to comfort me even if she won't say a word.

I am feeling better from the second shot, though I'm not sure if I feel this way from the new serum or from being able to see Jack if only for a moment. My anger starts to burn then, just like

Madge's. I can't help but wonder—and I'm sure it's the same thought she's working through—if the government doesn't give us contaminated shots on purpose.

I wish I knew more about medicine. I don't know enough to puzzle through this, to even understand if they did do it on purpose, why they would. I need to talk to Jack. I need to talk about the serums, but also about so much more. We have so many unfinished conversations, and they've been nagging at me. The glance this afternoon wasn't enough.

I get Madge's attention and point out the doors. *Do we have time outside?*

"Once a week." Her voice comes out in a hoarse whisper. None of us have talked much since the assembly.

When?

"Chicken jerky tonight means yard time in two days. Guess that's the good thing about a meal schedule. It's something to base your days around."

Do the men come out too?

"We overlap by five minutes."

Five minutes. Such a short amount of time, but I'll take it.

Madge is so lost in thought she doesn't question why I'm asking. Kai's eyes shift between Madge and me, but the mood hanging over us like a thundercloud can't dampen her spirits for long. She smiles and puts a hand to her belly.

"The baby kicked."

I have to smile too. She takes my hand and guides it to her side. Underneath my fingers, I feel a nudge that rolls across her skin and away from me. I grin at her.

Boy or girl?

She shrugs. "I don't know. They didn't tell me."

This starts to ignite the anger again, but she smiles, and her smile is so blissfully content as she puts a hand on her belly that I have to sit back.

"As long as it's healthy, I don't care."

I'm expecting another movie tonight, but the intercom crackles on instead.

"We have located another reclamation site. Those of you working in the cannery, instead of your normal work assignments tomorrow, you will report to the yard and be bused to the reclamation site. You will receive further instructions there." Then the scratchy voice is silent.

Madge shrugs. "Guess we're going on a field trip. Anything better than being in here for a day."

Reclamation?

"They must've found a small town or farm or something that hasn't been picked over. We'll go out and pick it over." She smiles at me. "They make us be the vultures instead of them."

The next morning, soldiers line the hall every twenty feet as we file from the mess hall toward the yard. I have a pounding headache, and even the pale fluorescent lights make me squint. I didn't have any more hallucinations after the second injection Dr. Benedict gave me, but I'm not sure which is worse: seeing things that aren't there or waiting for my head to split open.

I lay in bed last night and couldn't even bring myself to put my pillow over my head once the anthem started. The percussion throbbed into my ears, and then the lights went out and the screams started. All I could do was clench my fists around my blanket and squeeze my eyes closed as tightly as

94

possible. Jane didn't move (again), and I wondered how long it took her to get used to the cacophony all around us. That might just be the thing that breaks the silence between us. *So, how long until I can actually sleep through the screams? Do you just have a major build-up of ear wax?*

So today I'm exhausted and feel like pounding my head against a wall, but falling asleep and bludgeoning myself aren't options, so I do my best to follow Jane down the hallway. If I look only at her head, the lights and noise don't seem quite so bad. She walks with her shoulders hunched, her head down, her arms wrapped around her middle like she's trying to hold herself together. She looks like the most pathetic thing I've ever seen, but the soldiers leave her alone. Hardly anyone notices her.

When the doors yawn open to the outside, I'm thankful that the sky is overcast. I long for another clear day like yesterday, but I don't think my headache could handle sunlight. One bus waits for us in the yard, spewing dark exhaust into the air. The bus is painted the same mustard yellow as our shirts. The engine sputters and chokes and then resumes roaring at us. A soldier sits behind the wheel and his mask is turned toward us. A few more soldiers board the bus, and then an agent steps beside the door, scanner in hand.

We line up and she scans each of our arms as we make our way onto the bus. Jane slides into a seat, and I sit next to her. Her eyes rest on mine for just a second, and I catch the faintest glimpse of more than the beat-down girl she always shows me. Then she turns to look out the window, and the glimpse is gone as soon as it began.

Madge sits across the aisle from us and grins maniacally. I guess she was serious about the field trip. I just don't know how she thinks it'll be a grand time out when there'll be soldiers and agents breathing down our necks. She runs her fingers through her hair, and the curls pouf out into a frizzy torrent of red.

"I've been waiting for another reclamation site for months." She grips the back of the seat in front of her and sits up as the bus chugs us out of the yard and beyond the fence onto the dirt road.

Simple pleasures.

We drive east. We wind on bumpy roads through the forest, and all I can see on either side is green and more green. The trees threaten to take over the road at some points, and the bus squeals between branches and grumbles over tree roots. My stomach lurches, and Jane leans further away from me. Just when I think I'm about to see my breakfast again, the trees open up and a small town appears.

It's nothing more than a handful of houses, a grocery store, and a school. It looks immaculately preserved, though, like the time between the Event and now never even occurred—like the gas station where I made bread for Jack. It's amazing the way some places are just skipped over as if they exist on a completely different plane. I'm astonished nomads or the government haven't found this place before.

As I step off the bus and into the gray, cloudy light, everything has a magical quality to it. I've never seen anything so untouched before: the windows are covered in grime, but they're intact. There are toys still out in the yards where children abandoned them ages ago. Granted the trikes are mostly rust and look like they'd crumble under my hand and the balls are all limp and deflated, but the sense of people having lived here is tangible. It looks like they all just went for a picnic together and they'll be back at any moment. They must have left quickly to leave it like this.

Down the street there's a truck. A ramp leads down from the back, and the inside is lined with empty shelves and boxes. I'm guessing we'll be loading what we find in there.

We stand in a line in front of the bus. The agent peers over us with small, brown eyes.

"You'll proceed through the town and collect anything that seems useful. You may go in twos or threes, but no groups larger than that. If you get too noisy or too spread out, the soldiers have orders to corral you back together and keep you under control."

The soldier standing next to her flexes his hands, and I shudder. What means do they employ to keep us under control?

"If any of you try to run, you will be shot without warning," she says while looking at a digital tablet. She doesn't even bother to look in our eyes. "You have four hours until it is time to load back on the bus." Then she turns on her heel and walks away, typing into her tablet. She finds a front porch, brushes it off with her hand, and sits down.

Madge leans in. "You, me, and Jane. Come on."

We follow her. She has a knack for this, either that or she's done this plenty of times before because she leads us to a house, opens the door (it isn't locked), and parades us through. I'm kind of weirded out because it's someone's home; someone used to live here, and we're just going through it like we own the place.

"Blinds are good. The agents think they're useful, the strings and slats and stuff. Let's start on those."

We were given screwdrivers. They're short, squatty things with barely enough handle to grip; the agents probably thought longer, more useful ones would be too weapon-like. It takes us a while to simply unscrew the blinds with the ridiculous tools, but we work our way through the house, making match-stick piles of blinds.

I watch Jane and even with the stubby screwdriver, her slender fingers move deftly, and she takes down blinds faster than even Madge. It's like with the corn-shucking in the cannery. Her hands fly over the task. While she's working, she almost looks confident. Well, as confident as Jane can look. She sees me watching her, and I expect her head to bob down, but it doesn't. She studies me appraisingly. I want to look away, return her privacy, but I don't. I look her straight in the eye and offer her a smile.

For just a second the right corner of her mouth twitches like it might just turn up. But then she turns back to the blinds she was working on.

"Life must have been pretty good before the war," Madge says, carrying an armful of blinds down the stairs and adding it to our pile. "Look at this place. Blinds to keep out prying eyes, a comfy sofa to sit on, plenty of food in the cupboard. Yeah, most of the cans have exploded, but can you imagine just walking into a kitchen and having all the shelves stocked?"

I'm suddenly very busy with a stubborn screw. This does seem like a decent place; the town could have been idyllic. But still there were people who left and built colonies on the bottom of the ocean—the very colonies I was born into. No wonder so many people on the Burn hate the idea of colonists. Sure they don't know for sure if the colonies even exist, but just the idea of anyone turning tail and running for cover while everyone else gets blown up raises my hackles.

"I wonder if there'll ever be anywhere nice ever again," Madge whispers, studying the blinds.

She's so full of hate and sadness right now that I have no idea what to say to her. Jane stands up and puts a hand on her arm. Madge tries to smile at her, but her expression twists into something ugly.

"Do you ever think they're real, Terra?"

I drag my eyes from the blinds. *What?* I mouth.

"The colonies?"

I shake my head. She must see how white I've gone. Every last ounce of color drains from me. This is the last thing I want to talk about, especially since Jack doesn't even know yet.

"Sometimes I wish they were. Just to know there's something a little better out there."

Then Jane speaks. "I hate them."

It's the first thing I've ever heard Jane say, and the sound of her voice—small and bird-like—startles me so much that I drop my screwdriver.

Madge guffaws. "Leave it to Jane to get right to the point." Madge squeezes her shoulder. "I couldn't agree with you more."

I expect Jane to say more, but her mouth clamps closed and she returns her fluttering hands to the blinds.

It's not that I don't understand how they feel, but to hear them say that, to hear the way Mary told me that Dave hates colonists, feels like a punch in the gut. I want to tell them that we're not all cowards and not all of us had a choice. But why in the world am I defending them? Didn't I want to run as fast as I could out of there? I think of Jessa and Brant and the genuinely good people there, and I know it's not always black and white the way I imagined it to be while I still lived there. Nothing ever is.

We've retrieved all the blinds from the house, so we each take an armful and carry them down the porch and to the truck. I grapple with mine, the blinds and cords slipping and swimming in my arms, but finally manage to dump them in a pile. There are three women at the truck sorting and boxing and piling, and they take the blinds off our hands and start loading them.

I look around and realize Kai's not here. I've never seen her in the cannery either.

Where's Kai? I ask Madge.

She pulls away and blows warm air into her hands. They're red and chapped from all the cannery work, and being out in the cold doesn't help.

"Since she's pregnant, the agents gave her special work hours. She works in the commissary—the staff's kitchen. You know, feeding the agents and soldiers all that jam and the other delicacies we'll never see."

I nod, glad the subject is off the colonies. Or so I think.

"Hey, Jane. Do you think they have jam in the colonies?"

Jane has assumed her hunched shoulders and drooping head now that we're out in the open again, but her eyes flick to Madge. They say *yes*.

I want to crawl under a rock.

We spend a few more hours finding small kitchen electrics: toasters, griddles, mixers—anything with heating elements or

100

gears—and bringing them back to the truck. Then the soldiers start rounding us up, and we file back to the bus.

Just as the agent scans my arm and I get ready to step up, a soldier leans to her and whispers, "A settlement was taken up north by the Sound. We'll have new workers tomorrow."

My foot freezes on the step and my muscles refuse to move. No, no, no, is all I can think. Please don't let it be the school. My eyes clench closed as I see the settlement in the afternoon summer sun: the bees buzzing lazily over the strawberry fields, Red in the kitchen helping with meals, Nell combing through my hair with her fingers, Dave's mischievous eyes sparkling, Mary leaning against one of the old trees out back, rolling bandages.

Please don't let it be them.

I get a sharp jab in the back from a soldier's gun. "Move, worker."

The pain pulls me from my paralysis, and I force my feet up the steps and into the aisle. I shake my head, trying to shake the memories loose, trying to convince myself that no, it couldn't be them.

I can't convince myself.

NINE

Jane leads the way back to our cell after dinner. As soon as we cross the threshold, she sits on the bottom bunk, her arms wrapped around her legs in the all-too-familiar posture. She looks like she has something to say, but then she bows her head and her hair forms a lank, yellow wall between us. I lean against the opposite wall, studying her. She's carefully not looking at me: looking at the toilet, the sink, the door, the light flickering from the ceiling, the window with its fading sunlight. It must face west. I feel the sudden need to see out the window. After spending the hours in the reclamation town under the heaviness of gray clouds, I leaned my head toward the bus window when the sun finally came out on the way back to the camp. I can't get enough of the outside. I miss waking up with dew on my sleeping bag and the green of pine needles hovering around me. I miss the sweet, rotten smell of decaying leaves stirred up under my feet. I even miss the smell of the government rations

Jack and I ate in the woods; I miss it because we *could* eat it in the woods.

The window is too high to stand on tiptoe to reach. The bunk is high enough, but I'd have to move it. I stand straight and wipe my palms on my pants. I need to tell Jane my plan so I don't frighten her. I've never even spoken to her so I'll probably scare her to death anyway, though I'm not sure how to reconcile her weak self with the confident, angry girl she became for just a moment today when she declared she hated colonists.

I tap her on the shoulder. Her head jerks up and her eyes are wide, the blue irises completely surrounded by white. I'm afraid if I touch her to spell my words she'll completely freak out on me. Instead, I point to the bed next to her and write the words there.

Jane?

She nods, understanding, but her eyes still look like a hunted animal's.

I point to myself. *Terra.*

She nods again and relaxes a fraction. She tucks her hair behind her ears like she's tearing down the wall between us. I venture a smile, but she doesn't look me in the eye now that I'm so close.

Move our bunk?

She looks away from my invisible words to my face, and she studies me. I try to appear calm, neutral, kind. I'm trembling, though; the same kind of nervous tremble I had outside the settlement for the first time when all I wanted was for them to accept me.

She mouths a single word. *Why?*

She *is* a ghost. Pale, waifish, and silent. Even now that our defenses are down, she doesn't speak to me.

To see. Do you know what's out there?

She shakes her head.

Find out. Help me?

She nods and unfolds herself. We both lean against the bunk, but it budges only a mere inch. It's much heavier than it looks. Jane shrugs. I hold up one finger. One more time. Then I mouth to her, *One, two, three.* We heave against the bunk and, together, we push it. It screeches across the linoleum and we freeze, listening for the soldiers' footsteps, sure they'll come running to investigate the noise. We stand that way for five minutes, and I feel ridiculous propped against the metal of the bunk, frozen like some child with her hand caught in the cookie jar. Honestly, shouldn't we be able to put our bunk wherever we want to? If they come, they come.

I count again and we push the bunk, leaving white gouges in the floor. By the time the bunk bumps up against the wall under the window, we're both panting and sweating. Jane gives me a goofy smile expanded by adrenaline and accomplishment. She has yellowed, crooked teeth underneath her thin lips, but her smile is the most beautiful thing I've seen since I got here. She feels like we got away with something too, and I can't help smiling back.

I climb up the bunk and crawl to the window. Our window does face west. There's a thick line of trees, mostly evergreens with deep green, pointed tops. They cut a jagged line into the horizon. I look beyond them and discover I'm holding my breath. The sun is setting, sending yellow-orange light skittering across the clouds in a rainbow of colors, and then the light bounces off the thin ribbon of water in the distance.

The ocean.

I wave Jane up, and she climbs beside me. She looks out and her smile deepens. I lean against the wall, and she surprises me by grabbing my hand. I squeeze hers gently, and together we watch the sun set. It disappears beyond the water and trees, but I can watch it again tomorrow. They can't take the sun from us.

Jane jumps when the anthem begins to play. She's usually asleep for this part.

Tonight I don't think about the government or the agents or the soldiers. The anthem playing is somehow suited to the majesty before me. I watch the violet haze creep over the building and toward the horizon. Soon the sparkling water is nothing more than a dark line between trees and sky. I reach and put my palm flat against the glass. It's cold and covered in a film of condensation. I pull my hand away, tuck it under my blanket to warm, and study the outside world through the shape of my hand print left there.

When the sky is completely black and the lights have gone out for the night, before the screams and moans begin, Jane's head droops and she falls asleep on my shoulder. Her thin frame is hardly a whisper leaning against me. Her breathing deepens. I'm awake, though, straining my eyes for the horizon.

I'm *this close* to the water. The spark I felt three days ago riding in the cattle truck to the labor camp returns. I'd forgotten it until this moment. If the ocean is only beyond that line of trees—maybe two miles at the most—how hard would it be to get a small group of people there and into a sub?

Gaea watches me; I know she does. I can picture her in her small cave of a room, the dozens of computer monitors all trained on the views of other satellites. I roll the stump of my tongue inside my mouth, close my eyes, and find I still have tears for that woman. Mother. I thought I had matured, moved past it, or whatever psych term my therapist in the colony would have used. Repressed it, more like. But I haven't; she still haunts me. The mother I should have known, but she was too afraid to face her problems and she ran. I can see that about her now. I feel a strange mixture of anger, sympathy, and pity, and I'm not sure which one wins out. I have every right to hate her, but I can't bring myself to do it. She acted so self-assured those few minutes with me before I left for the Burn. Now I think it was a mask. She ran from the colony, but wasn't courageous enough to run all the way to the surface. She hunches over those computers, drinking in the pictures she'll never be brave enough to see for herself. It's sad, really.

Does she watch me closely enough that I could send her a message? Could I tell her I need a sub—for how many? Five, six? Ten?—and would we be able to time it exactly right?

All of this would depend on escaping the camp. My gut clenches. I stare out the window at the guard towers. All but one is empty. In that one, in the northwest corner, there's a single soldier. The flare of a cigarette illuminates the dark silhouette. But there's no one patrolling the yard, no searchlights. Just the huge fence and the curls of barbed wire.

Do they really believe we're all so broken that no one would dare escape?

My heart leaps in my chest. Yes, yes they do. The steely glint in Madge's eyes tells me that. The soldiers and the agents never

106

see that, but she's shown it to me. How many others have that same fire they don't readily share with everyone? I'm hoping it's more than they can guess. If so, this could possibly work.

The first moan starts—low and throaty, and then it grows and becomes a wail. I've only spent two nights here, but I'm already starting to be able to ignore the awful noises now. Jane nuzzles into my shoulder, and I pull my blanket up over her. She's too frail. She would be the first one I get out of this place. Her and Kai. I frown. With her growing belly, would Kai be able to make the two-mile run to shore?

Jane's hand eases away from mine as she falls deeper into sleep, and I finally close my eyes. I won't put all the pieces of the puzzle together tonight. Tomorrow, though. I'll be out in the yard. I'll send the message to Gaea. For the first time, I feel like there's not just hope for me, but hope for the hollow people here. The colony couldn't hold me, but I'm willing to bet it has enough kindness in it to fill these people back up again.

TEN

I've picked up Madge's habit—as soon as I sit down, I look for the soldiers. One is by the cafeteria door; the other is by the food line. A quick glance tells me the agents are watching a hushed conversation a few tables away. I slide my canned peaches onto Kai's tray. She gives me her limp bacon in return.

Jane sits closer to us now, and she looks at me and almost smiles.

Madge nudges me. "Don't know what you did, but she's never been so down-right friendly."

I grin. Small victories.

I don't tell Madge about my plans yet. It's such a big announcement. Do I just lean over and write *I'm a colonist* on her hand? Follow it up with *I'm going to break us out and take you there*? I wonder when we can discuss it without all these watchful eyes. I'll need Madge's help; I'll need Jane's help. They've both been here far longer than I have, and they can tell me if my suspicions are right about how heavily guarded the camp is.

This is not a conversation for the mess hall, with the roaming soldiers and the hovering agents. But soon. It has to be soon. Kai tells me she's now thirty-three weeks pregnant and she says she has seven more weeks to go.

Time is running out.

Maybe in the yard today. There's no way they can monitor us closely enough to hear our traitorous words.

The mess hall doors fly open, and silence hangs over us. Two soldiers flank three new inmates. My fork falls onto my tray with a clatter that echoes in the hushed room. I ignore the eyes that fly to mine—eyes accusing me of breaking the silence and drawing attention to us—and I can't look away. I can't look anywhere else but at *her*.

Mary stands between the soldiers.

Her black hair has been buzzed, and her eyes flash defiance as she takes us all in. Then her gaze settles on mine—it's the only place for her to focus with all the other inmates staring at their trays—and her eyebrows shoot up, and the defiance softens into something I can't place. Almost sympathy or sorrow.

Then my eyes water because I know what it means. The conversation I heard at the reclamation site yesterday was about *my* settlement. How many others are here now?

The soldiers step away, leaving the three inmates looking like lost puppies. Mary shakes loose of them and threads her way between the tables toward me. Conversation resumes, and Mary is forgotten—just another prisoner in our midst. Nothing to bat an eye at. Though Madge hasn't forgotten, and she watches Mary stride toward me. Madge's eyes are too sharp, and I know she's wondering what it means.

Mary doesn't sit with me quite yet. She sidesteps the table and attempts to go through the food line, but the agent with the scanner just frowns at her. Eating will have to wait until dinner. Then Mary returns to me, clasping her hands together on the table and staring at nothing but her freshly sanitized fingernails. Her skin is still red from detox, and she has a length of gauze wrapped around the inside of her elbow. She's had a blood draw; I only hope she hasn't had an injection. Then I notice the tracker lump right next to the twisted scar from the one that was cut out. I remember her nightmares from Seattle, the way her "family" terrified her into submission and cut out her tracker. I wonder if she thought of them every second during her visit with Dr. Benedict.

I inch my tray toward her, offering my fork, but she shakes her head.

She finally looks at me. "How did you get here, Terra?"

I almost gasp with what I see in her eyes. They're filled with such churning emotions. She looks vulnerable for the first time that I've known her. I reach for her hand.

Rounded up. Looking for nomads.

She laughs, and the sound is humorless. "Probably a big change from what you're used to?"

She's referring to the colony, and a few months ago I might have thought the comment was meant to sting. But her eyes betray her.

Yes.

"Jack?"

They found us both.

She nods. "I was at the settlement. They found us."

I drop her hand. Please no. *Everyone?*

110

Mary closes her eyes and a tear slides out. She shakes her head. "Not everyone. Red and Nell got out. Sam, I think. A few others."

Dave?

Her eyes harden, erasing all the soft edges. "He's here too. They took us at the same time, loading us into that awful truck."

She looks down at her fingers again. I notice a thin, pale line around the fourth finger of her left hand. She rubs it absently as she looks out the window. I tentatively place a hand on hers— she who both ruined my life and set me free at the same time— and she gives me a rare smile. But her smile is so twisted with anger and sorrow that I blink and look down.

"We were married last month."

I see that pale line on her finger for what it is.

"Behind the settlement, underneath those two huge trees. It's not legal or binding in any technical sense, of course—Red officiated—but we're still married. We still have that commit- ment to each other. I still would do anything—" She can't finish the sentence before the tears well up in earnest, and though she fights them, they fall out and splash the table. She rubs the shiny streak off her cheek with the heel of her hand. "They took my ring when they took us. It wasn't even valuable. Just a nail Dave managed to make into a circle."

I sit back. They would take her wedding ring? It infuriates me, sending heat coursing through my veins as though all my blood has drained away and nothing but anger pumps through my heart.

Mary notices and nods. "The union wasn't legal, wasn't sanctioned by the government, wasn't documented. So they took the only token I had of it." Her jaw clenches, the small muscle along the firm line of it pulsing. "Though that's the only reminder they can take."

My hand burrows in my pocket until I find the bit of red thread from the rug in the cabin. The thread I clung to like it was my lifeline to the outside world. I take it out of my pocket and show Mary.

"What's that?"

Before she can ask another question, I grab her left hand and tie a bow around her ring finger, carefully turning the loops to face her palm, so all that is visible is the finest scarlet line on her finger, almost like a paper cut.

For you and Dave.

Her eyes shine when she looks at me, and I can't believe I ever feared or pitied her. She's too strong for pity and too kind to fear.

"Thank you," she whispers. She touches the thread with her other hand. That thread was my sanity the first night when I thought the screams would overwhelm me. But she's lost Dave, and he was her lifeline in so many ways. She needs it more than I do.

She lets the moment pass, and her facade settles into place and all her vulnerability is gone. "So what do we do here?"

Madge has been watching our exchange with careful eyes, taking it all in. There's no way she could know that Dave was a peace offering I gave up so I could remain on the Burn. No way she could know the love I have for these people we spoke of. But she's taken enough in to know there's a history between Mary and me.

112

"We work," Madge says, chewing on her bacon. "And work until the agents say stop. You're in for a treat."

Mary's eyes sharpen with the same anger as Madge's, and I know these women are cut from the same cloth. They'll understand each other perfectly. I'll just be sure to stay out of their way when they're on the warpath.

"What are you in for? Nomad like Terra?" Mary asks.

I never have asked Madge that. With the rage simmering just under the surface, I wasn't sure I was ready to face it, but I'm curious too.

Madge smiles grimly. "We were hiding from agents. We left Portland—our sanctioned city—and ran north. Funny how agents don't see that as innocently as changing residences. They see it as escaping. We found an old, abandoned town and stayed there a few nights. The agents found us there."

Madge stops and pokes the rest of her bacon. Her lip quivers. I've never seen sorrow from her. I'm not going to like the rest of the story, and I want to tell her to stop. She can keep it as her own if she wants to, but she rushes on like a dam bursting: once it starts, it won't be contained.

"My Danny—my husband—threw himself over the kids when the agents came. He tried to keep the soldiers off them, didn't want them to be touched or harmed or to see any of what we knew would happen. But the soldiers dragged him off of them. One of them smashed his head with his stick, and he dropped to the ground. My girl screamed, and I tried to shush her, tried to tell her it would be okay. It was the worst lie I've ever told her. I could tell by Danny's stillness that it would never be okay again. I held the three of them for twenty seconds before the agents ripped them from me. 'We'll relocate them to nice homes,' they said. 'They'll be taken care of.' I didn't believe a word of it. What kids are taken care of without their mother? Then they loaded me into a truck and brought me here. I haven't seen my children since."

I have no words. Neither does Mary. We exchange glances, and I know in that moment, when I choose to tell her about my crazy plan to smuggle people to the colony, she'll help me.

The intercom sounds again. "Yard time. You have thirty minutes."

Trays scrape over tables as everyone scrambles to their feet. They rush their trays—some of them filled with half-eaten food—to the windows where they're cleaned. There's a buzz in the air. It's inaudible, of course; they wouldn't want the soldiers or agents to think they were happy about something, heaven forbid. But I can feel the energy tingle along my arms and tickle in my ears. For the first time since I've been here, they're excited. I follow along with them, and I'm almost bouncing on the balls of my feet when the double doors open at the end of the hall and gray light streams in.

Clouds make a patchwork in the sky. The sunshine from yesterday evening tries to hang on, shining between clouds, but still the magic of being outside works its way into all of us, even if I do rock back and forth on the balls of my feet and blow air in an attempt to warm my hands. This is the only thing these women have to look forward to. I plan to enjoy it.

I look over to the fence that separates the yard down the middle and see that the men are already there. Our overlap comes in the first five minutes of yard time, so I work my way through a tangle of women who do nothing but stand with their eyes closed and their faces tipped to the sky. As I approach the

114

fence, my heart soars to see Jack already there, his fingers entwined in the links, waiting for me.

Waiting for *me*.

This doesn't unnerve me the way it would have a week ago. It's a relief to see him here, and I'm ashamed to admit I worried that he wouldn't wait. Ashamed to admit a few weeks ago I'm not sure I'd have waited for him. What's wrong with me? Of course I'd wait for him. We were partners, companions, together in the wilderness. Of course I'd wait. But what has changed? Why am I seeing him differently?

"Mind if I come with?" Mary asks, suddenly right by my side. I shake my head. No, I don't mind. Mary should be here for this, where this all begins.

Jack's eyes bounce back the pale light, and the hazel looks almost gray. His cheeks are round with his smile, and he has a bruise over his left eye and a cut on his jaw. He's surprised to see Mary, which worries me. Shouldn't he have seen Dave by now? But I didn't see Mary until about fifteen minutes ago. Maybe Dave hadn't made it to the mess hall yet before yard time.

I grab his hand, but he pulls away from me. My hand is barren without his.

"I don't think we should touch."

I raise my eyebrows. *Why?* I mouth.

He just nods his head toward a soldier patrolling the perimeter. "They're watching. I noticed that two days ago when we were all out here for the announcement. They're always watching. I don't know if it's to discourage relationships between men and women or what their reason might be, but they watch. We shouldn't do anything too close."

I nod and step back. I gesture to my own left eye, and his fingers gingerly touch his face. He winces.

"Just a little disagreement between inmates."

The nomads who were after us; it has to be.

Jack nods. "Yes, it was them. They seemed to think that beating me now would be some kind of justice for escaping them in the woods. The soldiers took care of it though. I don't think they'll bother me again. I never thought I'd be grateful to anyone running this place, but now I am."

Now that I know he's fine, I need to tell him who I am. I need to start the ball rolling toward this insane plan of mine. It's essential I tell him now. It's not the way I wanted to do it. I would rather have done it in the cabin, under the blackberry brambles, in the gas station, anywhere that I could have studied him longer, taken the time the truth deserves, been able to at least put a hand on his.

I study the dirt between our feet and the fence. There's no easy way to take away all the lies I've told. They weigh on me now. They never weighed this heavily when I was around Dave. But knowing how much Jack has trusted me, I can feel the burden of it pressing down on me, wanting to bury me. Mary sees the change and takes a step away from us. I've got to give her that. She knows how to read relationships.

"What's wrong, Terra? Are you okay?"

I laugh. I must look so sick to him. I feel sick. My stomach is churning, threatening to show me that the bacon is even worse coming back up. I shake my head and take his hand.

"Terra, I don't think—"

But I shake my head at him again, my eyes wide. This is important, and he sees it on my face. He quiets and lets me hold his hand, but he angles his body to shield us from the soldiers.

I lied about Arizona.

This doesn't surprise him. "Lots of people lie about where they're from."

I'm not from the Burn.

"What's the Burn? Is that what you call Arizona? It makes sense with the heat." He gives me a half-smile. That smile makes me sad.

The Burn is what colonists call land.

He drops my hand. "Colonists?" The thoughts race across his face and weave through his eyes, puzzling what I could possibly mean.

Mary's not far enough away to be out of earshot. At the word "colonists," her head snaps up. She's doubly alert now. She knows the truth, and she is surprised I'm telling anyone else.

"It's true then, what they say about the colonies?" Jack says.

I nod. I guess it is. I honestly don't know what they say besides the few snippets Mary's told me and what Madge and Jane talked about at the reclamation site. Mary steps back to us.

"Terra, what are you doing?" she hisses. She glances at the soldiers patrolling and the one soldier in the guard tower. There are no agents I can see, and they scare me with their silence more than the soldiers do with their guns.

I grab her hand and hold it so Jack can see what I write. *I have a plan. It's crazy. Might work.*

But Jack's not ready for that yet. His eyes hold the hurt I was expecting, but actually seeing it is completely different. What I wasn't expecting was the way it would affect me. It almost bowls me over to know that I could hurt him that much. How can I jump immediately to plans and dates and logistics when he's just had the wind knocked out of him?

Wanted to tell you sooner.

He shakes his head, trying to brush away the shock. "I know you did. That night in the gas station, right?"

I nod. His next question cuts me more deeply. It's a question I'm not entirely prepared for because I still haven't sorted out what he means to me, why things have changed.

"Why not before then?"

I shrug my shoulders, helpless. He always thought I was brave, but really I was a coward.

He turns from me, and as he does, my knees wobble. He walks away, and I brace myself against the fence. Mary puts a hand on my arm. Then Jack stops and turns back to me. He looks so much like he did that day next to the Puget Sound when he told me he'd come with me.

I'm so sorry, I mouth. I don't know what changes his mind, but he hesitates for a moment before walking toward us, and his face is guarded. He doesn't light up for me anymore.

"Not much time left," Mary says, and I panic, remembering what I had to accomplish here.

I want to bring people to the colony.

Both of them are so stunned that if I didn't feel like I'd just been punched in the stomach, I could almost laugh to see their identical expressions: jaws gaping open and eyes wide.

I can get a sub.

They do nothing but blink at me.

I'm not sure about escaping, but I'll try.

Mary is the first to compose herself.

"You're right. It is crazy."

I nod. The craziest thing I've done so far. Crazier than lying in a field of corn under burning UV lamps, crazier than allowing my mother to mutilate me, crazier than going on a thirty-mile hike in boots that don't fit. I laugh, though. I've definitely done crazy, and I think I can handle it.

"We'd need help," Jack says, and I see the look in his eyes. It's the same look he gets when he sees a patient and knows he can help: it's just a matter of coming to a diagnosis. He's right. This could heal people. But that look is not for me anymore, it's for the people we could save. It sends a shiver through me that splinters my heart. I ache now.

Then the intercom sounds. "Men, report to your work hours."

The soldiers file along the fence, herding the men back into their building. A soldier makes his way toward us. We have no time left.

Two weeks, I write.

Jack and Mary nod.

ELEVEN

Two weeks is going to both fly by and drag on forever. I hate the feeling of time being completely out of my control. There's so much to do between now and then, so much to plan for and take care of. It will take forever because I feel like I just might be marching myself and those who come with me to our doom.

First, I need to send the message. I squint up between the clouds. It's amazing how even a day like today can seem bright, especially now that the spark I felt in the truck has blossomed into flame. I have a plan; I am going to act; I am trying to save others.

I look at the sky, trying to imagine where those satellites are that Gaea watches so intently. They're out there, circling the earth in ever-decreasing orbit. I wonder when they'll just fall from the sky like meteors. I'm sure there will be more to replace them—Gaea can't be the only one who wants to keep tabs on what's going on down here.

Mary's standing two feet away, her eyes hard. I know from the way she said, "You're right. It is crazy," that she thinks it's the most insane idea ever, but that she's also willing to try it. Her hard eyes don't speak to me of mistrust, but thoughtfulness, her way of puzzling this out. What I'm about to do will probably look even more insane. I look down the fence. The soldiers march away, focused on getting the men back into their building. The soldier left on the women's side leans against the fence, one foot propped behind him. Almost bored. I'm safe for a moment at least.

Gaea, I mouth, praying that she's watching me, that she hasn't stepped away from the monitor bank right at this moment. This is one time her obsession will pay off. *If you're watching, I need help. A sub for seven passengers. Fourteen days. Midnight.*

But then I falter. Where? Where is the rendezvous point? I snag Mary's hand. *Closest shore?*

Mary's brows knit together. "The harbor," she finally says.

That's it?

She shrugs. "I don't know what else to call it. There's an abandoned airport right on the edge."

That will have to be enough. *The harbor, the abandoned airport.*

That's all I can do. I hope that my suspicions are right: that she watches me as much as she can because, despite it all, she's still my mother.

"That's it?" Mary folds her arms over her chest. If it had been four months ago, I would have said it was because she was angry or dissatisfied. Now I read it as concern that there's more that needs to be done.

Now we plan.

We walk back toward the cluster of women.

121

"You said a sub for seven. Who's coming?"

I point them out. *Madge. Kai. Jane. You. Jack. Dave.* Then I hesitate. I've never felt more unsure about anything. *Me.*

"You're sure? You don't look sure."

I shake my head.

"Well, I guess you have two weeks to decide."

Two weeks to decide whether or not I regret my decision to come to the Burn. Two weeks to decide whether or not I can cope with the blackness of ocean all around me after I've felt the sun and the wind. After I've been free. I look around: soldiers, chain link fence three times taller than I am, coils of barbed wire like snakes waiting to strike, agents who hate me for a reason I have no name for. Am I free?

"Take your time. It's a big choice."

Two weeks to see if Jack will ever trust me again.

Mary's rubbing the thread on her finger, and an uncertain smile plays at the corner of her lips. She watches the last of the men disappear into the building.

Dave?

She shakes her head. "I didn't see him. That doesn't mean he's not here, though."

No, it doesn't, but I worry that he wasn't out here with the rest of them and that Jack didn't mention him. Jack. Will he ever really look at me again? I chafe the sides of my arms. I'm cold remembering the way he looked at me like he was seeing me for the first time and what he saw was almost . . . repulsive.

I told him the truth, and now that hangs between us like a guillotine.

"You okay?" Mary asks.

I nod.

122

"You're not. That's the same look on your face the night I . . . "

She can't finish, and she doesn't have to. I know which night she's talking about. The night she confronted me with Jessa's letter. The sadness floods her eyes as she thinks about what she did to me. If I stayed at the settlement, I might have wound up here anyway, but I know she thinks it's her fault I'm here.

You didn't make me leave.

She laughs and shakes her head. "I may as well have, and you know it." She looks at the pathetic grass trying to fight the cold as it's trampled under our shoes. "I'm so sorry, Terra."

I know.

She grips my arm tightly and I wince, but she doesn't let go. "I don't think you do."

It's okay, I mouth.

Her eyes are tear-filled again. "I just wanted to fix everything, the way I wanted to fix Seattle. I couldn't do anything for that city, and I see that now—how hopeless it was. But I could fix what was wrong with me and Dave. I could fix that."

I know.

She releases my arm and puts both hands over her face. "I'm so scared, Terra. I'm scared why he wasn't out here today."

Jack would have said something.

She drops her hands, and her eyes are red. "He would, right?"

It's little comfort because I know how quickly the agents can take you away. Dave was born in the settlement. He had no tracker. They were rough with me, but I didn't take any damage because I've learned from Madge and Jane how to play the game. But Dave? Would he fight back, say something, get riled up? He could be in solitary confinement right now. I shudder, but quickly try to play it off as a shiver. I can't let Mary see my doubts.

She's moved on, trying to set aside the pain for now, focusing her mind on something else. But still she strokes the thread tied around her finger.

"How are we doing this?"

Madge and Jane. They've been here longer. They might know something.

"Well, let's figure out how to talk to them."

This proves trickier than Mary's simple sentence.

The next two days are filled with cannery work, medical exams, agent questions, meals, and time alone at night in my cell with Jane and the screams. Jane and I both sleep on the top bunk now. We spend the few minutes we have of twilight gazing out the window and dreaming before we pull the pillows over our heads for the anthem.

It's been two days since I sent Gaea the message—the message I hope she's received. If she didn't receive it and we can actually break out of here, I don't know what we'll do when we reach the ocean. So much can go wrong. I fully expect to have soldiers and agents on our heels, and if we come up against the water without a place to run to, we'll all die. But would that be a worse fate than what we do now? I'm alive but is this *life*? I'm tired from working, sure, but the work is just work. The rest of it—treating us like animals, like machines with no emotions—makes me feel like I'm living some kind of half-life, like I'm a zombie with only half of my brain functioning. But what the agents don't know is that it's the more dangerous half.

124

Has anyone tried to escape before? I look out my window across the yard. The shadows are a mile long as they reach east, like they're begging the sun to rise again. The sun dips beneath the horizon, and in the purple gloom flooding the quad, the soldier's cigarette flares in the tower. Still just the one soldier. The soldiers patrolling the perimeter have gone in for the night. There's an old searchlight on the tower—I noticed it in yard time two days ago, and it looked dusty with disuse.

If someone had tried to escape, there would be more security around this place. If there isn't very much security out there, sure we could get past the fence, but will we be able to get out of *here*? I think the inside will be the hardest part.

Jane is nestled against me so comfortably I hate to wake her, but it's time to ask. I nudge her shoulder, and she buries her head deeper into my arm. I bump her again, and her eyes shoot open. This is how she always wakes—like she needs to be up and running or else she'll get plowed over.

Ask you something?

Her eyes relax, but her body is alert.

Do you think we could escape? It all depends on this, whether someone like Jane—who's been here long enough to have hair a foot and a half long—thinks it's even possible.

She sits up and the bunk springs groan at her. She nods her head.

Anyone ever done it?

She shakes her head.

Anyone ever tried?

She shakes her head again, and I allow my heart to leap just a fraction. That's why they're so relaxed, and that's the biggest advantage we have. The government is arrogant and will never

125

suspect that a tongueless girl could engineer something like this. They're right—I can't. But with Jack, Mary, Madge, and Jane? Who knows what we'd be able to accomplish.

It's crazy, but would you come with me?

Then Jane speaks her first word to me. "Yes."

I want to wrap my arms around her right then, but I figure I'd better start slow. I grin instead, and I'm met with another one of her beautiful, crooked smiles.

"When?"

It seems now that the language barrier between us has been broken she wants nothing more than to speak.

Twelve days.

"Where?" Her words are music, like river water on rocks.

I look at my hands. This again is the tricky part. *I'm from an ocean colony. We could go there.*

She freezes, and I'm worried she'll disappear back into her sanctuary of silence and stone. The hatred I saw in the house at the reclamation site flits across her eyes, but she surprises me.

"I knew there was something different about you."

I can't help but laugh. I try to do it quietly. The screams have died off already, and the silence is heavy in my ears. The soldiers would probably think it was just another hallucination or side effect from an injection, but there's no way I'll raise suspicion now, not when I have plans to make.

I think I can get a submarine.

"I'll help you."

I remember how fiercely she told Madge her feelings about colonists. Jane sees it on my face.

"I hate them. I don't hate you."

Can you go there if you hate them so much?

126

"I hate why they left. I hate how they abandoned us. If they're willing to help now, I won't turn my back on them."

She squeezes my hand with her short, slender fingers. She has such nimble fingers. When I look at her I see a blade of grass shivering in the wind, but her fingers are strong and can do more than I can ever dream about. I need her help.

You've been here long?

She nods. "Three years."

Outside won't be a problem.

"No, it won't."

Inside?

"Yes."

I sigh and prop my chin on my hands. I lean back against the wall and strain my eyes to see the dark slash of ocean beyond the trees.

"The soldiers have never checked our cells before bed."

I perk up. *We could do it at night?*

She nods. "After dinner."

That has possibilities.

"Talk to Madge. She can help too."

I knew I would have allies. I squeeze Jane's hand again. *Sleep. Talk to Madge tomorrow.*

Then I groan. In the cannery with the soldiers so close, I don't know if we'll be able to talk, and this kind of conversation will definitely be too intense for the mess hall.

"What's wrong?"

Can't talk in the mess hall or cannery.

"I think we're done with the cannery. We finished the corn and the blackberries yesterday. There will be something new

127

tomorrow. Maybe the warehouse for the things we found at the reclamation site."

After breakfast Jane and I enter the warehouse, and it's filled with the murmur of voices. We have to talk about what can be salvaged, what can be disassembled into its various parts, what's worthless. The soldiers and agents allow these small conversations. They keep an eye on conversations that go on for too long or are too intense, but if we exchange a conversation over the course of the work hours, they will never suspect. I hope they'll never suspect.

Jane is too small for most of the jobs, so she does the more intricate work that suits her fingers. She usually takes strings from blinds and sorts the slats into piles by size or mends old sheets and pillowcases.

Jane doesn't do well in reclamation, but Madge is a force of nature here. Madge can find a use for just about anything, and I can tell by the almost approving look on the agents' faces that they appreciate her work. If they can appreciate anything, I think this is the closest they would come. They leave Madge alone because if they were to harass her like the other workers, she wouldn't get as much done, and they know how valuable she is.

Madge's curly red hair flames out behind her as she bustles down the aisles between work projects. She still has the flinty look in her eyes, but she's purposeful. I wonder if it comes from being a mother in a city—the need to make ends meet, to find new uses for old objects. I remember dipping candles with Nell and the way we used wicks made from the strings of blinds. It was much the same there.

128

Most days Jane pulls away from me as soon as we enter any work area and goes off to find a job of her own. Today, however, she stays at my side and scans the warehouse for a pile of materials. I'm doing the same. I want something that looks tricky or full of possibilities, something that the agents will expect we need Madge's opinions on. There might be enough time if I pretend to be figuring out a problem.

Jane lingers near me like a sparrow who knows there might be a few morsels tossed her way. She's so used to being on her own that she wants to fly as soon as someone comes too close, but she stays long enough to see what might be offered. It's a tricky situation to be in. I'm actually surprised she agreed to help me. Maybe the bread crumbs I offered were just tempting enough to keep her around.

I point to a pile of shiny metal and black electric cords. Jane smiles.

"Toasters. Perfect."

No one else has started working at this station, so we claim it and sort through them. Would they want them refurbished? Dismantled? I can see why Madge thrives on this so much, trying to save something from nothing. I don't focus on the problem too intently; I watch Madge wind up and down the aisles out the corner of my eye. She hasn't noticed where we are yet. She will once Jane gets her attention and we start our conversation that will take up our ten-hour shift.

Madge finally steps between a pile of old blankets and a stack of plastic pipes. She gives a half-smile when she sees us.

"Toasters, huh?"

I nod and raise my hands as if to say, *Any ideas?*

She shrugs. "Some of them might be able to be saved. They're a luxury in the cities. We didn't have one, I can tell you that."

Jane bends down like she wants Madge to examine something closer, her hair falling down to block her mouth from the soldier and the agent across the room, and I busy myself examining a toaster much too closely. Here we go.

"We're going to escape."

Madge goes rigid for just a second before assuming her normal posture. I've got to give her credit for the way she can handle just about anything.

"When?" She picks up a toaster and peers into one of the slots.

"Eleven days."

"Where?"

Jane glances at me, and I nod almost imperceptibly. I know that this part about me—being from the colonies—is essential to the plan and Madge needs to know it, but I don't know how much further I want the knowledge to spread. Mary told me so many months ago how much some people on the Burn hate colonists— and rightly so, in my opinion—and I've caught glimpses of that here. If the wrong people were to find out, I don't know what might happen to this web we're so carefully weaving.

I nod one more time.

Jane sucks in a breath. "An ocean colony."

Madge does more than just freeze then. Her eyes blaze, and there's such anger that swells over her face, I almost stagger back. I look around to see if we've drawn any unwanted attention. The agent by the door is typing something on her tablet. She yawns. Yes, she has nothing better to do than babysit us.

130

The soldiers are patrolling the opposite side of the warehouse. I will Madge to calm down.

"How're you going to do that?" she asks, her eyes trained on Jane.

Jane looks unflinching back at her, but she's done enough already. I grab Madge's hand. So many people have found out from other sources. I need to do the telling.

I'm a colonist.

She wrenches her hand away like I've burned her. She does very little to hide the rage boiling on her face. "What are you *doing* here?"

Jane comes to my rescue before I try to spell out the words that will take way too long and say far too little. "Move on for a few minutes, Madge. Please. Take a breath."

Madge needs no coaxing. She turns and stomps away to the next pile of junk. I can practically see the steam rising from her hair.

"That didn't go well."

Did you think it would?

Jane pulls her hand away so she can inspect a toaster. She grabs a screw driver and deftly takes off the housing. She talks to me out of the corner of her mouth, her shoulders hunching over again into her defeated posture. "No, but I wasn't expecting that. Madge is usually so calm."

She hides it.

Jane nods, staring at the guts of the toaster. I marvel at the change that's come over her. She used to look beaten down all the time. Now I see it as the act it is. She's a new person in the same body. That faint ray of a possibility, the hope I've given her with our plan, has invigorated her.

"She's trapped it for too long. She's a time bomb."

I peer over a toaster to where Madge stalks down the opposite end of the warehouse. She looks back at me, sees me watching her, and jerks away.

She hates me.

Jane shrugs and uses her screwdriver to take more of the toaster apart. "Maybe, but I doubt it. I think she just needs to cool down."

How will we do this? I gesture to the toasters, remembering we're supposed to be talking about our projects here, but Jane knows what I mean.

"She'll come around, Terra."

Before it's too late?

"She'll come around. She gets worked up quick and she fizzles quick."

Sure enough, she literally comes around. She won't look at me; she only looks at Jane. I can tell by the gleam in her eyes, though, that she's all for escape.

"I'll help you," she says. She has a clipboard now, and she's writing down what we've done with the toasters and what more use we could possibly get out of them. "What do you need?"

I move forward, ready to write the words, but Jane puts a tremulous hand on my arm. "We think the yard should be easy. We're worried about inside."

Madge writes down a few words on her paper and says, "Mm-hmm. That's right. So you're thinking that's my job?"

I nod, but she's still ignoring me.

"Yes," Jane says. "Any plan you can think of."

Madge pokes at toaster guts with her pencil. "I've been thinking about that for way too long. I just never had anywhere

132

to go." I hear the sadness in her voice. She has no idea where her children are or if they're even alive. Escaping wasn't really escaping if she didn't have somewhere to go.

Thank you, I mouth. She still refuses to look right at me, but I know she saw it.

Jane pulls the heating element out of a toaster, straightens the wires, and places it on a table. "We need a plan in place soon."

Madge nods brusquely. "I know. You said eleven days. For how many?"

Seven, I mouth to Jane.

She nods and glances around. As she spots the soldiers, she tenses like a deer that's caught the scent of a predator. She lowers her voice. "You, Kai, me, Terra, and three of her friends here."

"That's pushing it."

I grab her hand, and she doesn't pull away from me. She sees the burning look in my eyes. *I won't take fewer.*

"Fine, but no more. Seven's risky enough."

I nod.

"I'll talk to you about it in two days. Don't ask me any more until then. We've talked long enough as it is." She walks away, leaving behind her a strange wake of anger mixed with hope.

I can tell Jane wants to smile, but she won't with the soldiers and agents so near. For them, she's still broken. Her hair falls back around her face, and she hunches over the toaster. We don't say another word.

When the intercom speaks several hours later, I'm surrounded by a pile of dismantled toasters, and I swear I never want to see another one for as long as I live. Who needs a small metal box just for browning bread anyway?

A grin creeps across my face as I remember trying to swallow down the awful bread I made in the gas station, and the way Jack never complained. Funny things remind me of him and at the most random times. Then Jane offers an imperceptible shake of her head, and I quickly wipe the traitor smile off my face. I adopt her stance: head down, eyes down, spirit stomped into the ground. If I'm to last until the escape, I have to make them believe there's no more fight left in me.

TWELVE

As promised, in two days Madge talks to us. I'm sitting at our usual table, pushing around slimy eggs and limp hash browns on my tray, watching the way the yolk swirls out in abstract patterns. Jane doesn't speak. She hasn't spoken since reclamation after Madge left with her promise to help. I haven't pushed her. She's been nervous and fidgety, her hands and fingers constantly in motion, and as many times as I just wanted to tell her *Relax! For my sanity, calm down!* I didn't say anything. She's on edge about the escape. When it comes down to it, I'm on edge too. Madge was just so angry at me, and I haven't forgotten the scathing look she gave me when I branded myself a colonist.

She sat with us the past two days but didn't say a word. I glanced around, hoping the agents monitoring us would just chalk it up to drama—we are a huge group of women here—and not that something out of the ordinary was going on.

But nothing.

So between Madge's silence, the agents not doing anything, and Jane with her fluttering hands, I bit my nails down to the quick. Only nine more days and then we leave. There are too many variables. I'm freaking myself out.

Then Madge sits down, shoves a bite of egg into her mouth, wipes the yolk that dribbles out, and says, "I'll only say this once."

I sit up and listen, and Jane drops the napkin she's been shredding into tiny strips.

"I won't tell you here. I'll just tell you it'll take a few days, it will be risky, but there's a certain . . . poetic justice to it." She says it with relish as a wry smile crosses her lips. The anger against me might simmer under the surface, but the anger against me has no comparison to how she feels about the agents and soldiers here. She's totally on board with the whole thing.

"When will you tell us?" Jane whispers. It comes out as a croak since she hasn't been speaking. She clears her throat.

"Reclamation."

Thank you, I mouth, and Madge nods curtly.

"What're you talking about?" Kai asks. I slide her my tin of pears and take her hand.

Something important. I'll tell you later.

She senses our mood and nods gravely. Then she digs into the pears.

Reclamation comes quickly. Usually I dread the build-up to work hours, but today it can't come fast enough. Madge beats us there, is given her clipboard, and starts her rounds. Jane and I hover in the doorway, trying to watch Madge while

136

pretending to look over the piles. Our toasters disappeared yesterday. There's a pile of back packs and I nod to them.

"There could be lots of things in there we have to talk to Madge about," Jane agrees.

We sit cross-legged next to the pile. I choose the pack closest to me and watch for Madge as I unzip it. She's an aisle over, talking to some women working on unstringing blinds. She'll be here soon. I look into the pack.

Two text books, a notebook, a few pencils, and a note that says, *Have a good day at school, honey!*

My stomach is urging me to lose my breakfast.

"These were all from the school at that site," Jane whispers, holding a piece of blue paper covered in old, yellowed cotton balls. That small square of blue sky and clouds pricks something in her, and her eyes fill with tears.

"I had a little brother. He was eight. I have no idea where he is now. These poor kids. Do you think they were sent to a sanctioned city?"

I put a hand on her arm. She's asking if I think they made it, if I think—even though they're long gone now—they escaped what every country did to every other country out there.

Not everyone died. We're here.

Her face is grim. "That's why we're going to the colony. Because you're here. It's like the last safe place on Earth."

My churning stomach does another flip. Is it the last safe place on Earth? Possibly. But how much am I willing to pay to get us there?

Madge flicks her pencil on her clipboard, and the sound startles me and I drop the backpack.

"What's in them?"

Jane brushes a tear from her cheek and composes herself. Eyes down, head down. She shouldn't have enough fight left to be able to cry over this injustice.

"School supplies."

"Salvageable?"

I nod.

"Good. Here's what we'll do with them."

I lean forward. This is going to be Madge's plan.

"There are a few details to be sorted out." She gestures to the packs, her voice casual and even. Her eyes flick once, and she spots the soldier across the room and the agent by the door. They're too far to hear anything. "We'll give all the soldiers and agents serum the day of the escape. Hopefully the 'contaminated' kind, which shouldn't be too much of a problem. I think it's all contaminated."

I start back. She had said it was risky, but I think they'd notice if we injected them all. Madge waves it away.

"They're just school supplies, not a big deal. We can spike their dinner. It will take longer to kick in, which is perfect. When they're all incapacitated, we'll use the keycard we've swiped and get out."

She had said there were a few details to be sorted out. She wasn't kidding. But she was right about poetic justice. They'll finally see what we've been suffering for their stupid tests.

"How do we get the serum and the keycard?" Jane says. I nod.

"That's up to you. But this plan can work, Terra, if you're willing to take some risks."

I think back to a night months ago, when I was willing to leave my family behind, willing to face the darkness of the trench, and willing to give up speaking forever.

138

Madge reluctantly lets me take her hand. *That's how I got to land.*

"Then make sure it gets done. We need all the serum in place by the night before, so eight days. Ask your doctor friend how long it takes to work when it's eaten."

The keycard?

"I think you can figure it out."

Madge walks away to the next pile. A soldier patrols the aisles, his mask trained on us. I guess the conversation took a little too long for his taste. Jane and I sort the books, pencils, notebooks, and packs into separate piles. He stops a few feet away from us, his fingers tense around his gun.

He doesn't say anything, but I can feel his eyes as we sort. I expect him to shout or deride us or something, but he just stands there. I can't read him with that black mask in the way, and I remember all too well the way the soldiers looked like scorpions only a few days ago when I was drugged out of my mind. I shudder—not from the memory—but because of how accurate that hallucination was.

I bend my head down a little more, hunch my shoulders a little more. It feels so wrong pretending to be so weak, but I need to lay low. We all do. If Madge can hide everything from them, well then so can I. Jane has perfected the weak thing to a tee, and I take my cues from her.

Finally the soldier speaks, and his voice is softer than I expected. "Worker 7456, come with me to interrogation."

I pull my shoulders back and look him square in the eye. My act drops in an instant. I'm being reckless. If I'm to keep this up, I can't let them faze me. The soldier waits to make sure I follow him. I shrug once to Jane, drop the pack I'm holding, and

139

go out the door with him. I try to reassemble my face into something like helpless, but it's so hard to do. During my days with the settlement, I was free. I could be myself. No, that's not quite true. I was still hiding, really. I couldn't tell them what I was. I remember those hot, summer days with Dave. I remember the way he smiled at me, the way his blue eyes shined. The way I saw him starting to love me, the way I tried to return it but couldn't quite manage to. I wasn't sure why then, but I know now. I know how corrosive just one lie can be. A harmless lie really: I'm from Arizona, not from an ocean colony. But it poisoned things, poisoned relationships. The way I'm now almost friends with Mary shows me that. Now she knows the truth about me; now she can trust me. I just regret not telling Jack sooner.

In a way, I'm more free here than I was in the settlement. I've come clean with a lot more people, and it's liberating to be seen as I am. But the gloom settles on me again because I can't let the agents or soldiers know. That was the price of my escape to the Burn: the promise that I wouldn't speak of the colonies to anyone, and I know the soldiers and agents are the most dangerous people I could tell. In their hands, what might that knowledge do? Would it start a war? It could, I guess, if enough people were angry about it. I could see the government doing exactly that. They're so desperate for their citizens to be loyal, to engender some kind of trust that I could see them going after the colonies if for no other reason than to pretend they were seeking vengeance against the colonists for deserting everyone. It would definitely make quite a few citizens happy, I think. Then the government would study the colonists to see what makes us tick.

The soldier opens the too-familiar door of the interrogation room, and my agent waits there with her arms folded. Her eyes are hooded, and she looks like a cobra ready to strike. I'm surprised she doesn't hiss at me. She's getting frustrated with me. Good.

She gives a quick nod to the soldier, and he closes the door. There's something different about this meeting, and I can't quite place it. Then I realize: except for the two of us, the room is empty. No Dr. Benedict, no nurse, no soldiers. And suddenly, I'm very afraid.

"Sit."

She didn't even have to say it. I would have sat down under the weight of her gaze alone. I'm fighting between acting weak and throwing my head back defiantly, but I breathe deeply and try to remember. A little over a week. Then we fight.

"I'm getting tired of this, Worker 7456. Tired."

I look at the glossy buttons on her white shirt. Two show above where her jacket meets. The crooks of her elbows make three wrinkles in the fabric on her right arm, four on the left. I study these details as hard as I can to keep from jumping up, fighting back, and ruining everything.

"Did you hear me?"

The buttons. Looks at the buttons. I nod.

"I know there's something you're keeping from us, and it's only a matter of time before we rip it from you. Keep that in mind. You can willingly give it, or we can rip it from you. Which do you think would be more pleasant?"

I close my eyes. I doubt they'd rip it like a bandage. Their ripping would be more like slowly tearing.

The buttons. Focus. One gleams pink in the fluorescent light.

The agent makes an ugly sound in the back of her throat. "You inmates are all the same. You disgust me."

My eye twitches; her buttons can't hold me now. I meet her gaze with such malevolence, I kind of expect her to burn to ash on the spot. A smile creeps across her lips.

"Yes, there's more in there than you'd like us to know. You're unusual that way."

She stands up and stalks around the table. The sharp click of her heels reminds me of beetles, but she's a thousand times more deadly. She sits down on the edge of the table and leans over me.

"I think for you, ripping will be better."

Then she reaches back a hand and slaps me as hard as she can across the face.

"I'm done here."

I don't even have time to shake the stars out of my vision before the soldier pulls me to my feet.

"Take her to Dr. Benedict. I believe he has another injection for her."

The soldier drags me out of the room before I realize what she's said. I force myself to clear my head, to ignore the blazing pain in my cheek. Dr. Benedict. The serum. I have to start now, don't I? That will be the only way to smuggle enough of it out. I loll my head to one side. It's a little too dramatic, but the soldier doesn't seem to notice. After all, he has no idea what really went on in there, and with the way my cheek and mouth sting, I'm sure I have a huge red mark—maybe even a welt—on my face.

142

We stop outside the medical area, and the soldier props me up against the wall before swiping his keycard. He grabs me again, and as the door opens, Dr. Benedict looks up from his desk. I keep my eyes down, but through my lashes, I see his brows furrow.

"What happened?" He stands up from his desk where he's been pouring over some files.

"Interrogation," the soldier says.

"I knew she'd take it too far. She never knows when enough is enough."

"Not my call, doc."

"Of course it's not. You're as much of a pawn as the inmates are."

The soldier tenses next to me, but something passes between them, some look from Dr. Benedict's black eyes that I can't read. The soldier softens.

"I'll take it from here, soldier."

"Yes, sir."

Dr. Benedict reaches for me with both arms as the soldier lets me go, and I let myself fall into them. I feel like crying right now. I won't, of course. That's a little too much weakness, and I won't let them see it. But I need the comfort of a friend, and Dr. Benedict's the only thing remotely close to one right now. He strokes a hand over my hair.

"What happened?"

I reach for his hand. *She hit me.*

"How badly?"

Hard. Is it ugly?

He manages to laugh. "I've seen worse. Let me get you an ice pack."

He motions me into the equipment room with the serum fridge. He disappears behind a few filing cabinets, and a fridge door opens and he rummages around. I slip off the bed and open the serum fridge. The vials are marked with numbers and letters. I have no idea what they mean or which symptoms they'll bring on. I don't think it really matters. I haven't seen any of them produce anything close to a positive side effect, so I just grab one from the back and slip it under the elastic of my waist band. The cold glass brings goose bumps, and I worry for a moment. Do they have to stay cold? I think of my cell window and my hand print on it. That will have to be cold enough. I can't do any better.

Dr. Benedict comes back with an ice pack and eases it onto my cheek. His face is inches from mine, and the scent of woods is too close. I pull back, and he smiles at me.

"Keep it there for a few minutes."

I press it to my face, sighing as the cold works its way past the sting and numbs me. I tuck my shirt down over the vial just a little bit more, hoping the bagginess will hide the small tell-tale lump.

"I'll get your injection ready."

I'm paralyzed remembering the hallucinations. The color drains from my face, and the ice pack chills me to the marrow of my bones. How will I lose control of myself this time? I grab Dr. Benedict's arm, my fingers pressing into his skin. He looks at me and I shake my head. I'm suddenly startled by the sadness in Dr. Benedict's eyes. I don't often see anything there I can name.

"You know, Terra, I am sorry about all this. I'm following orders."

144

He fills up a syringe, and I grit my teeth, bracing myself for whatever horrors this one will bring. I watch as he puts the needle in me and feel the familiar burn as the serum works its way through my veins. Dr. Benedict lets his hand linger on my arm for another moment before he puts the stupid smiley face bandage over the pinprick of blood. Then he caresses my hand as he takes the ice pack away. I clench my fist. How long until my brain isn't in control? Could I ever do anything to convince Dr. Benedict not to give me another injection?

"I'm sorry about your face too. It should feel better soon. Might be bruised for a few days, though. Come back and see me, Terra."

I just nod. I have something to get done; of course I'll come back. I jump down off the table and go to the door. The soldier sees me through the small window and opens it. He takes my arm and is about to lead me away when Dr. Benedict clears his throat.

"I'd actually prefer it if you took her back to her cell. I think she'd better rest."

The soldier pauses for a beat as if he's unsure he's heard right. "There's still an hour of work hours left."

"True." Dr. Benedict looks down at his tablet and makes a few notes. "But she'd better get some rest if the agents would like her to still be of use to them."

The soldier isn't happy about it, but he leads me down the corridors and into the maze of cell doors.

Once inside my cell, I listen to the sound of his boots retreating down the hall before I move away from the door. When there's nothing but silence—and there's too much of that with everyone else on work hours—I climb the bunk, slide the vial from my pants, and put it on the window ledge against the glass. I wipe away a circle of condensation and look out across the forest. The frost-tipped pines are grayish green against the blue sky. There are clouds coming, though, across the ocean toward us. There will be a storm tonight.

I'm sure Dr. Benedict thought he was doing me a favor letting me come back to my cell, but just lying on the bunk for a couple of hours does nothing for me. I would rather keep my hands and my mind busy, and the nasty headache forming behind my eyes doesn't help. All I can think of is how our plan can fail—there isn't enough serum to go around, the keycard doesn't work, the serum actually isn't contaminated and all the soldiers and agents are at peak form, we can't move fast enough, the sub never comes. Kai can't move fast enough and is caught, Jack and Mary and Dave are shot before my eyes, Madge claws at a soldier who pops out of nowhere, Jane and her small frame can't contend with the obstacles placed before us. Every way I imagine it, it always ends in death. The tears prick in my eyes, but I can't let them fall. I rub my palms across my face. Stop thinking of it, I tell myself. Thoughts like this won't help. This is going to happen; we're going to try.

Finally the intercom lets me know it's dinner time. I slide off the bunk as the door opens and think maybe I do just want to lie on my bunk for the rest of the night. There's no one else in my hall—they are coming from work hours—but as I get closer to the mess hall, trickles of women converge and we go in to dinner. I sit by Madge and it's all I can do to fight back the tears and give her a hopeful smile.

One down.

"You look horrible." She grins and her smile is genuine. I don't know if she's still angry with me, but she's excited about the progress we've made.

Interrogation. I feel so pathetic at the thought of it that a few tears do finally spill over. *How many do we need?*

Madge raises an eyebrow at the tears on my cheeks. "No idea. As many as you can get."

"Are you okay?" Kai asks. She leans toward me, instinctively wanting to comfort, and I know she will be a good mother. The concern on her face for all of us just about breaks my heart. I think of Nell who could have been a mother too. Do she and Red have children? I never thought to ask. I never really knew any of them, my family at the settlement, and I'm so overwhelmed with grief for the family I lost that I bury my head in my hands and sob.

"Get a grip, Terra," Mary hisses, glancing up at the soldiers.

Madge studies me. "Did you see Dr. Benedict after interrogation?"

I nod and wipe the back of my hand across my nose.

"Get an injection?" she asks pointedly.

I realize. Of course. This overwhelming sorrow wouldn't come over me just from sitting in my cell for a couple hours.

How long does it last?

Madge shrugs. "I've seen it last a couple hours. Seen it last more than a day."

The tears start afresh because I can't imagine sitting for more than a day with this pit of grief inside me. I'm pathetic right now and I know it, but I feel so out of control of my body. I'm a sniffling, wet mess, and I hate the way everyone is looking at me with pity in their eyes.

I'm about to bury my head in my arms when the screen drops down again and the lights dim. The familiar male voice comes on, accompanied by a picture of a pristine white building.

"The third hospital offering free medical care has just been completed in Salt Lake City. This marvel of modern technology hosts private rooms for every patient, state-of-the-art diagnostic equipment, and a staff of skilled doctors and nurses trained to serve you. You are the citizens of New America, and you deserve the best health care available."

Someone snorts off to my left, but no one looks. No one wants to rat anyone else out. The soldiers look around, but we all keep our eyes carefully on the screen. Even me, while I'm bawling my eyes out.

"This new facility has a comfortable birthing center—" Kai goes rigid "—an incredible surgical ward, and all the amenities you could ever want from a place where you can come to heal. All brought to you by your government. Dedicated to providing for your needs."

The lights brighten again and the soldiers look around, seeing if anyone bought into it this time. No one moves. There are more glares than I've ever seen, and I hiccup with my sobs. The agents are really wasting their time, and it's just so sad that we all have to sit here while they do it. I wipe my nose.

Then I think of the conversation that the film interrupted.

Don't you get injections? I ask Madge.

"I did for the first few months I was here. Guess they figured they pricked me enough times, gave me enough mood swings. Who knows. They stopped though. Sometimes I still have the same nightmares I used to have from one of the injections." She leans forward. "It's stupid, but I dream the soldiers are bees stinging me."

I manage to smile, and salty tears drip into my mouth. *I thought they were scorpions.*

"Yours is better."

I nudge Jane. *You?*

She shakes her head and whispers, "Later." She's the one who rarely talks. She doesn't want to strike up a conversation now and break appearances.

"How come they haven't given me one yet?" Mary asks.

It's a good question. She's been here a couple days. I already had one by this time.

"Don't know. It's weird the pattern of who gets them and who doesn't. Not everyone does."

I'm a nomad. I needed inoculations.

"Not a good enough reason," Madge says, taking a bite of bread. "Most people here were nomads, and not everyone gets them."

But before I can work past the tears to try to puzzle it out, two soldiers approach our table and we fall silent.

"Worker 7488?" one says. With those masks on, I have no idea who they're looking at. No wonder Madge imagined them as insects too. Then I realize the number comes after mine. It would have to be Mary.

"Yes?" She doesn't look up from her stew. It's all she can do to keep an ounce of civility in her voice.

"Come with us to the medical area."

Mary's eyes dart to me. "Think I'll get some of the crazy juice?"

Madge snorts into her stew, and I grin. We try to wipe it clean off our faces—the soldiers shift their weight, looking like they're ready to pounce—and Mary jumps up to appease them.

She runs a hand over her scalp and says, "Lead on, boys."

We watch her walk out the door, and I wonder if she'll be crying into her pillow tonight or imagining the soldiers are some kind of insect. What other varieties of injections are there? The tears start flowing again when I realize it's just a matter of time until I find out.

As soon as the door of our cell closes, Jane sits on the bunk, draws her knees up, and announces, "I have a theory about the shots."

I pull the pillow off my bed, and sit on it on the floor against the wall opposite her. I nod for her to continue.

"I've never had a single shot."

Why?

She shrugs her shoulders. "Because I don't think they ever saw me as a threat. I'm too small and too skinny and too broken. They didn't need me. But they need you. The same way they need Madge and Mary. They see it in you, the anger and distrust. They're trying to force our loyalty."

My eyebrows shoot up and Jane half-smiles.

"I know—it sounds so out there. Injections to make us loyal." She tucks her hair behind her ears and leans forward, and the earnestness on her face tells me she's thought about this. A lot. "Think about it though. They've made you hallucinate and they've made you cry. I've seen other people get horrible paranoia or turn so mean they're like different people. If they can do that with a shot, why couldn't they find one that will make us trust them? They just haven't gotten it right yet."

She could be on to something. Her words stir a memory in my brain, something I had forgotten in the midst of one of the most awful nights of my life. Between being chased by soldiers and running for my life with Jack, I had forgotten what the agent said to me as the cloying sweetness of his breath mint washed over me. *Trust is always an issue. I shouldn't tell you this, of course, but seeing as you have no future left, I think it's safe. The trust is what we're working on.*

Is this what he meant? They know how hopelessly messed up their system of government is, so they're not trying to engender trust and loyalty. They're trying to force it upon us. I have to ask Jack. He'll know if it's possible. But a small part of me already knows it's true without even having to ask. It terrifies me, and I feel the urgency of escape more powerfully than ever. I have to get them all out before the government does find a way to force them into being loyal. They deserve to make their own choices and not have that one last remaining right taken away.

The anthem begins again, and I climb up next to Jane. I remember a lesson in Burn History. Mr. Klein stood at the front of the room and showed us a picture of the flag that the United States used before the Event. It was simple but beautiful. I loved the pattern of red and white, and I was especially drawn to the stars. I had no stars then, and anything from the heavens captured me. Then he played a recording of their old anthem, with words about the flag still standing even though their nation was being ripped apart by war. It was moving in a way I hadn't felt before, and I knew then I wanted to meet some of the people who belonged to such a strong heritage.

The anthem now is so slow it feels like a funeral dirge. How can they hope for people to trust them if every time I hear the music all I can think about is death?

THIRTEEN

I gather two more vials before the next yard time. I steal the first when Dr. Benedict says he needs to have a follow-up to check on my face. He prods the bruises and I wince, but he says there's no bone damage and the contusions are healing nicely. Luckily the never-ending tears only lasted until the middle of the night, and then I finally stopped crying and fell asleep. I'd be mortified if I had to sit on this exam table sobbing while he examined me. He asks about side effects from the injection, of course. I tell him it made me sad. I don't want to talk about much more than that. It might be his unreadable black eyes, but he looks disappointed when I tell him about the depression. I shake it off to not knowing him well enough. When he goes back to his office to get his tablet, I grab a vial as quickly as I can and tuck it into my pants.

I still haven't solved the problem of the keycard.

Drugging the agents and the soldiers won't matter if we can't even get out of our cells. Sure we could all have a laugh that they're seeing themselves as snakes or crying uncontrollably, but escaping is the only thing that will get us away from their needles and their psychological abuse. It's only a matter of time until their scientists perfect a serum that will make us all mindless followers. We have to get out.

Dr. Benedict comes back and makes a few notes. I look at his side, and his keycard is missing. I grab his hand. He smiles at my touch, his black eyes softening, and then he realizes I want to spell something.

Keycard is gone.

He looks down, and the closest thing I've seen to panic reaches his eyes. He pats his pocket and leaves the room. I hear him rummaging around in his desk, and he returns a minute later with his keycard once again clipped to his belt.

"Thank you, Terra. You scared me for a minute there. You know, I keep a spare in my office—"

I perk up and scold myself. Don't act so interested.

"—but the agents might actually have me killed for losing one."

He reaches out his hand again, and I think he just wants me to hold it. Instead I grab it and write, *You're welcome.* His smile turns down at the corners, but he recovers and the dimple returns to his cheek.

So that's the answer: I'll need to search his office. Great. And how am I supposed to find the time to do that? Maybe I don't have to do it alone; other people come in here. Mary's been started on the injections—though she refused to talk about what she went through yesterday. Kai comes in here for prenatal exams. We'll come up with a search plan, and one of us will find it.

154

"What are you thinking about?" Dr. Benedict asks. He has a bemused look on his face as he watches me.

Nothing, just reclamation.

"Well, it's nice to see you busy. Take care, Terra."

I hop down from the exam table and as I walk to the exit, I glance in his office. Files, papers, medical equipment. It's a mess. It could take a while to find anything in there.

Eight days left.

The second vial comes a day later when I get another injection. Madge told Kai the escape plan yesterday, and she's all in. I'll give her the vials the morning of the escape. She works in the commissary before dinner, and she'll be able to put the serum into the agents' and soldiers' food.

"I know the risks," she says when I raise my eyebrows and look at her belly. She's thirty-four weeks pregnant now, and I don't want to do anything to endanger her or the baby, but she's determined to help us.

I spend the next five minutes explaining to Jane, Kai, Madge, and Mary how Dr. Benedict has an extra keycard somewhere in his office.

Kai groans. "I've been in the medical area enough to know it won't be easy to find."

I nod.

"What's wrong with the medical area?" Mary asks. After just one injection, she must not have noticed the state of Dr. Benedict's office.

"It's an absolute wreck." Kai chews a bite of pancake.

"Guess we better get busy."

Then the soldiers come again to take Mary to the medical area, and from the determined set of her mouth, I know she's going to find some way to look for the keycard.

She hasn't returned yet before another set of soldiers comes for me. I could cry for real this time, thinking about the drugs coursing through my veins and turning me into something I'm not. But it means a chance at the office, and I can't pass that up. I sag a little bit between the soldiers, just enough that they think I'm compliant. I can't look at them, though—I can't hood my eyes the way Jane can, or the way Madge barely manages to— my eyes won't tell a single lie.

When I enter the medical area, Mary still sits in the injection room, and Dr. Benedict waves.

"Just sit in the waiting room please, Terra. I'll be done with Worker 7488 in just a moment."

Mary raises an eyebrow. Am I the only one he's on a first-name basis with? Surely not, but it seems odd that he would call her by her worker number when he made such a big deal about names in front of my interrogation agent. Dr. Benedict doesn't seem fazed by the slip, though, as he consults his tablet. Mary shifts on the table so he has to turn his back on me to face her. I grin. She knows exactly what she's doing.

I slip into his office and start in the cabinets above his desk. Stacks of books. I look in between each one and flip through a few pamphlets, but nothing falls out. I close the cabinets with a soft click and as I do, I hear the sound of feet on linoleum. I drop down behind the desk. My breathing echoes in my ears. It's stupid, really. If he can't see me in here, it means I'm not out in the waiting room either, and then he'll think I'm running loose somewhere. Better that he sees me. I stand slowly, willing my heart to calm down.

"Doctor, could you look at my tracker injection site?" Mary calls. The steps pause.

"What's wrong with it?" His voice is detached and impersonal, the warmth completely sucked dry. He never sounds that way with me.

"It might be infected."

I ease a breath out and look in the top drawer of his desk. Wadded up papers, pens, paperclips, a few markers. Nothing important, and I worry that the rustling of papers will bring him back. I listen as he scolds Mary.

"There's no trace of infection here, worker. Believe me, you'd know if it was infected. Don't waste my time with any more of this nonsense."

Mary's voice is hard but controlled. "Sorry, doctor."

I scurry from the office and find a seat in the waiting area. Dr. Benedict's back is turned as he reaches for a vial of serum, and Mary catches my eye. I shake my head and mouth, *Cabinets, top drawer.* She nods. She may just get a chance to look in there when I'm getting my injection.

Her gaze could freeze Dr. Benedict's blood in his veins as he plunges the needle into her skin. I almost put a needle in her once, and she was so soft that morning before the sun had even come up. Now she's nothing but stone, and I swear Dr. Benedict can't meet her eyes. It's not fair, really, blaming him. He's just another piece in the government game. Did they have to force him to be loyal? What was the price?

"Please sit in the waiting room for five minutes to see if there are any side effects." He dismisses Mary with a curt nod.

I stand and go into the room, and he shuts the door behind me. He's never done that before, but we've also never been in the medical area with anyone else. I try not to be nervous about it.

"Terra, good to see you again."

I nod. I want to reach for his hand and ask why he treated Mary so differently from the way he treats me, but I keep my arms folded across my chest. Maybe he closed the door to hide the fact that he shows a preference for me.

He smiles and runs a finger over my head, where the stubble of black hair is growing in. "I think you had beautiful hair, didn't you? Before they took it all?"

It's so unexpected that I can't say anything. He talked to Mary like he could hardly stand her, and here he is complimenting me and caressing me. I would love to lean into that touch, to know that someone here actually cares, but his double-sided behavior raises goose bumps on my arms, and it's not in a skin-tingling way—more like a skin-crawling way.

His smile fades. "I'm sorry, Terra, but I have to give you another injection."

I nod and my eyes burn. I blink hard. I raise my hands to ask *why?*

He rubs his hands over his face. "I've told you, Terra. You've been in the wild, and we need to make sure you're inoculated against infectious diseases. So you don't get them and you don't spread them to the rest of us."

He does make it sound so logical. And it would be logical if I didn't know the government was capable of so much inhumanity.

Why all the side effects?

"That's a good question," he says, turning to the fridge.

158

I close my eyes and silently beg him to turn back empty-handed. I can't stand another day being prisoner to whatever is in that tiny vial.

"Every day new medicines are discovered as well as new diseases. So new serums are created. We have to start using them quickly to protect us all before it's too late. It's unfortunate there are so many side effects, but sometimes that's the price you have to pay."

Yes, unfortunate indeed. I shudder as I offer him my arm.

The smiles and the dimple come back. "Thank you for understanding, Terra."

He slips the needle into my skin, and the burning crawls through my veins. I wonder what they'll turn me into this time.

I can't look at him with the empty syringe in his hand. I slide off the table, open the door, and find Mary in the waiting room, looking a little pale. She moves her head an inch to the side, her mouth in a tight line, and I sigh. No keycard.

"You'll want to wait for a few minutes, Terra, to make sure there are no side effects this time." Dr. Benedict smiles warmly, but he's angled away from Mary so she can't see that show of kindness. Her eyes narrow. What *is* going on here?

I sit down next to her. My head aches a little, but I don't have the dizziness and I'm still seeing everything for what it is. Then she leans into me.

"You're just his little pet, aren't you?" She sneers at me, her face uglier than I've ever seen it. I stand up and slide over to the next chair.

What's wrong? I mouth. I'd write it on her hand, but I don't really want to touch her right now.

Mary grips the arms of her chair until her fingertips and knuckles turn white. She laughs, avoiding Dr. Benedict's gaze. His hands are on his hips, and he can't decide if this is going to be an altercation he needs to break up.

"What's wrong? You're serious? Why does everyone prefer you? Dave did—until I sabotaged that whole situation—and now the handsome doctor does." She nods her chin in Dr. Benedict's direction. "What *is* the draw? I just don't get it."

I didn't expect her words to make me angry, but there's an inexplicable inferno in my chest, and now I'm grabbing the arm rests just like she is. My eyes narrow to slits. Is it really so astounding that guys would find me attractive? Sure I'm not exactly beautiful and I have no curves by any stretch of the imagination, but am I really that repulsive?

"Must be the mute thing. Draws their sympathy." Mary releases one hand and taps her chin. "Yup, that's got to be it because other than that, I'm coming up blank."

The inferno in my chest flares up my neck and blinds me, and all I can feel is heat lapping at her, just begging to be released. Before I even know what I'm doing, my hand curls into a fist and I punch Mary square in the face.

FOURTEEN

The next day during yard time, I make a beeline for Jack, and Mary follows. He's at the fence, his breath coming out in foggy puffs, and he's waiting for me like he already knows I need him, that I need to talk to him. But before I can reach for his palm, his hands are on my face, caressing me like he thought he'd never see me again.

"Calm down, Jack," Mary hisses.

"You're okay?" he asks, his voice hushed.

I nod. *What's wrong?* I still see a battle in his eyes—he hasn't forgiven me for lying all this time—so I wasn't expecting this reception.

He takes a deep breath. "I got an injection yesterday, and for hours afterward, I couldn't help thinking you were dead. That Dave and Mary were dead." He laughs humorously. "I know I can't trust myself after those injections. The side effects are horrendous. You've had one, haven't you?"

I nod again.

"Heh." Mary laughs and gingerly touches her black eye and swollen nose. "You should have seen her yesterday."

"Terra did that to you?" Jack gapes at her. He turns to me. "Then you know what I'm talking about."

I grab his hand. *Could a drug make us loyal?*

"What?"

The injections. They make us everything else. Could they make us loyal?

His eyebrows knit, and he's thinking so hard I can almost hear the gears cranking. "I'm not very good at neurology. There was never time or resources to get into anything that complex. But I think so. Different drugs produce different psychological side effects, depending on how they affect your neural transmitters. They can make your nerves send incorrect messages. That's the basic gist of it. So yes, I think so. If they're trying to find a drug that would make us loyal to them, it would take a lot of trial and error. And a lot of the side effects."

That's why we have to escape.

His eyes open wide. "Because if they force us to trust them, no one will want to fight ever again."

I motion Mary to tell him about Madge's plan.

Jack's eyes stay wide, and his head drops when she's done. "It's so dangerous," is all he can say.

I have three vials. How many more?

"I don't know. They only give us a small dose, so there's quite a few doses in each vial. Maybe one or two more, but I wouldn't risk taking more than that, or they'll start wondering where it's disappearing to."

162

All the soldiers in the yard make their way over to the huge gate and stand at attention while it creaks open. A truck rumbles back into the loading bay against the building. We watch as the truck's doors open to the center part of the building. It's shielded by fence and barbed wire, but I can see the boxes' labels: shrimp, oranges, chocolate. I know they're not for us, but that doesn't stop my mouth from watering any less.

Jack rips his gaze away and focuses on me again. "It will take longer to kick in because it's being ingested instead of injected directly into the blood stream. Maybe an hour or two. What time does the staff eat?"

Mary glances over to where Madge stands with Kai, Jane, and a few other inmates. She waves Madge over. Madge pretends to huff about it, but I know it's just a show for the soldiers.

"When's dinner for the agents and soldiers?"

"Kai says around seven-thirty. They eat when we're done."

"Then they should start feeling it around nine-thirty, maybe sooner, maybe later. But they all have to take it around the same time so no one sees the others start hallucinating and realize what's going on."

Madge nods and blows warm air on her fingers. "From what Kai says, just about everyone is in there. Some come in closer to seven, and then the majority at seven-thirty."

Jack frowns. "I think it's close enough. There's not much choice, is there?"

"How's it coming with the keycard?" Madge asks.

It's not in the cabinets or top drawer of his desk.

"Not in the bottom two drawers either," Mary says.

Madge frowns. "I don't know how much more access we'll get."

It'll work. I'm sure of it. Dr. Benedict will want to see me several more times before the day of our escape, and Kai has a prenatal exam somewhere in those seven days as well. *I'll see him before then.*

Jack can see the words I'm writing, and concern lines his face. He's about to speak when I put my hand on his.

I'll be fine.

"I don't think you can trust him, Terra."

I don't. That's not entirely true: I want to trust him. I know I shouldn't, but there's this insane part of me that wants someone here to not be all bad, someone who cares just a little. I guess it's the need to know that they're not all monsters, that somewhere there's some hope for the citizens of New America. It may be the tiniest fraction of hope—he's only a doctor after all, and he makes it sound like no one listens to him—but I need that right now. I think we all do.

So instead of spilling this to Jack, I write, *I'll be careful.*

He puts his fingers in my hair and gently pulls me to him so that our foreheads touch through the chain link. His hands are cold but his face is warm, and even though he's been through detox and living in a cell and working, I swear I can still smell the woods on him, and he smells so familiar, so like home, that I could stay this way forever. I want to do nothing but breathe him in and feel his skin against mine. How did I ever wish that he wouldn't touch me?

Jack doesn't let go until the intercom tells us the men's yard time is over. When he pulls back, I see him differently. I see the trust I need to earn back, but there's also loneliness in his eyes. I recognize the ache from my second injection, but it's real this time, not some bizarre imitation of sadness with empty tears. I

164

realize how much I've wanted Jack next to me, needed his words, the richness of his voice, the gentleness of his hands. How did I miss this? How did this sudden longing sneak up on me so quickly?

My fingers are laced in his. When he pulls away, our fingers are the last to part. He turns and joins the men filing back into the building. We walk from the fence before the soldiers sweeping the fence line can harass us.

Mary shakes her head and smiles to herself as we walk back to our group.

What?

"I had no idea how you and Jack felt about each other."

What do you mean? I've suspected he's loved me for a while. That shouldn't be a shocker.

Mary rolls her eyes. "Oh, come on. Are all colonists so *dense?* Well, I won't be the one to tell you if you haven't figured it out yet."

We spend the rest of yard time talking about where the keycard might be. Kai, Mary, and I come up with a strategy for searching Dr. Benedict's office. I hate conspiring against him this way. He's been genuinely kind to me, and I feel like I'm betraying him somehow. I have to turn my back on that thought. Getting all of us out is more important than worrying about hurting his feelings. I feel like I'm eight years old again when Gram lectured me about including everyone after I told another girl she couldn't play with me and Jessa. Dad tried to butt in with something about 'equity for all,' but Gram silenced him with a look. Even as a kid, I couldn't stand the rhetoric he spouted, and Gram—more than anyone else back then—knew it.

Still, I can't help the guilt that curls around my stomach. Ignore it, I tell myself. It'll just get you in trouble.

The piles in reclamation have dwindled, and they move us into the sewing room. Sewing room is pretty much a euphemism in this case. There are rows and rows of brown sewing machines. They look nothing like the sleek, silver machines used in the colony. These sit on tiny tables. The room has a low ceiling and a row of small windows along the top. Even though the weather is chilly and I could see my breath in the yard, this room manages to be hot.

"We're above the kitchen," Jane whispers out the corner of her mouth when I wipe the beads of sweat from my forehead. I see the heavy pipes that run from holes in the floor up into the ceiling where they vent out the roof. "Don't touch the pipes."

No. I can already imagine the blisters that would form.

We file in and each sit at a table. I stare at my machine. It's a brown rectangle with a few knobs and a needle above a small hole in the bottom. Two large spools of thread—one gray, one yellow—sit on spindles next to me. I have no idea what to do here. A few workers walk up and down the aisles, distributing armfuls of clothes.

Help, I mouth to Jane. She keeps the hopeless look in her features, but I see something different in her eyes.

"Mend them. Look for holes or split seams."

I pick up a yellow shirt. The seam along one of the arms has come apart. *How?*

But Jane doesn't see me because her deft fingers have already found the flaw in a pair of pants, put the pants under the needle, and fly it through the machine. I study her for a few minutes until there's a rough shove on my shoulder.

"Get to work," says the soldier behind me.

A girl in the desk next to me says, "She doesn't know how," without even looking up from her machine. I suck in a breath at her boldness.

The soldier grabs her arm. "Don't speak unless asked."

She doesn't say anything more, just hunches down and resumes feeding clothes through the machine, dropping the finished ones in a basket.

"This is not a sewing class, worker. Figure it out. Now."

I nod, so glad the serum from yesterday has worn off and won't make me do something stupid like try to bash his face in. I purse my lips in concentration and try to mimic Jane's movements, but her fingers fly so fast over fabric, thread, and knobs that I have no hope of keeping up. It doesn't help that the soldier looks over my shoulder, waiting for me to mess up.

Finally I manage to thread the machine and put the split seam underneath the needle. I watch Jane press her foot on the pedal and the fabric flies through.

Well, here goes.

I push down way too hard, and the shirt pulls from my slippery fingers and zips under the needle, bunching in huge puckers and completely sewn down the seam and then across the back.

"You have to wear these clothes, you know." I swear the soldier—and the soldiers here have no sense of humor whatsoever—laughs at me. He quickly snaps to attention when the sharp click of an agent's heels bear down on us.

"What's going on here?" the agent snaps.

"This worker doesn't know how to use the machine."

"And why is this amusing?"

I don't know how she knows he's smiling, but something about his posture changes, like the smile is wiped clean from him.

She looks at the mess of yellow fabric on the table in front of me. "Twenty-four hours solitary confinement. Maybe that will teach you to be more thoughtful in your work."

Jane looks up from the pants she's sewing.

The agent turns on her. "And if you don't mind your own work, you'll be there too."

Jane's head snaps down and she runs the pants through her machine. They fall into the basket with a thump, and it sounds like my heart beating against my ribs.

"Get up. Now." The agent turns and stomps away, and the soldier rips me to my feet.

He marches me out of the heat of the sewing room and down the corridor. The cool air would be a welcome relief if it weren't for where we are headed. I can't keep the broken-down posture about me now. I'm frightened and I really don't care if the soldier sees it. I've been bottling myself up for so many days here—I've lost track of them—and I'm not sure I can keep anything hidden for much longer.

The soldier leads me to a stairwell, and we go down three flights to the basement. It's cold, and I can taste the damp in the air. Bulbs hang from the ceiling every few yards, and the light they cast is full of shadows. It's not as hospitable, but the oppressive dark reminds me of the colony more than any other place I've been here.

Our footsteps echo down the hall, and every few feet metal doors hunker into the concrete walls. I hear moaning or scraping or *something* from one of them. I guess solitary confinement isn't really solitary; I'll have neighbors.

The soldier leads me to a door, swipes his keycard, and swings the door open. I instantly gag at the smell that slams up against me, and when I hesitate at the threshold, the soldier pushes me into the room and slams the door. The smell of human excrement forces my back up against the door. There's a small slit in the door that opens into the hallway, and the dim light shines into my eyes. The soldier retreats back the way we came, but I don't care about any of that. All I care about is the wisp of fresh air—well, as fresh as anything is down here—that wafts into my face.

The scraping in the cell next to mine gets louder, and then I hear the hushed sounds of controlled sobbing. The small hiccups in breath, the sniffles, the sighs. I want to curl up in a ball, but do I dare sit down? I take a deep breath of the dank hall air and then look around. The small sliver of light barely traces outlines on the cell.

There's a bucket in one corner—I don't have to wonder what it's for—and a drain in the middle. That's it. The floor doesn't look too bad, but I can't really see it very well. I'm not going to stand for twenty-four hours, so I slide down onto the floor, trying to keep my nose as close to the opening in the door as I can. As gross as it is, though, I'm starting to get used to the smell. I wonder if they'll feed me while I'm here. I doubt I'd have much appetite for it even if they offer.

I think the only good thing about being down here is I didn't see a single watcher in the halls. I study the seam where the walls meet the ceiling and don't see the tell-tale gleam of a watcher lens in here either. Maybe I'll go through this without someone spying on me.

I can hope.

I wrap my arms around my legs. The cold of the floor seeps through my pants, and I wonder how long I'll be able to sit here before my legs go numb. Maybe I will stand for more of the twenty-four hours than I thought. I wonder who's in the cell next to mine, and what she did to be put here. I feel so cut off, though, because I can't ask her a single question. I've never felt more alone.

I don't know how much time goes by as my mind drifts. I see Dr. Benedict softly touching my face, but I can't read his eyes. They hide everything from me, and there's something in them I'm supposed to be seeing, but I just can't break through. Then Jack appears behind him, and I can't help the smile that races across my cheeks.

I remember what Mary said in the yard about how I feel about him. I can't deny the pull to him, like swimming for the surface when my lungs are about to burst and he's my breath. But what does it mean? I remember the way Brant and Jessa used to look at each other, the way they were lost from the rest of the world. I don't feel that, though. I feel that when I'm with him, instead of being the only two people on Earth, the rest of the world comes into sharper focus, and I can see things more clearly. It doesn't make any sense.

Maybe colonists *are* dense.

A hoarse whisper cuts through my thoughts. "What's your name?"

The person in the cell next to me. The voice sounds vaguely familiar, but I can't place it. Even if I could, I can't say anything. I wish that I could so she wouldn't feel so alone down here either. Instead I knock twice on the door and hope she gets some kind of message from it.

She's silent for a long time, and I wonder if she's decided to ignore me. Then she says, "Can't talk?"

I knock again.

"You're not the first."

I lean my head against the door.

"I've been down here a week and a half."

So long? The only thing I can think of is *why?* but I can't ask her that.

"Stupid accidents. It'll get you thrown down here every time." Her voice creaks over the last word, and I wonder when the last time was that she spoke to someone. She coughs. "Not the first time. I stole food from the commissary after I had been at this camp for about a week. You know, the agent's dining hall. I just wasn't used to being quite so hungry."

I think of Kai working there tonight, making a dinner for the agents and soldiers that's a hundred times more extravagant than what we get in the mess hall.

"I took a whole roasted chicken. They knew it was me because the bird was so juicy it dripped all the way down the hall and into the supply closet I jimmied. I managed to eat half of it, though, before they found me. It was the best chicken I've ever had. I was in for three weeks that time."

I wonder if three weeks of being here in the stink and the darkness was worth half a chicken.

"I shouldn't have done it for the chicken. No few bites of food are *that* good. But I'd do it all over again just to have that sense of power over them. Knowing that for a few minutes, I was in control." She sighs and sounds almost content.

Her voice nags at me. I've heard it before, maybe once. I wish I could see her face. If she was older or younger than I am; tall or short; dark or fair. I imagine she looks a lot like Jessa, and the thought makes me sad. I wish I knew what Jessa was doing. I wish I knew if she was happy, if she was still with Brant, if she was planting new crops in Pod #3, if she let her hair grow out. I run my hand over my own scalp. The hair has grown longer since I came here. It's maybe a quarter inch long now and doesn't feel quite so prickly.

Why am I even here? Because I didn't know how to use a sewing machine, and the agents couldn't stand to teach me? That's not right. It would be more worth their time to let Jane teach me instead of letting my work hours waste away down here in the dank. There's something they need from me, something they want. There are so many things I could tell them. They'll never hear them from me.

I curl my hands into fists. They'll never hear them from me. I repeat it to myself again and again. When I was in the settlement, the only thoughts that I could repeat over and over to myself were thoughts about blood and death. I don't know if it's a good thing I've moved past that, but I have. Now the only thoughts I have are how to get away from *them*, how to get others away, how to keep us all safe. I'm not doing much good down here.

My neighbor's words ring deep into my heart. *Knowing that for a few minutes, I was in control.* That's what this escape is about.

172

Taking the power from the government for just a few hours as we race away from the camp, knowing that they'll have no more power over us.

I will get one more vial of serum, I will find the keycard, and I will get us safely out.

FIFTEEN

I must have fallen asleep—I'm amazed I did, with the smell and the cold and the hard floor—because I wake to the sound of boots.

"Get away from the door," a soldier says through the slot.

I scoot far back. I hear the keycard slide through the reader and the lock slide back with a click.

"Get up and follow me."

Has it really been twenty-four hours? I guess that's the good thing about solitary confinement: the sleep, even though every bone in my body aches from the hard floor. I didn't realize I was so unbearably tired.

I hunch after him, limping as the blood returns to my right leg. He must be smiling behind his mask at how pathetic I look. Let him smile. It's only five more days, and then for a brief moment, I'll be in control. I need to tell myself this because for the past twenty-four hours I've been completely at their mercy: having to use the bucket, sitting with that smell, hearing my stomach snarl at me so loudly there could have been an animal in the room with me. Even now my stomach growls, and I wrap my arms around my waist, trying to contain it.

As we pass my neighbor's cell, the gleam of two eyes peers at me through the slot in the door. I nod my head to her—just barely—so she knows that at least I know she's there and that I care.

We climb up the stairs that lead away from the wet and the smell and into the cold light of the corridors. The soldier leads me toward the medical area. Maybe it's standard procedure to have Dr. Benedict examine everyone who comes out of solitary, but I doubt it.

We go in, and the door to the exam room is closed. The guard motions me to a chair, and I sit. He waits with me for Dr. Benedict to come out. When he does, I'm shocked to see Jane behind him.

"Oh hello, Terra. I'll be with you in a moment."

I'm even more shocked when he steps away from Jane and I really see her. Her hair hangs down over both sides of her face, but it doesn't hide the hideous purple bruises or the way her left eye is swollen shut. When the guard turns to leave with her, she gives me an unmistakable smile. What is with her? She's been beaten to a pulp and she looks *happy* about it. It's the only communication she offers me, though, as she follows the guard.

"Sad, isn't it?" Dr. Benedict says, coming from his office. "She's your cellmate, right? Got into a fight with another worker."

That doesn't sound like Jane. I watch her until the door closes.

"If you'll just come in here for a moment." Dr. Benedict gestures to the exam room.

I sit on the table. I look at him in his clean white lab coat, his perfectly combed hair, smelling that faint smell of pine instead of the stink that must hang over me like a cloud, and I suddenly feel disgusting. I put my hands over my face, not wanting *anyone* to see me right now. My hands smell even worse, and I've been sleeping in it for twenty-four hours. How must I smell to him? I can't stop the tears.

"It's okay, Terra. Solitary is horrible. I'm sorry they put you there, really I am. If I had any power over those kinds of decisions I would change things. It's no way to punish anyone."

He reaches for me, but I just sob. I slept, but it wasn't good restful sleep, and now my brain feels both fuzzy and too sharp at the same time, and I'm so hungry I could eat the beef stroganoff and call it a feast.

He touches my arm, and I shiver under his touch. The first touch I've had since talking to Jack in the yard. He's not Jack, but he's more companionship than I've had for too long. I try to calm down. When the tears stop and I'm nothing but sniffles, Dr. Benedict smiles at me, but his eyebrows are turned down like he's upset.

"I'm sorry, Terra, but I have to give you another injection."

He bends over me—too close, he's always too close—and reaches for another needle. I try to tell him I don't want another injection, but he doesn't listen. Before he would tell me how sorry he was, but he had to do it anyway. He would never just ignore me. What happened that changed things? I think back, racking my brain for what could have set him off, changing the way he treats me. Then I realize. I saw Jack during yard time, and he had reached out to caress my face. I had touched his fingers through the chain link. It was all I could do. Did Dr. Benedict see that? Surely he doesn't watch me that closely, and that couldn't have been enough to change the way Dr. Benedict sees me.

I stare at his black eyes, but he's not looking at me. His shoulders slump as he fills another syringe with serum. He looks defeated and small. Could he really be broken-hearted? I want to laugh, to think it isn't possible. We've never really had a decent conversation, never spent more than ten minutes together at a time, and it's always been under the scrutinizing eyes of the watcher or agents or soldiers. Never a moment alone. Surely he can't have developed feelings for me.

Before he can stick that syringe into my skin and force the serum into me that will—what? What will it do this time? More hallucinations, nightmares, paranoia?—I grab his arm and don't let him go until he drags his eyes slowly to mine, and those reflective black pools don't give anything away. I open his hand.

What's wrong?

He shrugs it off. "Nothing. Can we proceed?"

It's not nothing.

He smiles sadly, only one corner of his mouth lifting, the dimple half-formed in his cheek. "Fine, if you want to talk. Have you ever thought you had something, and then it was taken away?"

I sit back. Yes, I have. The only place that felt like home— the settlement—and I left it.

It broke my heart.

"Then you know what's wrong."

I'm sorry.

He shakes his head, and his eyes glisten. His black irises show nothing but my own face, but there are tears in his eyes. I'm awash in guilt. I shouldn't be—it's absurd—but I am. Maybe I'm not thinking clearly between the hunger and being unearthed from solitary.

Can I do anything?

He turns from me and wipes his eyes. "I hoped that you might have been able to, but not anymore. Don't worry about it."

He puts the bottle of serum back in the fridge and then takes two steps toward me. I grab his free hand.

Please. No more.

He bites his bottom lip. "I have to, Terra. I'm under orders because you're from the wild and you won't tell us where you've been. It's for your own protection and the protection of everyone else here. I'm sorry."

It's a lie. From what I've figured out, it's all been a lie, but how much does Dr. Benedict know? He seems so good and so kind; I have a hard time believing he'd willingly give me nightmares. I can't stand another nightmare, another day not trusting anyone around me. If he gives me this shot, would even Jack look like a monster? I can't stand not being in control of my own mind.

I have to tell him where I'm from. If I want it to stop, if I want to have control of my own brain back, he has to know, and I can trust him. He's been the only one to treat me kindly, the only one to comfort me. He can stop these injections if he knows where I'm from. At least then maybe these lies about the serum can end.

178

Not from the wilderness.

"What do you mean? That's what you told the agent. It's where they found you."

Not from there.

"But you can't be from a city. You would've had a tracker. Where else is there?"

I look at him long and hard. His eyebrows raise in confusion, like he's trying hard to understand me. I sigh and look at my hand holding his. My finger trembles as I write the words.

I'm a colonist.

"You're a colonist?"

I nod.

"Thank you, Terra." His tone has suddenly changed. It's short, clipped, and completely professional. It's the voice he uses with everyone but me. "That's all I wanted to know."

I look up, bewildered at the change in our meeting. He nods to the watcher, and the agent who interrogated me marches into the exam room, followed by two soldiers.

No.

"If you'll come with me, Worker 7456."

Dr. Benedict watches me, and the hood he's kept drawn over his eyes suddenly vanishes, and I see him as he is: clinical and calculating. None of the kindness is there. He smiles once, showing the tips of white teeth, and then presses a few buttons on his tablet.

I want to scream at him; I want to punch him. He was kind to me this entire time just to get me to admit I'm a colonist? My heart wrenches around inside me, bitten and cut by the betrayal. I *trusted* him. I talked to him like he was a friend. I should have known better. I did know better—Jack knew better too and tried to warn me—but I needed a friend. I needed to know that all of the people here weren't bad. I'm so mad I could spit.

I follow the agent. Her heels rap sharply on the linoleum. I stare at nothing but where her heels strike the floor. The world feels like it's shutting in around me, like nothing exists but the sound of shoes on the floor. Everything else is dark and empty, and the sounds are hollow and soft and far away.

Those shoes lead me to a door and a small room with a table and bright lights. I sit in the chair, the chair where I get asked the questions. My mind is foggy, and I can barely look up to see the agent folding her arms over her chest and leaning against the back of her chair. I pull my eyes up to her face. She looks satisfied. She looks like she's *won*. I can't look at that face anymore.

"So you're the colonist."

The way she says it makes me curious. *The* colonist? Like they knew one was here all along, but didn't know who?

She laughs. "You're confused? Wondering how we knew you were here? There are indicators that add up, you know. You're not nearly as sneaky as you've deluded yourself to be." She starts ticking off her fingers. "You never had a tracker. Your bone density scans and blood draws revealed you've had exceptionally good nutrition your entire life—very unusual for someone who has been in a sanctioned city, let alone a nomad."

So that's what those tests were for.

"And most of all, you were too sentimental. Ridiculous, actually."

I don't understand her last clue. The fog over my brain hasn't lifted and I'm two steps behind. I hate this feeling. In all of our other meetings I've been on equal ground with her because I knew something she didn't. Now I have nothing.

She rolls her eyes. "I'll show you." She snaps her fingers, and one of the soldiers lifts a pack off the ground.

My pack. The letter from Jessa.

I lower my head to the table. That letter. Why didn't I get rid of it? Why did I keep it for so long? I've let too many people use it against me.

"You understand now." The agent reaches into the pack and removes the paper covered in plastic. She fans herself with it. "You know, we've suspected that the colonists were real for quite some time. We could never prove it, of course. All of our military submarines were destroyed during the war, and we haven't been able to build our fleet back up to explore the ocean floor. But to have it confirmed like this will definitely please certain officials back at the capital."

She curls and uncurls the letter, and I want to rip it from her hands and shred it into a million pieces. She doesn't deserve to touch those words from Jessa. That piece of her is too valuable for a place like this.

"And you know what else?" Her hands clench around the paper, and it crumples in her fist. "It would be in your best interest to answer any questions we have about the colonies."

No. I promised Gaea, and I truly see the reason for it now. It wasn't to protect the colonies from people like Mary or Dave or any of the other inmates here who despise the colonies because it's somewhere better they will never see. It's to protect them from people like *her*, with her greedy eyes and cruel smile.

She flicks her fingers to a soldier, and he steps over and tightens the collar around my neck that will allow me to speak.

181

"Now then, Terra. Just a few questions for today."

I clamp my mouth closed, my body burning with rage. I hope she can see it in my eyes; I wish that my gaze could burn her to a crisp.

"How many colonies are there?"

I fold my arms and stare back at her. She laces her fingers together and leans forward.

"How many colonies are there?"

I can speak with this collar, but it's not my voice, and she will never have the pleasure of hearing any of this from me.

"You're going to be difficult about it. That's not entirely unexpected, though it is still surprising considering you left the colony for some reason. Surely you weren't completely happy there? Some grievance you'd like to share with us?"

She's being almost conversational. I know this won't last forever, but I'll enjoy it while I can. I raise a hand, examine my fingernails, and pick out a speck of dirt from my thumbnail.

"This will become very unpleasant for you," the agent says, tapping a few words onto her tablet.

I ignore her and nip at a hangnail.

"Soldier, take her back to her cell. She doesn't get dinner tonight."

I fight to keep my face calm. I'm so hungry, and she knows it. And more than just the food, I have to tell everyone that I don't have one more vial of serum or the keycard. There are so few days left, and now that the secret's out about Dr. Benedict, I doubt he'll give me the time I need to search for it. This more than anything will crush me. I have so many people depending on me.

The soldier rips the collar from my neck and drags me to my feet. We're almost to the door when the agent clears her throat.

"I'll be seeing you very soon, Worker 7456. And our next little chat will be a bit more uncomfortable."

SIXTEEN

I lie on my bunk and try my hardest to stare at the vials of serum on my window ledge instead of listening to the pain in my stomach, but the pain refuses to be ignored. When will Jane come back? I need something to distract me. I roll on my side and study the wall opposite me. Then I scrutinize the crack in the ceiling. Then the fading light in the window. Where is Jane?

Finally, the cell door opens and Jane steps inside, her face still as hideous as when I saw her earlier. When the door closes, she rushes up the bunk to sit next to me.

What happened?

She shrugs. "I got in a fight."

It's not like her to fight. My eyebrows knit together, and I gently touch a bruise under her eye. She winces.

"It's nothing. I'll be fine. But you—are you okay?" She's the one hurting, and she worries about me.

I shake my head. *Hungry.*

"I figured. Why didn't they let you have dinner?"

They know I'm a colonist.

Jane is silent for a long time. There are too many implications in my words. The biggest one for her is that their eyes will always be on me, and the escape that seemed like a possibility just two days ago, now seems like the most improbable thing in the world.

"We'll still make it work."

How? We need a vial and the keycard.

Jane lips turn up, and it's the first mischievousness I've seen from her. She tugs up her shirt hem and takes out a vial of serum from her waistband.

How did you?

"You're not the only one who can snatch stuff while Dr. Benedict's back is turned."

His name brings the bile to my throat. She sees the look, and somehow she seems to guess most of what must have happened.

"You can't trust anyone here, Terra."

I know. I laugh bitterly. *Never much of a listener.*

Jane puts a hand on my arm. "The vial wasn't the best part."

I raise my eyebrows as she reaches into her waistband again. She pulls out the keycard.

"There's an advantage to being the weak, broken one. Dr. Benedict hardly ever gives me a second glance."

Was it a real fight?

"What?"

You and another inmate.

She gives me an impish grin. "Not at all. I had Madge rough me up a little, and then told the soldiers it was someone else. Of course they sent me to the medical area." She rests her head on my shoulder. "But don't ever let Madge hit you. It *hurts*."

I laugh and surprise both of us when I reach over and hug her. I flip the keycard over in my fingers, the pale metal strip flashing in the dim light. Only five more days. I swallow hard.

Five more days.

As promised, I'm summoned back to interrogation and it's not pleasant. The agent and Dr. Benedict sit at the far side of the table. There is no chair for me. I stand while their eyes probe me. Dr. Benedict approaches me with the collar, and I glare at him with everything I have. It's not enough—it's just a look, and I'm sure he's gotten hundreds of similar looks—but to show open contempt for him helps me feel better.

He laughs. "You know, Worker 7456, you didn't have to trust me."

I turn my head. He's right, I didn't, but his betrayal still stings. I've been wrestling with this very idea about trust. I've decided it may hurt more, but being willing to trust people isn't necessarily a bad thing. If you trust no one, then you're completely alone. After being separated from Jack and left in solitary, I never want to be completely alone again.

Dr. Benedict fastens the collar around my neck. The agent waves him back, and he sits by her.

"Now then. Let's resume where we left off yesterday, shall we?" She pulls out her tablet, ready to tap my words there. I don't know why she bothers—it's not like the watchers won't grab every one of my words and store them for later use. Maybe the agent just likes feeling more useful. It almost makes me smirk, knowing that she might feel superfluous.

186

"How many colonies are there?"

Huh. She really expects me to answer. Does she think I don't have people I love down there? Maybe she thinks everyone is as inhuman as she is. I fold my arms and start counting the ceiling tiles to myself.

"I promised this would become unpleasant. Dr. Benedict?"

She has my attention now. Dr. Benedict stands again. He does look a little harried, like the part he told me of not wanting to follow their orders might be true. Not because of some altruistic motive, but because he just doesn't like being bossed around. He pulls a syringe from his pocket. It's filled with a pale green fluid, and I clench my muscles as he approaches me.

He chuckles. "Just like the tracker, Worker 7456. It'll hurt less if you relax."

I finally speak, only because the words will scorch my throat if I hold them in any longer. "What do you care if it hurts?"

"Touché."

He jabs the needle in. I thought the serum burned, but it has nothing on the heat from this stuff. I gasp as it floods through me and white spots dance in front of my eyes. I clutch the sides of my pants, desperate for something to hang on to, something to keep myself together and stop me from falling to the ground. I can't give them the satisfaction of seeing that.

Dr. Benedict studies his watch, and after what seems like an hour of agony, the searing pain eases and he nods to the agent.

The agent smiles at me. "How many colonies are there?"

Suddenly my brain is completely out of my control. The words bubble in my throat before I can stop them. "Fourteen."

She taps on her tablet, and I squint my eyes and try to focus. Whatever they gave me is taking my willpower away. I can't let it. There's a small portion of my mind that's tapping against the walls they've put up with that awful green liquid, trying to burst through and reclaim me. It's such a small portion, though, and it's so exhausting trying to fight back. My eyes flutter closed for a moment.

"How many colonists are there?"

"I honestly don't know. In my colony there were three thousand two hundred forty-two."

The agent's eyebrows raise. "I had no idea there were so many," she whispers, her fingers racing across the tablet screen.

What am I doing? Why am I offering up information she didn't even ask for? That small part of me still in control redoubles its efforts. Seeing her surprised like that calms me somehow, makes me believe I can do this. She's not completely in control, or she wouldn't have had to use the injection on me.

"What defenses do the colonies have?"

This is an important question, and that small part of me knows it. It's put a crack in one of the walls, and part of me is leaking out, shouting to the rest of my body to stop this at once. I hesitate for a moment, my voice suddenly lost in the fight between the drugs and my own conscience. The agent looks at me expectantly. She thinks I'm not sure again or that I'm trying to remember.

"I, uh . . ." The *uh* sounds so moronic in the robot voice that I finally do laugh.

"Take your time," she says, and shoots daggers at Dr. Benedict. She covers her mouth with her hand to hide her whisper, but I can still hear her. "Is this expected?"

188

"The side effects of our truth serums are never predictable." He studies me over steepled hands. "Always fascinating, though."

"I don't care about *fascinating*, Benedict. I care about answers. Give her another dose."

He frowns. "Overdosing has never been tested or approved, even on inmates."

"I don't care." She enunciates each word, spitting them out at him.

He pushes back in his chair. "If this goes wrong, the watchers will show that you were the one to destroy our only evidence of the colonies."

She hesitates for a moment, but then she sees I'm watching. She raises her chin and scowls. She nods to Dr. Benedict. "Do it."

He shrugs. "It's your neck on the line."

As he stalks toward me, another syringe glittering, that small part of me screams and finally shatters the walls.

"It won't work," I say, more sure about this than anything else.

He stops, puzzled at my words. "I don't think you understand how truth serums work, Terra." He clears his throat, surprising all three of us with the use of my name. Old habits, I guess.

"And I don't think you understand how *I* work." The words flow fast and hot. They don't sound like me—they never will—but I'm grateful right now that I have a voice and they can hear the contempt in it. "You think I was tortured or abused and that's how I lost my tongue?"

The look in his eyes tells me that yes, that's exactly what he thinks.

"You're wrong. *I gave up my tongue.*"

The agent sits back in her chair, her eyes wide. My neighbor in solitary was right. It feels amazing to be in control, even for just a short while.

"That was the price to leave the colonies: to never be able to speak of them, to never be able to give them up to people like you."

Dr. Benedict hesitates, the syringe in his hand trembling. He looks to the agent to see if he should proceed, but she's just staring at me with her mouth gaping open.

"At the time I didn't get why that would be so important, but I did it anyway because I wanted to leave. Now I understand why I was asked to do it. And you know what? I would do it a thousand times over. That's the kind of loyalty you will never be able to reproduce with those serums of yours. I have nothing more to say."

I rip the collar from my throat and throw it at the agent. It hits her in the shoulder before she can even flinch. But when it does, it snaps her from her shocked stupor and she jumps to her feet.

"Give her the injection." Her words shiver all over me like ice.

Dr. Benedict doesn't object.

I'm used to the burning from just a few minutes ago, so the fluid doesn't hurt me like it did then. But as soon as it starts to do its thing, I have a splitting headache. Thankfully my mind is able to see it coming and it can't leech onto my brain like it did before, but it still hurts like nothing I've ever experienced. I grab my head and double over.

"If it kills her, you're responsible," Dr. Benedict says as he checks my pulse. I'm barely aware of his hands on the inside of

190

my wrist. "And I doubt she'll be answering any more questions today."

"Take her to her cell."

The door opens and two soldiers grab my arms. As the door swings closed behind me, I hear the agent say, "How did she know about the serum?"

I smile before the pain in my head makes me black out.

SEVENTEEN

I wake up to Jane's blue eyes, her face about a foot from my own, her blond hair making a waterfall around us. I try to blink away the aching in my head.

"Are you okay?"

I shake my head. I've never had a headache last more than a few minutes. This has faded to a dull throbbing, but it's not as paralyzing as it was right after the injection. That has to be a good sign.

"You were out for three days. I could barely get you up enough to get some water in you."

I sit upright. Three days? How is that even possible? I grab her hand. *When do we leave?*

"Tonight."

This isn't possible. I can't have missed these days. They were crucial to finalize our plans and get us out of here. Jane puts a hand on my shoulder and eases me back against the mattress. Then she hands me a piece of bread.

What's this?

"Bread."

I roll my eyes. *From where?*

"A soldier brought a few things to the door. Said something about one of the agents not wanting you to die."

I smile. Dr. Benedict was right. It probably just about killed the agent to provide me room service. I scarf down the bread, and it sticks in my dry throat, but I gag it down. I haven't eaten since before solitary. Jane offers me a water bottle.

Then something that's been nagging at the back of my mind, something the thought of solitary reminds me of, comes back to the front.

Is there a way out through the basement?

Jane frowns, chewing her bottom lip. "Maybe. Madge would know. Why?"

There's someone we need to take with us.

"Is there room on the sub?"

Yes. It's a lie, there probably won't be room, but I write it anyway. It's the only answer that will save my neighbor from her punishment.

"It's almost breakfast. Are you going to get up?"

I don't want to. My brain feels like it might explode out of my head, but the small bit of bread didn't do anything to fill me up. And what has Kai been eating the past few days while I've missed meals? I swing my legs over the edge of the bunk and instantly regret it. I don't know what exactly the overdose of truth serum did to me, but I feel like there's a fire in my feet and it's spreading up my legs. I groan.

"Are you sure you can do this?"

I nod. I'm not going to lie in bed all day. Not today, when I need to talk to Madge and make sure everything is in place. I can't just leave all of them to fend for themselves. I know Mary could take care of them, get them out of here until they could meet up with Jack and Dave. Then the three of them could more than get them to the ocean. But I took responsibility for them personally when I concocted this inane plan. I need to get them through it.

Jane offers her thin arm, and I lean on it to walk to the door. The light from the window swirls around my head three times before I cock my head, squint just right, and make the spinning stop. The vials are gone, and my heart leaps into my throat. Jane puts another hand on my arm to calm my panic.

"They're in my pants. We need to get them to Kai so she can have them in the commissary."

Of course. The plan is put into action today. I need to relax, take a few deep breaths—not that it will really help. I'm sure I'll be a wired mess today, but I need to do a better job so the soldiers and agents won't suspect something's going on.

Jane guides me all the way to the mess hall, and Madge starts to stand when she sees us come in.

"I thought they killed you," she says matter-of-factly.

I shake my head and take her hand. *Feels like they tried.*

"We still on for tonight?"

I nod at Jane, and she makes a show of putting an arm around me to help me sit down. Madge hurries around to join her. Jane slips Kai the vials of serum, and Kai slides them into her waistband. A soldier walks over.

"Sit down."

Madge hurries back to her seat without a word.

The soldier watches us. My heart thuds in my chest, and I wonder if he saw the vials. He isn't making a move, though, and I can hear him breathing behind his mask. The effects of the serum are still lingering through my brain, and my mind wanders from the immediate danger. Instead of wishing he'd go away, I start wondering if he fogs up his mask breathing like that. I stifle a giggle.

Finally he does leave, and as soon as he's out of earshot, Jane leans in to ask Madge my question. I slide a pancake to Kai.

Madge taps her fork against her teeth. "I've worked laundry down there a few times, and there's a chute that runs from the laundry room to a grate a couple feet behind the women's wing. Why? I thought we were going out the loading dock."

"There's someone in solitary who's coming with us," Jane says.

"How many are we taking, Terra?" Madge's voice is harsh, but not unkind. I know her concern. The more of us there are, the greater the chance of capture.

Enough.

She looks at me hard, her eyes narrowing. "You're planning something. I can see it."

I shrug, trying to look nonchalant, but it's so hard with my body not completely under my control yet. I feel like my face is going to spasm any second now. I glance at the observation booth. The agents aren't watching me, for once.

You have the cutters?

Madge's one task (besides coming up with the plan) was to steal a pair of heavy wire cutters from reclamation. We'll use them to cut through the fencing along the perimeter of the camp.

She rolls her eyes. "You really have to ask?"

I smile and one corner of my mouth sags.

Madge gnaws on the end of a dry sausage and laughs. "I don't know what they did to you, but you look horrendous."

Double dose of truth serum.

Her smile vanishes. "Do they know anything?"

I'm a colonist. I don't think they would dream to ask if I was involved in an escape plan.

"I'm sorry."

I can't tell how sorry she really is. The conflict rages all over her face: hating the colonists out of habit and coming to grips that she might just be living with them soon.

Mary's eyes harden. "What did you tell them?"

There are fourteen colonies. Nothing more.

"Nothing?"

I shake my head.

"You fought the serum?" Madge asks incredulously. "That's impossible. I haven't heard of anyone fighting the serum."

I got an overdose for it.

She whistles through her teeth. "You're tougher than I thought."

The intercom declares work hours, and we stand up. Kai leans in. "I'll give them the crazy juice at dinner time. Be ready."

We file toward the doors. My tray trembles as I put it on the counter. Red, rough hands take it and put it in hot water. I don't look at the face that belongs to those abused hands. I stopped looking at faces when we planned our escape because I knew I'd want to take them all with me, and there isn't room for that, and I don't know if there will be a next time.

My mind is cloudy as I work in the sewing room. I'm more careful this time, and Jane slows down so I can follow her every

196

movement. Jane threads her machine, and I imitate her motions precisely. This stupid machine is what got me in so much trouble in the first place; I won't let it beat me, and I thrust all other thoughts from my mind. I won't attract attention, and I won't give them any excuse to lash out at me. I need to get through this day unnoticed.

By the time the intercom crackles that it's dinner time, there's a pile of crudely mended work clothes in the basket next to me. I stand, flex my fingers, and follow Jane to the mess hall. Now my fingers ache. They were the one part of me spared from the truth serum, and now they hurt worse than the rest of me. My hands weren't made for such intricate work.

We sit at our table, and Kai is gone—on her work hours, and hopefully pouring vials of serum into the agents' and soldiers' food. My meal is tasteless. Well, more so than usual. I shovel each bite in, but it hardly registers in my mouth. I have no appetite for it, but I'll need the energy on our run tonight. I force myself to swallow it down.

Jane hands the keycard to Madge under the table. Madge is the only one who knows exactly where all of our cells are, and she doesn't have a cellmate, so she'll be able to get out without a tag-along. The plan is that she'll slip a magnet she stole from reclamation to put on the door latch as it closes behind her for the night. This is the riskiest part of the plan. Admittedly, the soldiers always have their back turned as soon as we're in our cells, but if she's caught doing this, there will be no escape tonight, the agents and soldiers will figure out who poisoned them, and Kai—if not all of us—will be severely punished. Madge knows the weight of this. For once, her eyes don't shine in defiance, but in apprehension.

The intercom dismisses us, and we don't look at each other as we file back to our cells. Jane and I go in and sit on the top bunk. There won't be any movement for a few hours now. We'll just sit and wait.

Jane wraps her arms around herself. On any other night, she'd nestle up to my side, and we'd sit and watch the sun go down, seeing our only glimpse of a world outside the camp for those few hours before we fall asleep. Now she sits a foot away from me, wringing her hands—she's a bundle of nervous tension. I start tapping my foot and put my head in my hands. I need something—anything—to keep my mind off of what we're about to do.

My memories flick back to Jack in the forest as we wandered, the way he watched me, but held back for me. He knew I needed that. The way he ate the awful bread and didn't complain. The way he held me in the dark hollow while we hid from the soldiers. The way his mouth curled up into the smile that told me he loved me even if he couldn't with his words. The way I crave that smile. My eyes widen in realization.

It's real. And I feel it too.

I would say it out loud if I could. The stump of my tongue aches to form the words that would tell Jack how I feel about him. How I always felt about him but was too scared to see it. I look to the window where the sun settles below the ocean, the last golden light illuminating dust motes in the room.

I love Jack. My heart swells and all I can think about is his kind face, kind eyes, kind hands. He would never hurt me. I would never hurt him. We're alike. That's what brought us together in the first place; it's what kept us together. It's what's going to get me through this escape tonight because, one way or another, I'm going to be with Jack, and we're going to be free together.

The anthem plays so loudly it cuts through my thoughts, and all I want to do is put my hands over my ears and get that song out of my head. I remind myself that this will be the last night I listen to it here.

The light leeches out of the room, replaced with violet dark, and Jane is a pale ghost next to me. The first moans of the night start up. These are in the cells in our hall, much too close to be the soldiers or agents. I grit my teeth and wait.

After what seems like days, another set of moaning begins, and then screams. These are men's voices, and they sound monstrous after only hearing the women's wails for so many nights. The serum has finally kicked in, and I can imagine what the soldiers are going through. Do they see themselves as the horrible insects both Madge and my brain conjured up, or do they see themselves as fluffy bunnies?

Jane tenses next to me as the crescendo swells, and we climb down to the floor. Madge should be here any minute. We grab our extra set of clothes and a water bottle.

Then there's a click and the door swings open. Madge peers in and waves us out. She's already collected Mary and Kai, and we make our way down the dark halls. Madge leads us. She knows these paths better than any of us. I'd be useless in the dark here, but as soon as we're out in the woods, then I'll be the one leading them along through the dark.

My heart hammers as a scream echoes down the corridor. The lights flicker on and off. Someone must be trying to get them on, trying to get rid of the shadows that just make things worse. Madge raises one hand in the air and we freeze. She peers around the corner into an intersection of hallways and then presses herself flat against the wall. We all do the same.

The lights go out again, and in two seconds, a soldier barrels around the corner, screaming and tearing off his mask. He stares blindly past us, and now that his face is revealed, I marvel at how young he is. He might be my age, maybe a year older. How young do they start training the soldiers to kill us? He pauses for a moment—maybe wondering why human faces peer back at him from the wall—and then he races past us, and his screams fade with him.

We start down the hall again, headed toward the basement door. I don't think I could ever forget the way there. The tile walls are pockmarked with bullet holes. I never heard a gun go off, but sometime between the screams starting up and now, someone took a gun to the wall. I just hope we don't figure into anyone's hallucinations and no one pulls a gun on us. That's one thing we didn't account for: sure it would be fun to get the soldiers and agents drugged up, but no one talked about what would happen if we came across them.

When we get to the basement door, an agent slumps against it, blocking the way. Her eyes are closed and her breathing is shallow. I don't know if she's unconscious, and I'm not sure if we should move her. These people are dangerous if they have any kind of weapon.

Before I can stop her, Madge shoves the woman out of the way. The agent's eyes flash open, and they're bright with fear and aggression. I see the pen in her hand only a moment before she swings it and stabs Madge in the arm. There's no way she should be strong enough to do that on her own, but with the serum burning its way through her veins, there's no telling what she is capable of.

Madge curses, shoves the agent away, and sags against the wall. The woman falls to the floor and her tablet shatters into pieces. She scurries from us like a crab, her heels scraping across the linoleum. Madge clenches her teeth and pulls the pen out with a gush of blood. I grab my extra shirt and wrap it tightly around the wound, and Madge swears at me the whole time. There's still blood on the floor, and when people wake up around here and the serum wears off, they'll know exactly where we've gone.

"Hurry," Mary says. "This is falling apart."

I knot the shirt around Madge's arm one more time, and then we fly through the basement door, not caring if it clangs open. Everyone knows we're out; I just don't think they know exactly who or what we are right now. I don't want to wait for them to find out.

At the bottom of the stairs, I pause for a second, listening if my neighbor is awake. I hear steady breathing, no moaning. I knock on her door.

"You're not soldiers. Soldiers never knock."

I laugh grimly.

"Who are you?"

I don't say anything, just knock twice more on her door. Two eyes, wide and shining in the dim light, appear at the small slot. I press my face closer so she can see me, see I'm not an agent setting some cruel trap for her.

"You were down here before, weren't you?"

I nod.

"The silent one."

"As touching as this reunion is, *we need to go.*" Madge hisses her words through her teeth. Her hand is clamped tightly around the t-shirt, but a spot of blood has already appeared through the layer of fabric.

I motion for the keycard, and Madge hands it to me. I slide it through the reader. Nothing happens. No. I had hoped—I think we all did—that Dr. Benedict's card was some kind of skeleton key. I didn't even think he might not have clearance everywhere in the camp. I drop my head.

"It didn't work?" my neighbor asks.

I shake my head and hear her retreat to the other end of the cell.

"You tried. Thank you."

Jane puts a hand on my arm. "One more time."

I shake my head. It's pointless, but I slide it through the reader anyway, watching the red light blink at me. Nothing. But after a moment, a faint beep, and then the light turns to green.

"Always try again," Jane says, as the door swings open.

I would never forget the way to solitary, but I repressed just how bad it smells. I cover my mouth and force myself not to gag as my neighbor stands up. She's an older woman, hunched a little bit, and the faint gleam of silver hair bounces back to me. I wasn't expecting this; she sounds so young.

"Nell?" Mary whispers, thinking the same thing I did. I know it's not Nell. I would have recognized her voice anywhere, but still my thoughts drift to her.

"No, dear. My name's Lily."

"Lily?" Madge whispers, recognizing her.

As she steps into the light from the corridor, I realize I do know her: the woman from the cannery who spilled sugar. She's

202

been down here this whole time because of some wasted sweetener. I think of that day on the Juice Deck with Brant and Jessa and how I told them about smoothies on the Burn sweetened with sugar. I almost bragged about it. I look at Lily, and I'll never look at sugar the same way again.

I offer a hand to Lily, and she squints and covers her eyes as she steps out from her cell. She wears the same yellow shirt and gray pants that we do, but hers are so dirty they can hardly be called clothes. The smell from them permeates over the half-freshness of the damp hallway. Her hair hangs in matted clumps.

"How long were you in there?" Kai asks.

"I don't know. Too long. Not long enough for them." She runs her gnarled fingers over each other, and her eyes flit across each of our faces. "Where are we going?"

Madge barks a laugh and starts back down the hall. "About time someone remembered we have somewhere to be."

Lily steps in beside me. We made some kind of connection for the twenty-four hours I was down here—even though I couldn't say a thing to her—and she doesn't stray far from my side. She hobbles, not used to being able to walk more than a few feet in any one direction. Speed isn't something we can sacrifice, but I slow down anyway. It annoys Madge, but I don't care. We're all coming. Lily's legs loosen up after a few minutes, though, and she moves in a quick shuffle.

We follow the hall to a door marked "Laundry," and Madge swipes the keycard and we all slip in. Enormous laundry baskets on casters take over the room. They're filled with sheets, shirts, pants, socks, and soldiers' uniforms. Not agents' suits though. I wonder if they have a special laundry facility for those expensive clothes. Two giant washers and three dryers stand along the far wall. The smell of detergent and bleach stings my nose. The room is humid and warm.

"So where's the chute?" Mary asks. She closes the door behind us and blocks it with a few of the laundry baskets, locking the casters.

Madge walks over to the wall to the left of the washers. "Over here. It's for getting some fresh air in here, getting rid of some of the humidity."

There's a metal grate in the wall, maybe three feet square. The chute goes back maybe three feet, then goes straight up.

Climb? I write to Madge.

Madge nods. "It's narrow, so I figure we can brace ourselves against the sides." She sees the look on my face. "Don't forget it was your idea to come this way."

I know. Oh, I know. But I didn't think about pregnant Kai having to shimmy up a chute or poor Lily having to do it either.

Kai puts a hand on my arm. "Don't worry, Terra. I'll do it."

I run a hand over my head. She must see how hopeless this looks.

"If it means I can have my baby somewhere other than here, where they might snatch her away from me before I can even see her face, I'll do it. A hundred times over."

The fierce determination carved into her sweet features startles me. She will do it. I turn to Lily, and she looks offended.

"Don't you worry about me, young lady. I just need to shake the rust off these old joints. I'll be fine."

"Now that's settled." Madge squats down and pries at the grate with her fingers. She only works at it for a moment before she sags back and squeezes her arm over her wound. The spot

204

of blood on the t-shirt has spread to the size of a lemon. Jane rushes forward and works on the grate with her nimble fingers. I kneel by Madge.

You okay?

Her face is paler than usual, but there's color in her cheeks. "I'll be fine." She smiles, her lips tight over her teeth. "Just can't stand the sight of blood. You mind the others."

She wouldn't tell me even if she were dying. Madge grasps Mary's outstretched hand, and Mary hauls her to her feet just as the grate falls to the floor with a crash.

"We better hurry," Madge says. "Don't know how much time we have."

She goes first, folding into the chute and shimmying along it until she comes to the bend and she disappears. The thuds of bending metal echo down to us.

"We shouldn't go too close together in case one of us falls," Mary says.

I point to Kai. She'll take the longest, and she's the one I care most about getting out of here.

She scoots along on her side, and I push her feet with both hands, trying to give her some help in her awkward position. She flips on her back to navigate the bend, then her feet disappear. The sounds of her progress are painstakingly slow, and I grow more worried with every second that someone will come and batter down the laundry room door. Finally the sounds fade into silence, and I motion Jane up the chute. She jumps in and slithers up like a lizard. I send Mary next. Then Lily will go and I'll be last.

Just as Lily nears the bend, the beep of a keycard swipe pierces my ears, and the laundry room door rams into the laundry baskets. My heart leaps up my throat, and I grab the grate. I growl as one of the sharp metal corners cuts my finger, and a drop of blood splashes on the floor. The laundry basket screeches against the floor as the door opens a few more inches. The tip of a gun and a gloved hand creep through the opening.

"They must've come this way."

"How can you even tell? There's blood in front of every door!"

"Don't trust your eyes."

"Then how do you know they're here?"

"Because none of the other doors were blocked, idiot."

I swipe at the blood on the floor with one of the sheets in the laundry basket. There's a smear, but not as obvious as the dark spot. It'll have to do. I back into the chute, pulling the grate behind me. I try to pull it back into place. I can't get it wedged in the way it was before, but at least it doesn't fall back out. Then I slide back as quietly as I can.

The soldiers ram against the door a few more times, and the laundry baskets give way. I'm to the bend and have just climbed high enough so my feet aren't dangling down when the soldiers fall silent. I freeze.

"Did you hear that?"

"Hear what?"

"Metal bending somewhere. It sounds like it came from the walls."

"I think you're hearing things, man."

"I'm fine."

206

"Yeah right. Like the way you were fine when you saw the dancing cows back down at the end of the hall?"

"No, I heard something."

"They're not here. I looked in the washers and dryers. There's nowhere else to hide."

"What about there?"

"That chute?"

I stop breathing when I hear their boots step toward me. My muscles ache with keeping myself so still. One wrong move and the metal of the chute will tell the whole world I'm here. There's nothing but pale moonlight shining down from the hole about twenty feet above me. At least there's no one else still in here. A face appears at the edge of the hole above me. Please don't say anything, I think. I'm pressed against the sides of the chute for dear life.

Then the soldiers pull off the grate.

"Is it supposed to come off so easy?"

"Don't ask me. I've never been in here before."

"Think they could go through there?"

The beam of a flashlight flickers below me.

"Like that pregnant girl could fit. I doubt we could even squeeze through there with all our gear. I don't see anything in there anyway."

"Where does it lead?"

"Dunno. Like those suits would give *us* a blueprint of the place."

"What do you want to do? Hey, are you listening?"

"Do those look like rats?"

"Where?"

"Over there, by that laundry basket. There's hundreds of 'em. Give me my gun back!"

The soldiers struggle and grunt. The gun goes off four times before the other soldier stops it.

"No rats, alright? Pull it together. Told you that you weren't okay. I don't care if we're supposed to be looking for those idiot girls. You need to see Benedict. Let's go."

The boots fade away; the door swings closed.

I resume climbing, my muscles screaming with relief that I can finally move them again. Each rumble of the metal makes me cringe, but there's nothing else to do. The face above finally hisses at me.

"What's going on?"

I wave Madge away. If some of the soldiers are already recovering, either they didn't get very much of the serum, or it's already wearing off. We don't have much time. I climb faster. After a few more feet, I pull myself over the edge into the cold night air and flop on my back, my breaths coming fast and heavy. We're in a narrow space between the women's wing and the fence.

"What happened?" Mary asks. I can only see the planes and shadows of her face in the dark.

Soldiers. They know we're gone.

EIGHTEEN

"Hurry." Madge leads us along the fence to where we're going to cut the chain link. It's in the far corner and hopefully the last stop on a perimeter check.

Madge pulls the cutters from her pants and grunts as she uses both hands to cut through the metal. I watch our backs. The night is silent and cold, only the forest noises crackling across the fence at us. It's only a matter of time before the agents find out about the soldiers in the basement and start to suspect that we've gone through the chute. Maybe everyone's questionable mental state will give us enough of a head start.

I help Mary and Madge peel back a section of fence just large enough for a person to slip through. The metal twists against me. My arms shake as I struggle to hold it back long enough for all of us to worm through. Lily squirms on her belly through the hole, and she gives a quiet laugh.

"Never thought I'd be doing this at my age," she whispers.

I love that she can find the humor in these frightening moments. It makes me miss Nell terribly.

Lily stands up on the other side. "I definitely prefer crawling through the dirt than the stench of solitary."

Everyone's out, and I'm trying to wriggle through without slapping the sharp ends of the metal down on me when the alarms start blaring. It stuns me, and I let go of the fence. It hurtles down on me, the cut ends digging into my legs. I want to scream, but I only let out a moan.

The alarms have to be for us; they know we've gone.

Mary kneels by me and carefully pulls the fencing off me, and I pull my legs out. Blood wells up through the rips in my pants. I don't think the punctures are bad, though. It wouldn't matter if they were. We have to move.

The forest comes right up against the fence, and we retreat several feet into the trees and skirt around the edges of the camp. We are just nearing the southeast corner when suddenly the abandoned guard towers buzz to life. Soldiers scurry up the ladders and into the nests. The searchlights hum and then shine their stark beams down on the yard. I cower into the shadows of trees. Mary's eyes gleam, and the pin-pricks of her eyes are much too bright. The searchlights don't rove beyond the fencing, though. We creep onward, keeping a covering of brush between us and those lights.

Soldiers line up in the yard next to two trucks. Several agents consult tablets. One shakes her head and wipes her eyes like she's convincing herself of what she sees — or she's trying to erase it. She must still be hallucinating. A man yells at her and looks like he's going to tear her to pieces before two soldiers subdue him. They're still under the effects of the serum, then.

210

That will be in our favor, but for how long? They'll still be able to hunt us down, and if they're delirious and they catch us, they might kill us thinking we're some kind of monsters before they realize what's going on.

We scurry along the south fence, and the searchlights sweep by, closer and closer to the fence line. If they finally reach the perimeter and start shining in the woods, there's no way our yellow shirts will hide us. They gave us neon clothes for a reason.

About two dozen soldiers load into the trucks. I wish it meant that would be all that are following us, but there's still what seems like an army in the yard. They heft their guns in the crooks of their arms and stand at attention. Some of them waver in their ranks; a few of them whisper to each other. It's definitely not as precise as usual, but they're still just waiting for the order to hunt us down.

Madge hisses at us. "Hurry. If we're this close they'll find us in no time."

Lily can't move as fast, and I hold her arm and help her along. Every step on every twig makes me cringe, but with the way the agents are barking orders and the soldiers' boots stomp the ground, I know they can't hear us.

We've just reached the southwest corner when the huge gates slide open and the trucks hurtle out and down the road to the west. If they get in front of us, we'll have soldiers and agents coming at us from two directions.

My heart pounds against my ribs so hard it feels like it could bruise, and we plunge deeper into the forest. We've gone about a hundred yards when two shapes detach themselves from the trees and step toward us and I gasp.

It's just Jack and Dave.

I knew it would be them, but I'm too keyed up. Jack puts a hand on my arm and I shiver. If only I had a moment to tell him how I feel, but there are no moments to spare.

Dave eyes me warily. Jack had to have told him the truth about me to explain where we would escape to. But I'm still not used to the skepticism and mistrust people feel for me. After a minute, though, the creases between his eyebrows ease up and he nods at me. His eyes aren't clear, but he isn't openly hostile. I haven't seen him in months, and I wasn't sure what I would feel when I saw him next. I laugh at myself for thinking I was in love with him. Now that I know what it really feels like, I look back at how pathetic I was with him. All I feel for him now is warm affection. Mary rushes for him and kisses him. I don't think they ever saw each other in the yard. I wonder why.

As we jog away, I study him. He looks much too thin and his skin is sallow. His whiskers have grown into a scraggy beard, and the hollows under his eyes turn his face ragged. He was in solitary; he had to be. And why not? When the agents captured the settlement, what else would they do with the leader? And that would explain why he never made it to yard time and Jack hardly ever saw him.

"Who's this?" Dave asks as I pull Lily along with me.

"I'm Lily. Terra found me in solitary."

Dave raises his eyebrows, and Jack runs closer to me. "You were in solitary?" they both say at the same time.

I nod and stare straight ahead, not wanting to talk about the miserable hours I spent crouched on the floor trying to sleep without getting who knows what all over me. And then there's poor Lily who just gives me a slight nod as we keep jogging.

212

She was there for so long. She was there more times before that as well. I can't begin to imagine how she's stayed so human. Dave looks like he wants to ask more questions, but Jack shakes his head and simply touches my arm.

I pick a path through the trees. I never thought I had a good sense of direction because in the colony I never needed one. From the months of wandering with Jack, I discovered it came innately. I know without even thinking about it that we're heading straight west.

Jane wraps her arm around Lily's waist and she helps her along. Her eyes turn to Dave. "She didn't know how to sew."

Dave laughs between breaths. "I could have told 'em that. She barely knew how to weed."

Jack looks long at me, and I warm all over under his gaze. Then he turns to watch the path. Now, more than ever, I wish I could speak. Spelling the words would take too long, and I don't know if he can see it in my eyes as we're covered with tree shadow.

"How far?" Dave says.

"Terra thought two miles to the ocean. She could see it from her window." Mary lopes along beside him. "It'll be tricky when we get there, though, to know where exactly the sub will be."

"If there is a sub." There's a note of bitterness in Dave's voice.

My eyes flash at him. I hope that's aimed at colonists in general and not just at me, but his eyes are shaded, and I can't read them.

"There will be a sub," Jack says. I smile gratefully.

We run parallel to the road and it worries me. I don't know where those trucks were headed or when they'll stop, but the closer we are to the road, the closer we'll be to them.

The road veers to the southwest, and I lead us more sharply south. It'll add some time to our run, but I don't want to be so near the road. Jack must understand because he simply nods at me.

Behind us, Kai sucks in a breath. She's stumbled, but Madge catches her and helps her find her feet again. Kai's cheeks puff in and out, but she's still running well. She smiles at me. "I'm fine. Keep going."

There's a small clearing up ahead, and the moonlight filters down on the ground and is almost blinding after being in the trees. It instantly sets me on edge.

"Let's go around it," Jack says.

I nod and we cut a path to the east of it. I don't want to be caught between this bright spot and the road.

"What time is that sub coming?" Dave asks.

"Midnight," Mary says.

"What time is it? How are we supposed to know if we've made it?"

Madge holds up her wrist. "Kai stole a watch when she was in the commissary today. Guess I'm designated time keeper. It's ten-thirty. Hour and a half."

I wave my hand down.

"Not so much noise," Jack whispers.

We fall silent and pick our way past the clearing. I hear a noise and freeze. The others stop behind me, and all I hear now are the sounds of breathing. It's much too loud.

Across the clearing, a shape separates from the shadows: a single soldier creeps, and the plants shush-shush around his legs. I put a hand over my mouth. Luckily, he's not wearing his nighttime goggles. They dangle from his neck, and he closes his eyes and shakes his head before opening them again. He's dazed, and it doesn't look like he has anyone else with him. He has to be one of the soldiers from the truck, so there are others out here somewhere.

Dave motions us forward, and we take tentative steps, placing our feet carefully. The others aren't as practiced at this as Jack and I are, and we're like a stampede going through the forest.

The soldier doesn't turn, though. Not until we're almost out of sight, and Mary steps on a twig.

"I hear you!" he shouts. His voice quavers. "I know you're out there."

We keep going, and my body is on fire with the tension cutting through the night.

"I'll shoot you! I'm not afraid of monsters! Monsters aren't real. There's no such thing." But he doesn't sound sure. Then there's a deafening click, and his gun is up and ready at his shoulder. We stop mid-stride. He thinks we're monsters, and while he may not shoot people point-blank, he'll definitely shoot a monster. I press my eyes closed, counting silently in my head. One, two, three. Still nothing, and my hands tremble.

"I can't see you, but I can hear you!"

Four, five, six. I don't breathe, and my lungs ache for air. Seven, eight . . .

The gun goes off, and the bullet cracks into a nearby tree.

"Run!" Dave shouts.

We take off before the soldier has time to think about what he's hit, before he has time to get his head right and realize what's going on, before the other soldiers come running toward the sound of gunfire.

We crash back into the darkness of tree-cover, and we're nothing but shadows after the brightness of the meadow. We're too loud—the soldiers will hear us coming from a mile—but we're too scared to care. That bullet could have taken down any one of us, and I've seen too many bullets and too much blood, and I can't even dream what I'd do if it had hit someone. I am a wild animal flying through the woods on nothing but adrenaline.

Kai holds both hands under her belly to support it; Mary and Dave run in unison; Madge has a wild glint in her eyes; Jane looks radiant. Freedom agrees with her, even if we are being hunted down. Lily can't keep up, though. She stumbles and catches at tree branches. I slow with her and Jack grabs her arm.

In the distance there's a faint glimmer of light, and I hope it's not another meadow with more delusional soldiers. This light is funny though, slashed through and quavering. Maybe my eyes are going nuts after squinting through the dark. I don't want to veer even further east. We've already gone too far from the ocean, and I don't know how much time we'll have at the end. We plunge straight toward the light.

The trees thin and the brush thickens around my churning feet. We stumble now as brambles and thick plants grab our legs. I don't hear the heavy tramp of boots, and I hope we've outrun the trucks. I don't get too optimistic. Dr. Benedict effectively taught me that optimism always leads to trouble where agents and soldiers are concerned.

216

We break through the last line of trees, and almost slam into buildings. They're houses, old and rundown. In the darkness, the bricks pale to ghostly gray. Landscaping has long since gone, and it's all a tangle of tall grass and weeds. Windows are smashed in almost every house I see. This isn't where we came for reclamation—that town was still too pristine, even as dilapidated as it was—this town is a disaster. Was this the first town searched for reclamation when the labor camp was built? It looks like it's been picked over a hundred times too many.

The houses are close together, with skinny side yards separating each one by only a few feet. The streets are narrow but open. They'd be easy to walk through, giving us all a break from the obstacle course of the forest. But this easy route makes the hair on my neck stand up. It's too easy, too open. We only saw one soldier back at the meadow, which means there are almost two dozen still unaccounted for. They could have set up here in the streets, waiting for us to materialize out of the woods. We'll wind through the side yards.

Dave nods when I write to him. "I'm with you. Too open."

"Just what they'd like," Madge says, hands on her knees to catch her breath. Even though the air is chilly, her curls hang limp with sweat. "Us to come prancing down the street."

The side yards are filled with debris: boxes, crates, trash cans, all kinds of junk that must have been tossed aside. After Madge's astute lessons, I see a million uses for each of these, but when this town was first picked over, they didn't have Madge. I wonder if the agents keep people in the labor camps for life just because they're cruel or because they're selfish and want the skills they can imprison indefinitely. It doesn't matter now. Our skills are ones they'll never have again.

I smell the tang of sea water mingled with dead fish. This place isn't healthy in any sense of the word, but we're close. Then I hear the boots.

Dave holds out an arm, and we run up against the side of a house, all of our faces painted with fear. We're at the front of a side yard, next to a house that might once have been painted blue. Now the paint peels in long strips like a snake shedding its skin. I sag against the house with Lily as the tramp of boots echoes down the corridor of the street, bouncing off all the windows, the constant rhythm telling me, "We're close, we're close, we're close."

They're hunting for us.

We need to hide. I see an open window leading into the basement of the blue house. I squeeze Jack's arm and point. He taps Dave and nods toward the window. We all slither through the space. I panic for a moment as Kai gets stuck in the opening, but then she rotates half on her back and slips through the rest of the way. Mary closes the window and locks it.

We're in a small, dusty space filled with old furniture and boxes, and the scurrying and squeaking retreating into the corners tells me we share this space with smaller creatures. The smell is horrible: moldy, dank, and with the stink of animal excrement. But for a brief moment, we're safe. No one was chasing us, so they may not even know that we've made it to this town.

My mouth is so dry I feel like I'll choke on the stump of my tongue. I look around, hoping for some sort of provisions like Jack and I found in the gas station, but there's nothing but rot here.

Kai leans back against a stack of moth-eaten blankets and sighs deeply, rubbing her belly. Jack goes over to her.

"Are you okay?"

218

She nods. "The baby's really moving. I think he felt too sloshed around out there, and now he's letting me have it." She smiles and closes her eyes.

Lily leans into me. "I didn't know your escape would be quite so . . . vigorous."

I smile, and she rubs my arm.

"That Mary called me Nell back in solitary. Who's Nell?"

My smile fades as I wonder if Nell's safe, if Red is still there to protect her. I gently take Lily's hand. Her skin is wrinkled and soft.

She was like a grandmother.

"Well then I'm honored to be confused with her. So where are we going?"

I can't help but laugh. Madge glares at me, but I shrug. Lily followed us, pushed herself to breaking, and she has no idea where we're going. I don't know if I deserve the faith she's put in me. Now I have to get her to the beach and the submarine and the promise of peace.

To the ocean. I'm a colonist.

Lily studies me, her eyes glinting. I smile at her, glad I don't see open hostility on her face. "I always hoped those bedtime stories I told my own babies were true." She takes my face in both hands, and cradles me there for a moment. "I'll never get them to safety. I don't even know if they're alive or dead. But thank you, Terra. You've jump-started my old heart, and I feel like we could run another mile."

Jack steps beside us and gently places two fingers on Lily's wrist. His eyes close in concentration. "Good because that's what we're doing next. And your heart is going strong. As long as you let us help you, you'll be able to make it."

Lily gives him a stern look. "Of course I'll make it, young man. If they couldn't kill me in solitary, you certainly aren't going to do it by running me ragged."

Jack grins, and I can tell he sees the similarities too. I have to know if Dave knows anything more than Mary did. I take his hand.

Nell and Red?

His eyes are tired, the blue surfaces dull in the dim light. He puts a hand to the back of his neck. "As far as I know, Red got her out of there. We saw the choppers coming from across the Sound, and Red took her and ran. Sam helped him. A few minutes later the trucks came. Mary and I were loaded onto one truck, but it was overflowing. Everyone else was loaded onto an empty one. I didn't see any of the others at the camp. I don't know where they are."

I can only hope that Nell, Red, and Sam are safe somewhere, out of harm's way. I picture Nell's silver hair, her arthritic hands, her sweet smile, her way with growing things. She would shrivel and die just like one of her hydrangeas if she were in a labor camp. I wonder if she'd like the colony any better, or if she'd be like me: hating the artificial lights and the dark ocean that presses in on everything. If she'd only be happy in the open air, even if it does mean danger at every turn.

"She'll be fine, Terra," Jack says softly. "Red will take care of her."

I know it's true. If anyone can protect her, it's Red. And Sam is there too. He's young but he's strong and helpful. I turn to face the room. Everyone looks at me with expectation all over their faces, and I don't know what to do for them. What do they want from me?

220

I take Dave's hand. A flicker of doubt gleams in Jack's eyes as I do, and I'm not sure why. Dave's the most natural leader among us right now, and Jack knows that. Is he jealous? Still unsure of how I feel? And why not? I realize I haven't given him any indication of how my feelings have changed—not changed, exactly, but how I understand myself now. There just hasn't been time. We'll get a free moment soon. We'll have to.

How long do we stay?

Dave and I peer out the window. From here we can just catch a glimpse of the road beyond the side yard. It looks vacant, but we still hear the sounds of marching soldiers, barked commands, and trucks.

"I don't know. Madge, Jane, Lily, you've been in that camp the longest. How do these soldiers act? How long will they patrol?"

Madge snorts. "You're sure a young pup to be in charge."

Dave crosses his arms over his chest, but he doesn't look angry. "Tell me about it."

Madge smiles. "They're out there because they think we'll come this way. Which means they won't leave until they find something that tells them otherwise."

Mary smacks her hand against a box. "This is insane sitting down here and hiding like penned animals. We'll miss the sub if we just hide out here, waiting to be captured. We need to go."

Madge nods.

"But we can't just go through the streets," Jack says. "There are soldiers everywhere. They'll either shoot us on the spot, or worse we'll be captured."

"I'm not going back." Lily's resolute voice startles me. "I'm not going back to solitary."

The way her eyes shine from the slice of moonlight coming through the window hardens me. I had been wavering before, wavering between putting all their lives in danger and just hiding for the rest of our lives. But we can't hide. Hiding is just sitting still without reaching for something. We have to move. I have to move. I can't be in this limbo any longer; it sets every one of my nerves on edge.

As I head for the stairs, Jack grabs my arm.

"Where are you going?"

I pull my arm away and head up. Jane sees my face and she knows. We've been cooped up together long enough that she knows. She follows me.

Madge laughs. "I think we're finally moving. About time. I was getting the itches."

Jack trails behind me. "Terra, are you sure? It's so dangerous out there. If anything happened to any of us, if anything happened to you—"

I whip around to face him, wishing I could just let all the words spill out of my mouth. There are so many words right now and not enough time to write them. The pain on his face, the worry and heartache, cut at my heart. But there's never enough time. Maybe he'll see it in my eyes. All I can do is squeeze his hand and then continue on to the back of the house.

The back door faces south and opens out to another backyard. I pull a tattered curtain back, but it doesn't look like the soldiers are patrolling the yards, only the streets. There's so many of us—and with a pregnant woman and a geriatric— maybe they think all we can do is stick to the streets. I smile grimly. If only they knew how badly Lily and Kai hate them and want to get to the ocean, then they'd never underestimate them.

Jack touches my arm—he doesn't dare grab it this time. "Are you sure?"

There is time for words now. *You want to hide forever?*

His eyes instantly show his hurt, and I know even in writing it sounded harsh. But I can't help it. He has to know that I need to do this. This is a way that I can help these people, give them a chance for a future. It is something I can do and no one else. He falls behind me, and I feel cold without him by my side.

NINETEEN

As I open the door, it creaks on its hinges. I wince, waiting for gunfire to erupt, but nothing happens, so I yank the door open, ripping it off like a bandage. I try to smooth the cringe off my face. I poke my head out and peer around. There's the house behind this one and then the street beyond that. It doesn't matter if the soldiers have made it that far. We're going.

I creep down the three steps into the overgrown backyard. There's a swing set in one corner, and I wonder how long ago children actually played here. Come to think of it, I haven't seen very many children on the Burn at all, only the few at the settlement. I hope they're kept safely tucked away. Madge looks at the swing, her face wistful. My heart breaks for her. She'll never have those children back. Kai grabs her hand, and Madge accepts the unexpected gesture.

We walk through the grass, leaving trails behind us. There's a gate separating the two backyards, but it's so rusted shut we have no hope of opening it. I hop over the fence and then turn to help Lily down as Jack boosts her up. Once we're all across, we make our way through the yard and to the back of the next house. It's a single story and feels so much smaller than the house we just came from. It's stupid, really, feeling more exposed next to this one, but I'm psyching myself out. I press into the shadows of the house and inch along the side yard to the front and the street.

I stop behind an overgrown flower bush. It's more wood than leaves, and the leaves are shriveled and rasp against each other as I bump up against them. I wait until we're all here, all in a line. I peer up and down the street. I don't see any soldiers, but that doesn't mean anything anymore. The moonlight offers me only so much visibility. They could be camped out on rooftops or sitting on the front porch in a rocker, their guns across their knees, just waiting.

I'm ready to sprint across when Dave grabs me.

"We can't all go at once. We'll be too big of a target."

I'm too twitchy right now. I'm glad someone here is thinking straight. I grab his hand. *Me.*

Mary whisper-laughs. "Right. You're the only one who can get us to the sub. I'm quicker anyway. *I'll* go first."

Dave's eyes linger on her but he nods his head. "Be careful."

She puts a hand to his cheek. "Always," she says with a smile on her face, like it's some kind of joke. I guess it is. I haven't known Mary to ever be terribly careful about anything.

She hunches over and steps a few feet beyond the front of the house. She swivels her head side-to-side, but nothing stops her as she suddenly bursts across the yard, her legs pumping and her feet slapping across the concrete to the next patch of lawn. Something crashes a few houses down, and I jump out.

225

Mary's still running, not safe yet behind brick and wood. I run out, heedless of Jack grabbing at my shirt, trying to stop me.

I run, my heart racing and my breath coming in gasps. Mary still tears across the lawn. The crash comes down the street again, and I squint against the darkness. Out of the gloom comes a feline shape with a waving tail. Just a cat. I could almost laugh at myself, but then the manic grin disappears off my face as I hear the thud of boots rounding the corner.

I wave frantically, and my friends pour out from behind the house in a ragged line, racing across the lawn, the street, the lawn for the cover of the next house. The first soldier appears at the bend of the street, and there's no way he'll miss our rag-tag bunch streaming across the moonlit open space before them.

Lily just makes it to the shade of a sprawling tree when the boots pick up speed and I can hear guns readying. Jack's eyes are as wide as mine.

"Keep going!" he hisses, and we fly down the side yard, through a pile of boxes that tumbles to the ground with the shattering of dishes. Loud, much too loud. If we keep this up, we'll never lose them. I just hope that in their formations they'll be too slow to pursue us down the side yards and they'll have to stick to the open streets. Please, oh please, I whisper to myself as I fumble across an overturned wheelbarrow buried in the grass. Please let them all stay together. Don't get orders to separate and hunt us down.

There's no time to stop and catch our breaths. We race to the back of the house. There's no fence separating this yard from the next. I look west, and there are no fences for several houses. I cut a course that way, heading toward the ocean where we

226

were supposed to head in the first place. The weird sense of direction kicking in. Small miracles, I guess.

The grass whips and tangles around my legs, but my legs tear through it, and I plunge on, leading us west, away from boots and guns. All I hear is blood pounding in my ears and my heart racing up my throat. Lily gasps, and I want to stop for her. I want to stop for Kai, but there's no stopping. Only the race away from death.

Then the thudding is louder and more insistent in my ears. I know that sound. I haven't heard it in months, but it's been etched into my brain and it will never leave.

A helicopter.

The rest of them hear it, too, and Dave yells, "Down!"

We flatten ourselves into the grass and weeds, and there's a prickly plant next to me that scrapes into my cheeks and palms, but I can't move. I just freeze with the prickers in my flesh. Around me is nothing but panting and fear. Above us, the helicopter comes, and I see the searchlight before I see the huge metal bird. I pull the grass around me, closing the opening that exposes me to the sky. There are too many human-sized depressions all around me. There's no way they'll miss us. I only hope when the helicopter flies over, the long grass will billow and hide us well enough. I can pray.

The beating becomes unbearably loud, and I want to scream just to be heard above the noise. All I see are stars and grass and the flash of the searchlight. I wish I knew where Jack was. He could be two feet away or he could be miles. The grass shivers and then waves frantically as the helicopter gets closer, and I don't know if I can keep it in my palms. My fingers ache with clenching.

The helicopter flies over me. I can barely make out the shape of one or two soldiers with their heads out, looking. Their guns are silent and for now, that means we're safe. As the light and the helicopter passes, I finally urge the panic down and convince my body to twist around and look where the helicopter is going. It flies to what must be the edge of the town, and then it begins a sweeping arc around the perimeter. They definitely know we're here. They wouldn't spend so many resources otherwise. I stand up just enough to see over the grass. When my head pops up, so does Dave's, Mary's, and Jack's.

I point west, and Dave nods.

"Let's move before it comes back this way."

We half-walk, half-crawl through the yards. I see no more than the disembodied heads poking up over the grass. We skirt around playgrounds, old cars, sheds. We've gone five houses down when I see a dark silhouette making its way toward us, a gun cradled in the crook of its arm. I hiss and drop, and the bodies thump to the ground around me as the others do the same.

"What is it?" Jack whispers.

Soldier, I mouth.

"How many?"

I hold up a finger.

Jack rolls over to face Dave. "Soldier. Just one."

Through the weaving of the grass, Dave gets up to a squat, one hand planted on the ground, his whole body tense and quivering. The soldier is close now. He'll be here in a few seconds. "You grab his legs. I'll tackle him."

Jack nods. I can't see his face, but I can imagine the deadly serious expression—the way his eyebrows furrow and his mouth turns down in a slight pucker. I hold my breath. If they don't take the soldier out quickly, then everyone will know exactly where we are.

His boots crunch on dried grass. I hold my breath. He'll be here in five more second. Five, four, three, two . . .

I haven't finished my count when his boots appear between Jack and Dave. Jack wraps his arms around his legs, and Dave springs from the grass, hurtling into the soldier's stomach and throwing him to the ground. If he weren't caught by surprise, I know he could have done a lot more damage to us. But Dave is already on top of him, ripping off the mask and helmet and pummeling his face.

I turn away and listen to his fists thump into the man's head again and again, and I have to close my eyes and cover my ears. I know this must be done, but it's so much like what *they* do. Then there's a soft moan, and even though I'm not watching, there's a release of tension in the air and I feel the soldier go limp. I finally turn back, and Dave is threading the gun strap off the man's arm and fitting it over his own. Dave's left eye is already swelling shut, and Jack has a nasty gash in one arm.

Madge creeps up from behind. "We need to kill him. He'll tell the others we attacked him."

Dave cocks his head, considering, but Jack sizes me up in a glance and then shakes his head. "No. He's out for a while. It'll be too late by the time he wakes up."

I'm grateful to him for that. I can't watch another person die.

Dave frowns but turns and motions us forward. He leads now, the gun always ready as we hunch through the yards. In a few hundred feet, though, the grass runs out. There's a chain-link fence with a sign on it, but I can't read what it says yet. This must be where the helicopter turned and started its sweep around the town. What do we do when we come to the fence? If we climb, we'll be up high for all to see.

Madge slips in next to me and grins. "Don't stress about it, Terra. I have my cutters, remember?"

I didn't remember. It feels like a lifetime since we cut open the fence at the camp. Has it really only been—what? An hour? A little more? I smile, but I feel how wrong it looks on my face. Madge tries to look encouraging, but I probably look so messed-up there's no hope for me.

The grass runs right up to the fence and fades into weed-pocked gravel on the other side. The sign on the fence is scraped and dirty with age, but I can still read the faded red letters.

Warning. Low-flying and departing aircraft blast can cause physical injury.

The airport. Madge kneels down and grunts as she tears through each bend of wire with the cutters. Dave stands just above the grass, sweeping the gun side-to-side, watching for more soldiers; Mary is just behind him. She hasn't moved more than three feet from his side since we met up with Dave and Jack just outside of the camp. Jane creeps next to me and squeezes my hand. Lily's bright eyes crinkle at the edges, and even though I can't see her mouth, I know she's smiling. Kai sits with her back against the fence. We're all here; we've made it so far.

I look back toward the town, and the helicopter's searchlight swoops west as it turns on its circuit, coming back toward us. It will be on us in a matter of seconds. I wave frantically, and we drop into the grass and scurry a few feet from the fence. Madge curses loudly, squeezes the cutters through one last wire, and then flops on her belly next to me.

"Just a few more seconds. Can't they just leave us alone for a few seconds?"

"When did they ever leave you alone?" Mary says.

One corner of Madge's mouth turns up. "True. Should be used to it now, I guess."

Then our lips are drawn up tight with silence. I breathe into the ground, the smell of dried grass filling my nostrils. I remember lying in the corn field in Pod #3, raking my fingers through the dirt just to feel what it was like to be alive for a few miniscule minutes. The best minutes I ever spent in the colony. The heat from the solar lamps warmed my body until I was wet with sweat. It's so much the same, yet so different now. I was a prisoner there; I'm a prisoner here. Sure I wasn't locked in a cell, but I didn't have my freedom. Not what I'd call freedom, anyway. And now here I am, face-down in the dirt, my fingernails crusted under with so many layers of grime I don't know if I'll be clean again, and I'm trapped under the watchful gaze of a flying machine and soldiers who don't even know my name.

The helicopter veers closer, and the shadows cast by its searchlight waver through the grass, sneaking through all the crevices, casting snakes of dark and light across my arms and hands. My breath comes out in puffs, and for the first time since we left, I shiver from cold and fear. We're so close. I can feel it. We'll cross over the airport, and then we'll be to the water. The sub will be there.

Then Madge says, "Ten minutes," more loudly than she should because we can't hear anything over the helicopter.

What? I mouth.

"The sub comes in the ten minutes!"

There's no time to wait for the helicopter. I risk the movement and roll over and peer into the sky. The tail of the helicopter glides over us, and I jump to my feet. Jack grabs at my ankle, trying to keep me down and keep me safe, but I shake him off. There's no time. Madge senses it too. She rises with me and flies to the fence, cutting through the remaining wire to pry it open wide enough for us.

Jack bends down and holds up the chain link, and I get Lily and Kai through first. As the rest file through, I look at the open expanse before us. The avian shapes of a few old aircraft and the hulk of a few buildings are the only cover until the ocean. My heart sinks. We'll have to run for it.

I slip through the opening, and Jack shimmies through behind me, letting the metal fall, fitting it as best he can to the existing fence, trying to make it look to the casual observer that it hasn't been tampered with. But as he does, the helicopter's light swings back one last time, and Jack's hands illuminate, pale and pink with cold, in a blaze of light. The helicopter freezes in mid-air.

"Run!" Jack hollers.

Horror is etched on all our faces as we turn and run as fast as we can. The brilliant look on Lily's face is gone, replaced by the haggard realization that solitary might be closer than she thinks. No. I won't let it happen. I race to her, wrap her arm over my shoulder and my arm around her waist, and practically heft her up onto my hip as I'm running. She's thin enough, but so am I after so many weeks at the camp. I can't keep it up for more than a few yards before Jack is next to me and takes her other side. Lily hop, skips, and jumps to keep up with our churning

232

legs, and suddenly I'm back in the forest with Jack before all of this madness began, and I'm loping alongside him, easy and even, the way we did so often. Our strides match and lengthen, and though the sweat pours down my face and soaks my shirt and the goosebumps rise and my breath comes in short gasps from Lily's extra weight, I'm back where I belong, running alongside Jack.

I smile. But even as I do, I hear the gunfire start.

We dive behind a small airplane, and before I can even blink, it's pockmarked with so many bullet holes I can't count them. Kai sinks next to me, grabbing her belly. Her face is twisted into a grimace.

Jane kneels beside her. "Are you shot?"

Kai shakes her head, but what she says next almost sends me into a panic. "I'm having contractions. I think I'm in labor."

Jack crawls over. "It's all the stress—it might not be real labor. Kai, take a deep breath. You've got to get oxygen to your baby. Try to breathe normally while you can." Then his eyes find mine. "We need to get to that sub."

Kai lets out a small moan, trying her best to be quiet. Jane clasps her hand.

The helicopter hovers over the runway, its light sweeping side-to-side, trying to figure out where we've gone. The soldiers in the side hang out, tethered to the bird, and as I look back, more shapes bob through the grass on the other side of the fence.

I point, and Dave nods. "They're all coming now. We've got to move. When that light swings the opposite way, we run. Everyone ready?"

Madge and Jane help Kai to her feet. The light swoops away from us, and Dave shouts, "Go!"

We race down the length of the runway, and the ocean swells in the distance, and I can barely see white foam tossed on the waves. The smell is strong now, the smell of salt and water and gunfire in the air. We're just to a pair of hangars when another burst of gunfire erupts, and we dive in the narrow space between them. Kai has her eyes closed and breathes deeply as Madge whispers in her ear. It's Mary's face that's carved into a grimace. Dave faces away from her, pointing the gun out, and it's Jack that notices her first.

"Mary?" he says softly.

Her hand clutches her side, just under her ribs, and blood oozes between her fingers. Jack drops beside her, pulls his shirt off, and ties it tightly around her torso.

"Dave!" he calls, and Dave looks back. He sees the blood, and even in the darkness, I see how white his face becomes.

"Mary?" his voice is more uncertain than I've ever heard it in my life. There's no touch of confidence, and he looks like a little boy. She reaches out her other hand and touches his face.

"I'll be fine," she says. There's such determination in her eyes that I don't doubt her, but she twists up her face when she tries to stand.

"Don't try," Jack says. "I have no idea where that bullet is. Dave, you'll have to carry her. Carefully. This could do more damage."

Dave nods and stoops down, putting her arm around his neck, cradling her into him so her wounded side is pressed firmly against his, trying to stop the blood. She buries her head into his neck, and then her tears slip out. She still has the thin,

234

red thread around her finger. He holds her so tightly, I wonder if he could stitch her wound back together just from loving her.

Then there's a whistling in the air. I haven't heard the sound before, and it pierces me. My brain sets off all kinds of warning signals, but my tired body just doesn't process it. It's Jack and Dave that give meaning to the sound.

"Go *now!*" they both yell. Jack's command cuts through the exhaustion and sends my legs churning again. The whistle grows louder and changes pitch. We've passed both hangars and are beyond another airplane when the whistle ends in a blast so loud it deafens me and throws me to the ground. My cheek grates along the concrete, and I gasp with the burning that fills me. Every inch of my skin that touches the ground feels like it's on fire. I roll to one side. My palms are skinned, bleeding, and small pebbles are ground into the flesh. I feel dizzy seeing more blood. We're all sprawled out, but Kai is already getting to her feet and stumbling toward the water. Jane trails after her, limping. Madge looks disoriented as she wobbles after them.

Dave shakes his head and then scoops up Mary. Her head lolls back, and I think she's unconscious. Please, just let her be unconscious.

Lily still lies on the ground, and her leg is twisted at a funny angle. "I can't get up," she moans.

"Don't worry about it," Jack says as he picks her up as softly as he would a baby. "I'm sorry, this will hurt." She groans once, but doesn't make any more noise.

I grit my teeth, put my wounded palms on the ground, and push myself up. Run, Terra, my brain yells at me. I sprint after them all, looking behind me once. A fire blooms, and even over

here I can feel the heat of it. The two hangars gape open, pouring out smoke, and their roofs send long streams of flame into
the sky. The helicopter hovers near the site, its light trained on
the inferno. The soldiers from the grass have finally made their
way over to it, and they carefully pick their way through the
rubble, shining lights into the buildings. They're looking for our
dead bodies.

TWENTY

My legs burn and my head throbs, but we have a few minutes now until they discover we're not there. I catch up to Jack and Lily and run beside him. Lily tries to smile, but her hand clutches her thigh, and her face is too tight for smiling.

Beyond the silhouettes racing, the water opens up before me, and I can finally hear it over the thud of the helicopter. The waves call as they scud across the sand. They don't beckon me home, but offer greeting and promises of peace for my friends.

I'm amazed I can still hear peace in this world.

I search left and right down the narrow stretch of beach, and to the south in the waves, hovering just under the surface, the faint lights of a submarine glow blue. It's there; we made it. One hundred yards to go.

I make a guttural noise. Everyone looks at me, their eyes confused at my wild call. But I'm pointing frantically, my hand waving through the air toward the water, and they follow it and look to where the dark shape breaks the surface and glides to rest in the shallow water.

Madge lets out a whoop and leads the charge toward the water. She splashes in—it must be so cold now—without even breaking stride. I wasn't sure how she'd react to this moment when it came. The distrust and bitterness toward the colonies burned so deep in her, but she's surprised me once again. She thumps her hand against the sub's metal belly. It lets out a deep, hollow echo. Then there's a hiss at the top and the hatch opens slowly, propped up with a dark hand.

I recognize the halo of wild, curly hair before I even see the face. Gaea has come. I try not to look at her as I help Lily and Jack into the water, but I can't help it. Gaea's eyes are wild as she takes in the ocean, the fire burning in the distance, the figures racing through the foam toward her, and Madge yelling at her to let us up. I know it's true what I always suspected: she's never been on the Burn before.

She's a creature caught between two worlds. She despised the colony and longed for the Burn, but she could never go all the way. Why? Then her eyes settle on me, and I know. There's such churning emotion there: grief, regret, guilt, and love. She could never leave the ocean because she could never leave me and Jessa behind. It's little comfort for the motherless years she put me through. I can see the love there, the need to be near me. I can't bear it, knowing I can't return that feeling. Not yet, maybe not for a very long time. Then another face appears next to hers, and my heart soars. Jessa. She's here.

She pushes the hair out of her eyes. It's long enough now to be bothersome, just long enough to touch the tops of her ears. She looks annoyed by it, but I know she'll keep growing it out

238

until it's her black waterfall again. Her face is radiant as she turns to me.

"Terra!" she calls, waving. Then she sees Madge, still trying to find a way up. "The ladder there, those rungs."

Madge smiles and climbs, turning to offer a hand to Kai. Kai grunts and hefts herself up, having to turn to the side so her belly doesn't hit the rungs. Dave approaches the sub, still clutching Mary tight to him.

I look back to the runway and the flames, but I don't see any figures silhouetted by the fire, and I think our luck has finally changed. My friends will all get away.

"What's wrong with her?" Jessa says. I look up. Dave is trying to get an unconscious Mary up the ladder.

"She's shot!"

Jessa's brow furrows, and she disappears from the hatch.

"Is that your sister?" Jack asks. I nod. "I never knew you had a sister."

I'm not sure if Jack intends it this way, but it comes out as an accusation. I hear the layers of meaning — the things I've kept from him, the lies I've inadvertently told. My stomach hits bottom when I see the pain in his eyes. I love him, but he doesn't know it. I haven't let him know it; I haven't done enough. The realization hits me and I stagger back. I have to tell him. I have to show him.

I muster my courage and take two steps forward through the water swirling around our legs. The cold bites into me, but I ignore it, hearing only my heart beating for him. He watches me warily. Then I kiss him. He's stiff against me, his lips hard. I thought the water was cold, but the way he's so unyielding now chills me to the bone. This is too little too late. I know that and he does too.

Jessa appears with a sheet. She tells to Dave to use it as a sling, wrap it around Mary, and together they'll hoist her up. I watch the slow process in a fog, watch Dave gently wrap the fabric around her limp body, touching her so tenderly my heart breaks with it. I watch Jack turn from me, his eyes steely. He climbs the ladder, Lily's arm still wrapped around his neck as she uses her good leg. I watch him climb farther away from me. If only I could say something, but I can't say anything now. I don't think it would matter.

Jane wraps her arms around me and hugs me tightly, more tightly than I ever would have dreamed she had the strength for. "Thanks, Terra." There are tears in her eyes, and she doesn't dash them away like I've seen so many times before. They linger on her cheeks and shine like crystal. She climbs the ladder.

"Come on!" she yells, beckoning me forward.

I shake my head and step back.

"What are you doing?"

I can't ever explain to her why I'm staying. Sure, there's the easy reason: there's no room on the sub. Gaea and Jessa will be quick to tell her that too many bodies equals not enough food, not enough oxygen. But my real reasons would take far too long to explain. Life down in the colony is too crushing for me. Here there might be terror, but I'm breathing fresh air, and I still haven't gotten my fill of that yet. And bigger still: I can't see Jack every day and know how much I've hurt him; I'm still not ready to face my mother; I could never go back to my father. There are still so many things I don't know how to make right. There's no time for such words. Jane must see some of it in my face,

240

though, because she closes her mouth into a half-smile, nods once, and disappears into the hatch.

Then Jessa comes up. She tosses me a pack. "You'll need this."

I smile. She guessed before this night even happened that I wouldn't be coming. I thread my arms through the straps.

"I've missed you." Her eyes are wistful and shiny.

I love you, I mouth. She smiles brilliantly.

"Don't know when I'll see you next, but I'll say see you later anyway."

I grin at her optimism. Jessa never let me down.

She waves and then pulls the hatch closed behind her. It snaps in place, and the sub slips beneath the surface, with only a few bubbles and the eerie blue light to let me know it was here.

I wade out of the surf and finally slump to my knees in the sand, the damp soaking through my pants and shivering me all over, but I hardly register the cold. Jack left. It's my fault for not telling him. Love is too important to wait for the right moment, to wait for what might never come. I needed to make the time. I see that now, and I touch my lips where they pressed against his. The rest of me is cold, but my lips are on fire. I hope to remember the taste of him for the rest of my life.

I wipe my nose and my eyes with the cuff of my sleeve and blink the tears away. I tighten the pack's straps on my shoulders and take in my surroundings. The fire in the hangars is shrinking, and billows of smoke plume toward the sky as the soldiers douse the blaze. I don't have much time left before they realize there are no dead bodies. The forest reaches to the north, beckoning me with its green fingers. I know the woods. They're the closest thing I have to a friend right now. The best of my time on the Burn was spent in this sprawling forest with Jack.

I sprint to the woods but not out of fear. I have no fear of the soldiers or the agents and the physical pain they can inflict. They can't take anything from me now. Jack is gone; my friends are on their way to the colony. I'm running because the only thing I have left to lose now is my freedom. Again. After losing that for so many weeks, I know its value.

I jog through the spindly trees. Gradually they thicken into huge evergreens. I run through a wild marshy area that's crusty with frost. The running pounds a rhythm into my head, the constant *thud, thud, thud* of my heart and my feet helping me forget what I chose to leave at the water's edge. As soon as I'm under thick cover, maybe a mile from the beach, I sit down against a tree and unzip the pack. There's a plastic bag on top with a note stuck to it.

Cut out your tracker.

I open the bag and find a scalpel. From Gaea, obviously. She knew just as Jessa did that I wouldn't be coming back. Just as she knew she could never really leave the colony, she knew that I could never leave the Burn. We're both cowards in a way. Neither of us can face our pain.

She's right about the tracker. The idea that's been floating around my head would never work with a tracker. Just under the scalpel lies a capped syringe. *Anesthetic* is written on it with marker. How thoughtful. She doesn't want me to feel it. But the thought of feeling something, *anything* right now beside the heartache and loss wins over. There's a roll of gauze in the bag. At least I won't have to use clothes for a bandage.

I grit my teeth as I take the blade. I bite down on a pair of socks from the pack as I place the tip of the scalpel carefully at one end of the lump. I'm shaking so hard from cold and sadness that the point wavers and I draw blood in about five different spots before I slump back against the tree, take a deep breath to steady myself, and try again. Better this time. At least my hand isn't trembling. I bite the socks harder as I slice through my flesh. Then I use the scalpel tip to fish out the tracker. The tears slide down my cheeks before I can stop them. And once they start, I don't just cry for my aching arm, but also for Jack and for my friends who are gone forever now. I cry until my eyes are blurry and I can't clearly see what I'm doing anymore.

I use two butterfly sutures to close the wound and then wrap it with the length of gauze. The blood spots through the layers of cotton, but it doesn't spread. I cut out the tracker shallowly, carefully—the way Jack would if he were doing it for me. I hold the sliver of metal and computer guts between two fingers and watch the small blue light flash off and on, off and on. This is the last time the agents will know where I am. I place the tracker on a stone, and then crush it under the heel of my shoe. Small shards of glass glint in the moonlight, and the blue light flickers to nothing. I'm now as free as I'll ever be here.

I dig through the pack, find a sweatshirt, and pull it over my head. I lean back against the tree that's nothing but skinny trunk and tangled branches. For the first time in weeks, I'm surrounded by silence. There's nothing but the wind singing through the trees. It's too quiet.

I'm up and running again before I realize it, finding my rhythm again, listening to my blood and my footfalls. I think of my idea, the only thing that can keep my mind off of what I've lost.

Could I get Gaea to send another sub? And could I find more people to put on it?

TWENTY-ONE

I slow to a steady trot. After the weeks in the labor camp, I've lost the endurance I gained through the months in the woods with Jack. My arm throbs, and I'm tempted to pull out the syringe of anesthetic. I'd better save it though. There could be worse things ahead than slicing out a tracker just a few millimeters under my skin. The blood pulses through me, hot and heavy with every step, and it pounds in my wound, reminding me of what I've lost. Again.

My sister. The settlement. Jack.

I've lost and lost for the Burn. It was the decision I made all those months ago. Maybe five by now? I've lost count. There's so much I've paid to be here, but is it worth it? The answer will always be yes. Yes and yes again. My heart aches with loss and yet that's what makes me alive. I never felt so much until I had my feet firmly on the ground. I never knew there was so much to feel.

I wander northeast and by the time sunlight filters through the trees and turns everything green-gray, I think I'm about fifteen miles away from the beach. Maybe ten or eleven from the labor camp. I hope it's far enough to be safe.

I keep walking.

There's something driving me, pushing me on. There's a goal that tingles in the back of my mind, but it hasn't surfaced into full consciousness yet. I'll know it when I see it.

The sweatshirt keeps me warm, despite my breath that fogs in front of me. I tuck my numb fingers into the sleeves, and in a few minutes they tingle as they warm up. The ground is iced in frost. No snow, thank goodness. Jack and I could have dealt with snow together, but by myself it could be deadly. I know what I'm capable of alone and I know what I can do with help. That's probably one of the most valuable things I've learned.

I can barely make out the watery sun in between breaks in the trees when I see the first scanner. I know they've been here, but it's been too dark and shadowy to make them out. I shy away from it at first until I realize there's no way they can see me now. And I won't let them cow me with fear. That's happened too much. Not anymore.

I walk right by the scanner without a second glance, and that liberates me so much that I can finally smile. I start to hum. Singing's no longer an option, of course, but I can hum. I find my mind wandering back to a fire-lit night in the forest when I was surrounded by friends, and Sam's lovely tenor drifted up into the trees. *Amazing Grace.* I should be more careful, but I suspect the agents and soldiers are concentrating their efforts to the south. By myself I made more ground than they ever would have dreamed.

246

I play the words to the song over and over in my head as the music flows from my lips. It's a good song for humming, a simple clear melody.

I have nothing but myself to listen to now, and though I wish Jack were next to me, matching his stride to mine, humming along with me, catching my hand as we walk, I feel free knowing it's just me. It won't last long. When the grief really hits—and it will, soon—I'll be crippled for a while. I know what the price is for feeling so much.

When my stomach grumbles at me, I sit against a tree and unzip the pack, rifling through it to see what Gaea provided me with. She may not have been much of a mother, but the instinct is still there. Energy bars and dehydrated food, water pouches, first-aid supplies, an emergency blanket, clothes, extra underwear. A toothbrush. Oh, a toothbrush. I haven't brushed my teeth in days. I squeeze a stripe of toothpaste on and brush my teeth as I walk. I've never brushed my teeth so long in my life. I hum through the brushes, and some foam dribbles down my chin. I laugh, wipe it away, and keep walking.

Northeast. My inner compass keeps me on course.

When night falls, I stow my pack up a tree and pull the emergency blanket from the pack and wrap myself in it. It crinkles but keeps me warm, and I lie listening to the sound of wind tiptoeing through the tree branches. There isn't much animal life out this time of year, and the woods are pretty quiet. The wind's lullaby sings me to sleep.

In the morning I keep walking, and the trees start to look familiar. There should be a creek just over that small hill. When I find it, I break through the ice that's formed around the slow-moving edges and fill my canteen. I'm close. I can feel it.

247

An hour later, I find the cabin—the one Jack and I found the sleeping bags in, the one with the rug that gave me Mary and Dave's wedding ring. It's even more cold and barren than when we stopped here, but to me it looks like home. I go inside and rifle through the cupboards. Still all the same. There's a creak I don't remember when I step on one of the floor boards, though, and when I bend to examine it, I find I can lift it. Three other boards come up with it, and inside the dark hiding hole, there's an axe, a tin of matches, a can of oil for a lamp. Funny and providential things to keep from sight. Now I can get firewood.

I spend the rest of the afternoon finding small trees to cut down. It's all I can manage to hack down three of the smallest, and I'm sweaty and exhausted by the time I'm done. I don't want to leave the wood outside where it could get wet, so I stack it neatly against the wall opposite the fireplace. The fireplace smokes fiercely when I try to light the fire, and the next two hours are filled with soot and bird nests as I clean out the chimney. It stinks awful up there; there's so much excrement that I don't think I'll be clean for a month. Once I get the fire going properly, the cabin warms up in a matter of hours. I keep the fire low—I don't want to attract too much attention with the smoke, though with how high the evergreens tower over me, I don't know if any wafts that high up.

I empty my pack and lay out my supplies. I have enough for maybe three days. I'll have to figure out more food soon. That'll be my first job tomorrow. As much as I want to lie down and not move for a very long time, the rest of today is spent with any available container I can find—two old buckets and a metal bowl. There's a cast-iron pot hanging on a hook by the fireplace, but it's too heavy for me to heft down to the water. I take them all to the stream, fill them, and walk them all back. The stream is far, and it takes me so long. I'll see if I can find water closer. When I'm finally done my arms tremble, but still I keep moving, trying to keep the grief at bay. I fill the pot next to the fire and boil some water to rehydrate a meal pouch.

I sit in front of the fire on a moth-eaten upholstered chair. I'm all too aware of the empty seat next to me. I don't really taste my dinner. I sleep fitfully that night.

In the morning I search for food, and a gnawing hunger starts in my stomach and then goes to my heart. I find a few acorns, the surprising remains of government-issued supplies (probably from a nomad stash), and a den of sleeping rabbits. I don't know if rabbits hibernate, but they looked pretty sleepy when I came upon their home, and I was able to snare two of them before the rest dashed away.

The rabbits satisfy the hunger in my stomach, but the hunger in my heart doesn't go away.

I sleep in the chair again and as I fall asleep, I imagine Jack dozing off in the chair next to me. Here it comes, my heart tells my brain. We're going to be out of commission for a while.

The next morning, my eyes are dry and gritty when they flutter open. I must have been crying in my sleep, and I have no will to get myself out of the chair. Instead, through the slits of my eyes, I watch the last of the coals burn down in the fireplace and feel the cold creep into the cabin again. My stomach growls.

I don't move.

By midmorning I hear a heavy thump outside. I turn my head just enough to look out the window, squinting against the white brightness. It snowed last night, and heavy, wet hunks of snow fall off the roof and onto the ground. I should feel more about the surprising beauty something so cold and deadly can bring.

I don't move.

The next morning's brightness fills the cabin, and my dry, swollen mouth aches for water. I manage to crawl to the pot and ladle out a scoop. I fall asleep under the emergency blanket.

I don't move.

The third day and finally my body wills itself to get some food. An energy bar. It's tasteless and dry. I practically choke it down. I lie down next to the table and don't move.

The fourth day and there are footsteps outside the cabin door.

I move.

I drag myself up to the window sill, my fingers clawed into the wood to keep myself propped up. There are three people out there—two adults and a child. They're hunched over and wrapped in so many shirts I can't tell if they're male or female. They look cold, and they're struggling to find a way into the cabin. The sight of people shakes me out of my stupor, and suddenly my numb heart, numb limbs, and numb brain begin to thaw and I stagger to the door and open it wide.

They look up. All I see are three pairs of eyes that are so afraid that I'm afraid for them. I try to smile, and I don't even know how scary I look. Probably very, and my smile doesn't help. I try again, and one of the adults steps forward.

"Who're you?" A woman. Her voice is dry and scratchy, full of distrust, but it's not hostile.

I point to my mouth and shake my head. She eyes me for a moment with green eyes the color of spring buds. Then she takes another step forward.

250

"We'd just like some place to warm up."

I nod. I can give them that. I motion them forward and hobble toward the fireplace. My joints are creaky and stiff, but I manage to squat down and build the fire again.

As the cabin warms up, the three slough their layers and I see two women—probably sisters—and a girl who looks exactly like the younger one. A family. They stare with wide eyes at the cabin. I've left it a mess in my days of paralysis. I avoid their eyes as I warm up a can of beans. I still feel the hunger in my heart, but it's an ache that will always linger, and I can work around it now. I can't believe I let myself get that way. I still see Jack in the chair, but he smiles at me, and though I can't yet smile back, I don't let grief overwhelm me.

"You here alone?" the younger woman asks.

I nod.

"Where'd you come from?" the other says through a tiny mouthful of beans. They saw how bare the cupboards are, and they're desperately trying to eat slowly. Except the girl. She's all angles in her skinniness, and I dish her up another spoonful before she's even done with her first helping.

The woman lets me write on her hand. *A camp.*

Their eyes go wide. "No one gets out."

I did. And seven others.

"We heard from another nomad about some activity south of here. Something big. That was you, wasn't it?" The woman laughs, and shows her yellowed teeth. I nod. "Good for you."

The girl looks up from her bowl, and her eyes are big as saucers. "Where'd the others go?"

I'm not ready to tell them the whole truth. Not yet. *Someplace safe.*

The younger woman snorts. "I'd like to see that."

I won't contradict her. I don't know them at all.

I let the women sleep in the chairs, and I make a pile of ratty blankets into a bed for the girl. I climb up to the loft and sleep on the floor. I lace my fingers over my chest and stare at the faint outlines of the rafters. The sound of the fire crackling and the soft breathing of the sleepers soothes me, untangles the knots that cinch my heart so tightly it feels like a small, shriveled thing. It aches as those knots loosen and my heart expands to where it was before. It feels like when your arm falls asleep and the blood shooting back through your veins sends pinpricks all over your skin. But it's a good feeling. It means my heart might just survive.

In the morning we talk more. As the older woman builds up the fire and I dig through the cupboards to make us a meal, the women confirm that they are sisters, and the girl is the youngest's daughter. Just like Kai, she had an unregistered pregnancy, so the women cut out their trackers—they both have the twisted, puckered scars—and fled their city. The woman had the girl in the woods, with only her sister to help. I marvel at their courage. In turn they marvel at mine when I painstakingly take the time to spell out my story from the time I left the settlement until now.

I put bowls of oatmeal on the table. Then I decide it's time to tell them the truth. My heart is opening, and I need to trust them.

"You put your friends on a submarine to a colony?" the older woman asks incredulously.

I warm my fingers on my mug and nod.

"How long have you been here?"

252

I'm not sure what she means, so I write, *About five months on the Burn. Four days here.*

The girl's eyes shine as brightly as the foil wrapper on her granola bar, and I think I know what she wants.

"Why did you leave?" she asks, folding her wrapper around the remains of her granola bar. She's a meticulous little thing for someone so young. It comes from living a life in the woods, always watching for agents and soldiers.

To me it was a prison. Here is scary, but here I'm free.

My answer does nothing to dim her shining eyes. It's coming, just there on the tip of her tongue.

"Can I go on a submarine too?"

Her mother closes her eyes, and her aunt's black eyes narrow on me so fiercely I think she can see the way my heart has been hurt. I think of Dr. Benedict's black eyes, and the way the only thing I could see in them was my own reflection. This woman's eyes are so deep and full of emotion that they might swallow me whole.

I take her little hand in my own. *Yes. If your mother does too.*

She turns to her mother, all wide-eyed innocence. "Can we go there? I'm so tired, Mommy. I want to see a field of corn in a pod. I want to see the elevator that goes out by the ocean." She even giggles. "I want to see the funny fish."

Her mother stares at her folded hands. No one speaks for ten minutes, and the time presses in on me as I see the expressions painting her face with every emotion I can think of. She sighs and then asks the important question.

"If we did go—if it's even possible—would my girl be safe?"

As far as I know, yes.

That's the one thing I'm not sure of—what kind of a reception my friends received at the colony. It's never been done before, land-dwellers coming down to the colony. I'm sure they were put in quarantine at the minimum. I remember my dad's fear of the Burn, which would also mean he would be terrified of its inhabitants. I hope he can see them as people and not monsters. I hope they can see him the same way; I always had a hard time with that.

She looks at her sister, and the hesitation is written all over her face. But her daughter tugs at her sleeve.

"Please, Mommy."

I smile. I don't know if I'd be able to resist that voice either.

Her mother turns back to me. "How do we do it?"

A woman watches me by satellite. I don't even go into how Gaea is my mother. That whole situation is way too messed up. *I tell her when. Then we go to the ocean.* In theory, at least. It worked once before. It could work again.

The older woman laughs hollowly. "You make it sound so easy. Like getting out of here is as simple as snapping your fingers."

I think of all my friends climbing the sub ladder, Jack disappearing into the hatch, Jessa waving goodbye as I stood on the beach and watched them all go. *It's never easy.*

The younger woman stares into the fire, her fingers splayed on the table, trembling. "We'll go."

I take a deep breath. *It'll probably be about a week.*

Gaea has to be back by now, and I'm not sure how soon she can get a sub. But she has to know about this plan. She gave me supplies, and I saw the look in her face as she disappeared into the sub again. She looked proud.

The next day I find a clearing in the woods, one where I have an open view of the sky. If Gaea's been watching me, she'll know I'm here. I hope she knows. I'll do this again tomorrow, just to be sure.

A sub. One week. West. Two adults, one child.

There. Message sent.

The women, the girl, and I spend the next four days gathering firewood and scrounging for more food. My pack of supplies won't last the four of us, and they feel bad enough that they've already gone through half of what I had before. I hide the firewood outside under a tarp and a layer of snow. I put as much of the food as I can back into the hiding hole under the floor boards. I scoop down to the ashes in the bottom of the fireplace, stirring them so they look old. It's the best I can do so that if anyone finds the cabin while I'm gone, it'll look abandoned.

We take a straight route west. I don't want to go anywhere near the labor camp. I'm guessing it'll take us about three days to get to the ocean. I could probably do it in two, but I don't want to push the girl. I realize I don't even know their names. I don't ask. If they wanted me to know, they would have told me.

The girl smiles at me and holds my hand sometimes. She chatters about anything and everything, and she reminds me of a bird. She's so different from the sunken-in, haggard thing that came to the cabin doorstep. I wonder if I've given her wings.

On the third day, I see the ocean through the trees, and we descend the hill and stop along the forest's edge until nightfall. We've seen the occasional scanner in the woods, helicopters flew overhead twice, but saw no soldiers or agents. When the helicopters flew over, both women and the girl shrank to the ground, desperately covering themselves with wet bracken. I felt so sorry for them. That was me not too long ago. Only a few more days and they won't have to cower again. I wonder if the helicopters were looking for me, looking for my friends, or if they were just a routine patrol scouting for nomads. It doesn't matter anymore. I won't let them scare me.

At midnight, we make our way to the beach, staying hidden among the trees, but watching the ocean for the lights of the sub. I tell the girl what to look for, and she's on her tiptoes, her face beaming as she scans the water. She wants to be the first to see it, and I want her to be too.

She squeals suddenly, and her mother whips a hand over her mouth, silencing her. But the girl jumps and points, and I see the lights. She's ready to burst free, but I hold her back, waiting for the sub to surface. As soon as it glides to a stop and the hatch hisses out a breath, I let them go and we race across the sand to the water's edge. Jessa appears above the hatch.

I'm so glad she came again. She motions the girl up the ladder, and I help the mother up the ladder. Jessa turns to me.

"I told Dad what I'm doing."

I freeze. *What?* I mouth.

She smiles. "He flipped."

I smirk. Of course.

"But after a few days, he couldn't keep up the purple-face look. He's not happy, but he's okay with it."

My friends?

A tremor flutters over her face but disappears just as quickly. "They're fine. Dad put them in quarantine and then isolation, *of course.*" I can't help but smile at her tone. She's breaking up the remaining ice that lines my heart. "But the council met and decided we couldn't keep them prisoners. They're not terrorists or anything."

I breathe out in relief.

"Kai had her baby. A girl. With a shock of black hair. We're all pretty smitten."

My heart expands. Kai had her baby safely, and she wasn't taken away from her. Then I remember Mary's wound.

Mary?

Jessa's face falls. "She lasted for the sub ride home. Dave held her the whole time, and all she did was smile at him and tell him how lucky they were. She died as we pulled into the sub dock. We just didn't have the supplies we needed on the sub. Dave hasn't said much since then, but he wants to stay. He asked if he could work in agriculture."

I bow my head. At least they had those few days of peace.

"But Gaea helped me outfit the sub better. I don't know how often we'll be doing this, but I think we ought to have the supplies, just in case."

Jessa helps the older woman into the hatch, and then they're all safely aboard. Still no word about Jack. I won't ask. I don't want to know how happy he is, if he's found a vocation as a doctor, if he's settled in just fine.

I hear the thud of a helicopter in the distance. I jump away from the sub, the icy water sloshing against my legs, and motion Jessa down. She smiles and waves, closes the hatch, and the sub disappears into the ocean.

The searchlight flickers through the trees as I make my way back to the forest. When I'm safely covered in shadow, I hunch down in the brush and shiver as I change out of my wet clothes. I watch the helicopter swoop by, lingering for a moment on the beach. The sand is pocked with footprints, but hopefully the soldiers won't know how recent they are. I turn my back on the helicopter and the ocean and retreat back into the woods.

Terra's story concludes in *The Reaping*

The government is on the verge of perfecting the loyalty
serum, and Terra knows exactly what that means—the
agents will have absolute control. Terra has survived the
labor camp, the agents, and the soldiers who hound her
as she brings nomads to the water's edge. But now she
faces her most daunting challenge yet: she must return to
the colony to ask the council—and her father—to help
her destroy the loyalty serum. With the aid of old friends
and unexpected allies, Terra races toward a confrontation
that will decide her fate on the Burn forever.

Away from her writing, Annie is the mother of the awesomest girls in the world, has the best husband in the world, and lives in one of the prettiest places in the world (the Wasatch mountains are breathtaking!). She loves to cook, sing, pretend she's artistic, play the piano, and participate in community theater.

Learn more at annieoldham.com

Made in United States
Troutdale, OR
03/12/2025